# *Earthly Spirits*

By Ed Konstant

PublishAmerica
Baltimore

© 2006 by Ed Konstant.
All rights reserved. No part of this book may be reproduced, stored in a retrieval system or transmitted in any form or by any means without the prior written permission of the publishers, except by a reviewer who may quote brief passages in a review to be printed in a newspaper, magazine or journal.

First printing

All characters appearing in this work are fictitious. Any resemblance to real persons, living or dead, is purely coincidental.

At the specific preference of the author, PublishAmerica allowed this work to remain exactly as the author intended, verbatim, without editorial input.

ISBN: 1-4241-4727-1
PUBLISHED BY PUBLISHAMERICA, LLLP
www.publishamerica.com
Baltimore

Printed in the United States of America

*For Barbara*

# PROLOGUE

Four months after leaving the monastery where he had spent most of his adult life, Brother Gerald thought he had found a way to help him forget what had happened there. He tried to find something new to hate every day.

It was easy at first because his targets all were people. He had started by hating Nicholas. And why not? It was Nicholas, who had claimed to be at the root of the deaths of Brothers Matthew, Bruno, Anthony and Leo. Then he began hating the four dead monks for leading lives that were so flawed that Nicholas deemed their tragic endings necessary so that he could regain his lost memory and prevent the world from sinking first into apathy and then chaos. He hated his father for abandoning the family. Gerald's hatred reached its peak when he decided to hate himself for his own indecision. After that, he turned his sights away from people and his targets became increasingly less important: the cup that held his morning coffee, the glass that held his dinner wine, the bed in which he slept. Finally, he hated the door to the Vatican Secret Archives, where he worked in labyrinthian solitude every day. As the days droned on, his new pastime seemed to be taking on a life of its own. It went from routine to hunger to addiction. It became so bad that he broke his nearly lifelong love affair with time and decided to hate his alarm clock and wristwatch.

By the third week of his obsession, Gerald was having as much trouble working as he was trying to find new things to hate. So, he began hating the pages of centuries-old books and yellowed papers in musty file folders, which he had started to merely browse without knowing or caring what he was reading. Devils, demons, spirits, spectres. Each one became like the other and that other always was Nicholas.

Was Nicholas really Lucifer, as he had confessed to Gerald in the dream that night at Blessed Skyline Monastery in Virginia seven months earlier? Gerald had tried so often since then to believe that it was a dream. Each time that he had denied that it had not been a dream, because anything else would have been unthinkable, he had to face the probable reality of being in denial.

The reality that made him uncomfortable was the work. If it was simply a matter of researching and writing a new history of the Devil for the Vatican that would have been appealing. But it was discomforting, in the least, to realize that an obscure monk with no credentials recognizable to the rest of the world should have been chosen for the task. It was his reward, Father William had insisted, for being kind to Nicholas, the amnesiac drifter who had been sent to Blessed Skyline for spiritual and mental rehabilitation. If true, that would mean Lucifer had influence at the Vatican. No matter how hard Gerald had argued against that, he had little choice but to grudgingly and secretly accept it. At least until he could find a more acceptable reason.

Perhaps all the time he was spending in the Secret Archives only was adding to his malaise. Father William had been badgering him to get out more, to see the Rome that Gerald had mostly ignored since being assigned to the Vatican. William seemed content, even happy, roaming the streets in search of recollections of supernatural events that somehow missed being recorded by the Vatican or were buried too deeply in the all the books and documents of the Vatican Secret Archives that chronicled the dark history of religion. And, Father William was aware of all the circumstances that had jarred their lives in Virginia and eventually brought the two of them to the Eternal City. The only difference was that William did not experience them, but Gerald did.

*EARTHLY SPIRITS*

Lately, Father William had been lecturing Gerald about how his cloistered existence in the Vatican Secret Archives seemed to be affecting not just his morale, but his physical being. Had he really breathed in so much dust from all the old paper and wood and stone that it was giving birth to a cough? Were the muscles that he had developed in his back, shoulders and arms from years of ringing the old bell at Blessed Skyline Abbey starting to turn to flab? Had he added to the one-hundred-and-seventy pounds of weight that for so long had clung tightly to his five-foot-ten frame?

Damn it. Why did Father William always have to be so right?

# CHAPTER 1

The squat old man in the shabby brown suit and black rumpled beret opened the door. He paused for a moment as though he was uncertain that he was in the right place, letting the street noise of roaring scooters and shouting voices shove their way past him like a ravenous mob in search of prey. Only when he seemed sure that he was where he wanted to be, he closed the door behind him.

"I never thought I'd live to see a miracle."

Brother Gerald speared a marinated anchovy with his fork and lifted it from the appetizer plate in front of him. What was left of the tiny fish dangled on the suspended utensil halfway between the plate and his lips. He raised his head and looked with one eye cocked across the table at Father William, but not to question the priest's claims of bearing witness to a miracle.

"Me, too," Gerald said. He shoved the anchovy into his mouth, let his tongue and palate savor it briefly before chewing, then sent the mass on its way down his throat. "This is one of the rare times we're in agreement. This food is miraculous."

"Not our dinner," Father William said. He smiled and waved the fork he was wielding in his right hand over Gerald's head in the direction of the old man who had just entered the small family restaurant. Gerald

*EARTHLY SPIRITS*

pretended to duck out of the way of the utensil. "I was referring to 'Il Professore'."

"The retired old teacher you told me about? The one who's been eating here every night for, what, twenty or thirty years?"

"Yes, the man who wears the same brown suit, brown cap, one of those old red and gray striped neckties, and limps along with his cane. And the same frown on his face. For twenty-seven years."

Gerald shoved another anchovy into his mouth.

"Okay, so he's a creature of habit. I knew that already."

"If you'll stop stuffing your mouth like a barbarian and take a look, you'll see there's something different about him tonight."

Gerald watched the old man hobble slowly past their table, then turn right between two others, his legs carrying a body that looked like a soccer ball that had been kicked around the field once too often. Il Professore carried himself in the classic mood of a retired teacher, clinging to the despair and loneliness that were his constant companions. He stopped at the only empty table in the restaurant next to an old stone wall hung with empty bottles of Chianti whose wicker wrappings had been signed by tourists with black markers given to them for the occasion by the restaurant staff. The old man turned his face toward them as he removed the beret from his head and hung it over one of the backposts of the chair. He gave the two clerics a brief smiling nod that seemed almost alien to his sagging cheeks, drooping eyelids and lonely brown eyes. Then he sat down and reached for the napkin on the table that was set for one.

"I still don't get it," Gerald said.

"God, it must be happening to you again," Father William said, lowering his voice.

"What now?"

"You're spending too much time in that medieval labyrinth they call the Vatican Secret Archives. It's probably having the same effect on you as that the musty old room where you loved to hide at the bottom of the bell tower back at Blessed Skyline Abbey. You spent hours a day there alone for years, mostly reading, I suppose. What do you do now at the Archives?"

"Spend hours a day reading."

"Exactly my point. It's dulling your observational skills, maybe even that fine memory you used to have. I think you avoid going outdoors even more here than you did back in Virginia."

"Father William, I've listened to a lifetime's worth of your lectures. So, could you spare me just this once and please get to whatever point you're trying to impress on me this time?"

"For one thing, 'Il Professore' never gets here after seven-thirty, probably so he can beat the nightly dinner crowd and get his favorite table. I'm somewhat disappointed in you. You've always been such a fanatic keeper of time I thought you would have recognized that."

Gerald glanced at his wristwatch.

"It's ten-to-eight. So he's late. Maybe he took a nap and overslept. More likely he had a long one for the road at that bar around the corner where you've seen him standing along with the rest of the neighborhood winos when he's not in here."

"We're sitting at his table, you know."

"You told me that tonight when we came in. It was the only table they had left. I didn't see a placecard reserving it. Either we took it or went somewhere else. I'm glad we stayed here."

"But he never looked upset that we were sitting here. One night when I was here a couple of months ago the place filled up early, too. Someone else got his table and when he arrived at his usual time, he looked confused and upset because he might have to sit somewhere else. Tonight, he just took another table. Not only that. He smiled at us, to boot."

"I don't understand what's such a big deal."

"He never smiles."

"He probably recognized you as a regular."

"No, you don't understand. He never smiles at anyone. Not at Giorgio, the owner, not at the waiters, not at Carlo."

"Carlo? Isn't he the pudgy guy you told me about? The one who pulls up outside on his scooter around eight o'clock every night to get a take-out pizza? He should be here any minute."

"Yes, that Carlo. I only discovered this place about three months ago and he's been a regular a lot longer than me."

*EARTHLY SPIRITS*

"I still think your 'Il Professore' was just being friendly."

"Did you notice his eyes?"

"Only that he still has two of them."

"They weren't dull and lifeless like they've been before. They were almost sparkling."

"He probably got a good night's sleep."

"Under other circumstances, I might grudgingly consent on that point. Except, there's his necktie?"

"What about it?"

"He's wearing a new tie. Solid red."

"Maybe he bought it at a street market or someone gave it to him as a gift."

"There's something else. Did you notice the way he was walking."

"Yes, he was limping, as usual."

"So, you noticed something after all. But, that's not what I meant."

"So, what else am I supposed to have missed?"

"He didn't have his cane."

"He probably didn't need it tonight."

"It's comforting to know that in the uncertainty of this ever changing world, the predictability responses of Brother Gerald remain as solid as the rock on which Saint Peter built the Church. On the other hand, your skill at producing a mundane answer for everything can be frustrating."

"Whatever you think is wrong with the old man doesn't seem to have affected his dining skills. Look at him."

Father William shifted his eyes to where the old man was sitting. He had tucked the large white cloth napkin under the collar of his shirt so that it hung down across his chest like a baby's bib. He took a sip from a glass that the waiter had filled from a bottle of red wine that had been placed on the table along with an appetizer of marinated anchovies. He did it all with a pause here and another there, almost like an artist studying a canvas before applying the next brush stroke to a masterpiece.

"Well, at least he's got good taste," Brother Gerald said. "Until tonight I never knew anchovies were anything more than salty strips of mush that were used to ruin pizza back in the states."

"He's got more than just taste," Father William said. "He has style. You could learn a few table manners watching him."

Brother Gerald shoved the last of his appetizer into his mouth and deliberately chewed it with just enough noise to be annoying.

"Very funny," Father William said.

"You've become quite the snob in the four months we've been in Rome," Gerald said. "Not that you weren't already on the way toward becoming one after you retired as abbot. But at least that cabin in the woods where you were living while all Hell was breaking loose at our old monastery helped you keep things in perspective. It's as if the one mystery we had wasn't enough, so you've got to go looking for another wherever you think it might exist."

"I've got to admit you're right about that. This outdoor café lifestyle, all these old Roman ruins and Renaissance buildings, the churches with their frescos, they all get to you after a while. This whole city is like a giant outdoor museum. And that doesn't include all the cultural and material wealth of the Vatican. Then there's all those odd occurrences that I've heard about from local priests who have no answers. Sometimes I feel like a kid who's been given free run of a candy shop."

"It's partially my fault. You're supposed to be my assistant on this project that I was summoned here to do after our old Virginia abbey was closed. I should be giving you more to do than an occasional assignment at a neighborhood library. I've been so busy trying to find my way around the Vatican, especially at the Secret Archives, that I haven't had much time to come up with a plan to keep you busier."

"I don't need a plan to keep me busy. There are enough churches, nunneries and cemeteries around here to keep me busy for the next couple of years. All I do is ask questions and sometimes even get interesting answers. It seems that you're more in need of a plan. Do you even have one?"

"Not really. I'm not even sure exactly what I'm supposed to be doing that hasn't already been done on the subject."

"Cardinal Verano hasn't been much help, I suppose."

"He's helpful in his own way."

"Verano's pleasant enough, but from the Vatican gossip I've picked up, I don't understand how he ever got this far. He's no mover. He's a greeter, a clerk who somehow managed to convince the pope to elevate him to the rank of cardinal. More likely he has a friend or two who has the pope's ear. I expect Verano probably will end his career as a Vatican ambassador to some third world country."

"Now you're adding gossip to the wealth of sins you've started accumulating late in life."

"Not gossip. Information. You never know when it will come in handy, like it did back in Virginia when we were trying to figure out who was killing the brothers at the abbey."

"A lot of good that did us. Not only did it fail to save anyone, we never learned how whoever was guilty was able to commit the crimes."

"You're not going to relapse into denial again, are you? When you think about all that's happened since then, there can't be much doubt, even in your fixed mind. Otherwise, I'd be sitting in a wheelchair waiting for God in one of those dreary places they send penniless retired priests. Look at us. We're in Rome. For the first time in my life, I'm not penniless. It's not much, but I actually get a salary and a place to live, though my room across the hall from you isn't as elaborate as the quarters you were assigned. There probably are priests who've spent most of their careers at the Vatican who don't have half the living space you've got. During all those years at the abbey all I ever got was bare walls and bland meals. On top of it all, you've got a plush job, being paid to read all the history you can absorb. Where do you think you'd be now if you didn't have that special friend?"

"Christ, Father, not so loud. I hope you don't talk about that with your Vatican cronies. Especially using the word 'friend'."

Father William lifted an eyebrow, accentuating the wrinkles of age that added character to his face. He lowered his voice another notch just as the owner, Giorgio, brought their main dishes to their table. At the same time, as if on cue, Carlo arrived to order his pizza.

"All right, 'friend' may be a poor choice of words," Father William said. "But it's pretty obvious that whoever you want to believe he was had enough influence to save you from spending the rest of your life in some dying monastery or parish church in the middle of nowhere. The Church has plenty of places just waiting for clerical bodies that they can suck the life out of. I'm not saying that the Lord has forsaken them, but I'm sure He knows better than anyone when to cut his losses."

"Father, are you going to relive that subject every time we get together?"

"I try not to, but can you think of anything that's happened in your life that's been more significant? You were privileged to meet a legend, a myth in the flesh. Neither of us can ever forget it, least of all you. I can't forget it and all I have is your story. It's a whopper of a tale, but considering what happened back in Virginia, I can't help but believe it. You now know more about the faith than anyone I've ever met. You'd be the envy of the pope. Maybe you are."

"I'm still not one-hundred percent convinced that the myth wasn't a bad dream. And don't start giving me another denial lecture. Even if it wasn't a dream, I can't forget it, either. How could I? The Vatican won't let me. All I do is research and more research on that subject every day. There's so much material to go through that even with your help it would take both our lifetimes to study all of it. And that timeframe would apply only if we started on the day we were born."

"You're right. So, I'm going to insist that you get away more often from that tomb of papers where you go almost every day and do some of what I do. Sooner or later you're going to have to do some field research."

"You want me to become a tourist and café junkie?"

"That's not a bad idea. But, I mix a lot of business with those pleasures."

"Talking to librarians and parish priests?"

"And nuns and monks, even an occasional Church layman who's got a story to tell. That doesn't include the Protestant ministers and Jewish rabbis in this city, as few as there are. They're on my list, too. Some of them have to have seen or heard a lot that doesn't make it into the Secret Archives. Whatever answers you're supposed to be looking for might not even be there. I'll bet you won't find any mention of your own encounter with Nicholas in the Archives."

"Of course I won't. You're the only person I've told the full story to."

"I thought you also confided in Teresa Lucci, which means that her husband Christopher almost surely also knows."

"I did, but I withheld a few things, including that final detail about the missing tattoo."

"The big red letter 'N'?"

"Yes, the one that was on his left arm when he was alive, but wasn't there after he'd died."

"Well, if nothing else, that should've been the clincher for you. By the way, why didn't you tell Teresa about the tattoo?"

"I wasn't sure that she could handle it. Anyway, in the end I think she and Chris figured it out for themselves. Why else would they have packed up so soon after it was over and moved three-thousand miles away?"

"I suppose you never worried that one of them would've told anyone else. They'd have been fools to do so. Who would've believed them?"

"No one. Besides, they wouldn't tell even if they knew they'd be believed."

"There, you've made my point for me. Maybe no one else has had quite the same experience, but I've heard some pretty wild tales on my rounds in this city."

"And I'm sure not all of them have anything to do with why we're in Rome."

"I won't deny that."

"Score a rare one for me."

"Getting back to what I was trying to say, take a good look around you. This may be the best restaurant in this city. And there are plenty of good ones as long as you stay away from those pricey tourist traps near the Via Veneto. Eating here is more than just dining. It's almost a philosophy."

"I suppose you're going to tell me people tell you ghost stories here, too."

"Again, your body is in the right place, but your brain isn't. You recognize our 'Il Professore' but no one else. Most of the people who eat here live in this neighborhood and come here more often than they go to church or probably even pray. Even though it's halfway between the Vatican City and the Roman Coliseum, this side street is just enough out of the way so that only the occasional adventurous tourist finds it. And,

'Il Professore' certainly is a living advertisement for this place. He started coming here when Giorgio's father ran it. By the way, he hasn't been here every night for twenty-seven years. Once or twice a year he asks Giorgio for permission to try another restaurant, but always comes back after a few nights because he likes this one better. Do you know why?"

"He likes the food and he can afford the prices."

"Yes, but it's also his comfort zone. He's lonely. Never married, no family. But he can talk to the owner and the waiters here. He pays a lump sum for his meals at the end of each week. Probably gets a frequent diner discount. Everyone here is relaxed, the way they might be at home. The amazing thing is that even with every table taken and so many people talking and laughing, the noise level isn't bad. It's so inviting that even the most discriminating cat would have no problem curling up wherever it wanted."

"You want me to relax? After all that's happened. I can't forget it so easily. It happened to me, not you.

"Rome can have a relaxing effect on you, even with those annoying scooters and the cars. It's amazing how easy it is to find what you're looking for when there's no sense of urgency. I can't talk to more than one person in a day and sometimes it takes two or three visits just to convince some local priest that I'm not on a Inquisition witch hunt before he'll trust me enough to tell me what I want to know or at least point me in the right direction."

"I told you that you enjoy playing detective."

"Sort of. But, if we do this together, say once or twice a week, we can cover a lot more ground together than I can by myself. And who knows? We just might pick up a few interesting tidbits."

"I'll think about it. But for now it's somewhat academic. Cardinal Verano either won't or doesn't want to talk shop with me. Except for Father Shane, I get what seems to be the polite brush-off by anyone else I try to talk to at the Vatican."

"How is Father Shane these days?"

"Apparently not the boy wonder he once was. He seems to have come down a peg or two since Virginia. He could be a great help, but he always says he's too busy with other projects. I think he's reluctant to get involved. Maybe he's afraid to step on my toes. Ironic, isn't it?"

*EARTHLY SPIRITS*

"What is?"

"He was so eager to step all over me back in Virginia. Before you ask, while he knows a lot about what happened, I didn't tell him everything. So he doesn't know as much as he'd probably like. Which isn't much different than my situation. I still don't know exactly what they expect me to do here that hasn't already been done."

"Maybe tomorrow you'll know more."

"My meeting with Cardinal Grosetti?"

"What else? Anything you write will have to go through his office at some point."

"For Vatican approval? Or clerical censorship?"

"Both. If the head of the Congregation of the Doctrine of the Faith can't explain it all to you, who can? It's amazing how you can bury the Church's sins of the past with a name change. I wouldn't be surprised if some of those robed relics you see walking around the Vatican corridors would like to see its name and purpose changed back to what it was ages ago."

"The Holy Roman Inquisition."

"Just be careful what you say when you go there."

"Why? Have they brought back the rack and the iron maiden?"

# CHAPTER 2

Interviews can be intimidating.

Cardinal Grosetti discovered that he had a natural talent for intimidation early in his clerical career, listening to confessions as a parish priest. Over the years, he had molded it into a personal art form so subtle that not even his targets were consciously aware that they were being intimidated. He always practiced his art with a cordial smile. In his younger days it was mostly in the confessional where penitent sinners could be threatened with damnation by his utterance of a carefully chosen word or in the rectory where recalcitrant altar boys could be cowed with a stern glance. At the Vatican, it had been in mostly whatever office he was given to occupy. Now, aging with a body that had not responded kindly to years of physical neglect and a mind that had been ripened by years of expertise in games of Vatican political intrigue, Grosetti always tried to choose the moment when he would have a home field advantage.

The cardinal's home field was his personal office. It was the power center of a small bureaucracy that officially was known as the Congregation for the Doctrine of the Faith. Like a few others before him and some in other Vatican bureaucracies, Grosetti had made it into a personal fiefdom. It was the kingdom that he had come to believe that he had been born to inherit.

*EARTHLY SPIRITS*

Only the Secretariat of State was more important than the Congregation for the Doctrine of the Faith in the departmental pecking order of the Vatican's Roman Curia. Beneath them was an assortment of offices such as the Institutes of Consecrated Life and Societies of Apostolic Life and the Congregation for the Causes of Saints. A judicial division included the Apostolic Penitentiary and the Tribunal of the Roman Rota, which heard appeals. Lastly, was a variety of commissions and pontifical councils whose many responsibilities included economics, property administration, migrants, the media, special events and even relations with non-believers.

In the end, all had to bend to whatever orders the pope might issue. But, like all government leaders, even the pontiff was subject to making decisions sometimes based on the whims of advisers, then later enduring the delays of implementation that were forced to navigate the red tape webs woven by Vatican bureaucrats.

Despite its ranking below the Secretariat of State, the Congregation for the Doctrine of the Faith was the ideal place for a man of Cardinal Grosetti's talents. For Grosetti, it was the only place.

The Congregation's primary duty was to promote and preserve the Roman Catholic faith. It issued documents defining morality. It investigated anyone claiming to have experienced divine revelations. It even dared to clarify statements made by the pope, making certain that what the pontiff really meant did not reflect negatively on his infallibility. It would not be good form to leave the interpretation of papal pronouncements to outsiders or even to other Vatican experts. Most important was the section staffed with trained zealots who studied every word written, and many of those spoke, by Catholic theologians for meanings that could be considered harmful to the Church. When found, these infractions were called "erroneous" or "perilous," depending on their severity. Clerics who refused to recant faced discipline ranging from rebuke to defrocking. Still, those penalties were less harsh than those the Church had meted out to heretics of the distant past.

Everyone at the Vatican and most visitors to the Congregation for the Doctrine of the Faith knew that it had experienced several name changes over the centuries. In its early days, it had been called the Holy Roman

Inquisition. Those whose historical education was lacking were casually informed by Grosetti of the Congregation's past while being careful to distance it from the more notorious Spanish Inquisition. This casual reference was complemented by the powerful subtlety of the trappings of Grosetti's office, which he had personally chosen and arranged.

The most striking feature was the cardinal, himself. He never greeted anyone standing. Instead, he sat behind a massive desk set as far back as possible from the entrance door to his office. Some of the cardinals who had visited him there caustically remarked to each other that he was trying to recreate the torturous long walk that Christ was forced to take while bearing the cross of his crucifixion on his shoulders. When visitors reached Grosetti's desk they were supposed to feel that they had arrived at Mount Golgotha, where invisible cross, hammer and spikes awaited them. The cardinals kept these remarks to themselves. In the Vatican, some forms of humor could be hazardous to ambition. Though the office was substantial, Grosetti's physical bulk had grown so large that it seemed to overflow from behind the desk and spill into the room. The cardinal would ask visitors to sit opposite him in front of the desk on chairs whose numbers were pre-arranged to accommodate just those who were expected. There were no extra seats and no unscheduled visitors.

Cardinal Grosetti would have preferred spending this late afternoon on what was a perfect late spring day in the Campo Santo Teutonico in the Vatican Gardens. But he was expecting a visitor. He could have arranged the meeting for his favorite outdoor retreat, but had calculated that he could leave a more lasting impression of authority on his visitor if they met at his office. Because the visitor, an unassuming Benedictine monk from a failed monastery in the backwoods of the United States, was coming alone, only one chair was set. Four months earlier, Brother Gerald would not have gotten more than a simple nod had the two men passed each other on the street, let alone an invitation to come to the cardinal's office. Eventually, the two would have to meet. For Grosetti, curiosity and anxiety ruled that it should be sooner than later.

Brother Gerald could not be intimidated. Years at a dead end in the now demised Blessed Skyline Abbey in the foothills of Virginia's Blue Ridge Mountains had taught the monk that survival was nothing more

*EARTHLY SPIRITS*

than a routine. He was forty-eight years old and believed that everything that could be done to him already had been. Still, when he arrived he could not help but be impressed.

A self-trained expert observer, Gerald took measured steps into the room, quickly taking it all in on his way along the mottled brown-and-white pattern marble tiled floor to the only chair other than the padded throne-like seat that held the bulky red-robed frame of Cardinal Grosetti. The smiling cardinal was aware that his visitor was scanning the surroundings and kept quiet until the monk stood just in front of him. He extended his right hand and Gerald responded by kissing his ring. He asked his visitor to sit in the chair across the desk from him. Grosetti then waved an arm in a sweeping motion.

"Take your time enjoying it," he said in perfect English. "I personally supervised the décor. I wanted it to look more like a den with character than one of those colorless offices. That was years ago. Of course, a few modern touches have been added since then. Even the Vatican has to go with the times."

A laptop computer and a cell phone on the desk were the only recent touches Brother Gerald noticed. But then, neither seemed out of place, especially the cell phone. Everyone in Italy seemed to have one. They had become so annoying that many restaurant owners in Rome insisted that they be turned off. In some eateries, they hung on racks at the door and were returned to their owners on leaving like pistols once were in the American Old West.

A picture of the pope should have dominated the room, but it did not. The pontiff was there all right, as large as life and framed in gilt on the wall behind the monk, to the right of the door where he had entered. On the wall where the pope should have been enshrined, an oversized copy of the center panel of the Last Judgment by Hieronymus Bosch, the late medieval painter of the grotesque, rose halfway up to the high painted ceiling behind the cardinal's desk. It was an eye-catcher for any visitor. The heavenly saints and angels that had been depicted centuries earlier in a wall-to-wall living color mural on the ceiling were no match for the demons of Bosch.

Gerald had little doubt why the Bosch work was set facing him. It was intended, he reasoned, to remind visitors where they were. He wondered if the pope's placement on the wall behind him skirted on the fringes of Vatican protocol.

"Are you familiar with Bosch?" Grosetti asked.

"Somewhat, your eminence," Gerald answered. "I've seen some of his works in books."

"Nothing quite as impressive as this one?"

"It's the Purgatory panel from Bosch's Last Judgment, isn't it?"

"Very good. Most visitors know it's Bosch's work, but not which one. There's no need to be culturally modest here, my son."

"It was an educated guess."

"The Holy Father also has an appreciation for Bosch. That's one reason his picture is on the opposite wall, so he can admire it from there, metaphorically, of course. The other is that having his picture on the wall opposite my desk allows me to look at it for inspiration from the Holy Father whenever the need arises, as it so often does."

Brother Gerald was surprised at how far the cardinal was willing to stretch the truth. Grosetti was either a blowhard or a game player. Maybe Father William was right. Gerald should be careful with his words. Before he could find something to say, Grosetti spoke again.

"Don't rush. Go ahead and soak up all the detail you want. It's not often that I receive visitors who have an appreciation for genuine art."

The monk knew that art appreciation was the smaller part of why Bosch's Last Judgment had been placed behind Grosetti. It was there only to remind visitors that they were in the presence of the head of what once was the office of the Holy Roman Inquisition. While the cardinal might not be able to order their internment in a dungeon fitted with torture devices, he could make some of them just nervous enough to be more truthful than they might have been otherwise.

The work depicted Christ in the center with Mary and Joseph above each of his shoulders, and six apostles on each side of the Messiah. The contrast between these holiest of images and the scene below is powerful in imagery and color. They look down from heavenly clouds on a fiery landscape of red earth and burning walls that reveal the sinister depths of Bosch's imagination. Demons are practicing dreadful tortures and

*EARTHLY SPIRITS*

mutilations on sinners. Liquid is forced into the mouth of a man from a cask being refilled from the bowels of another. A sinner in a large pan is fried over a flame by a demon with a whimsical sense of the horrific—the poor soul is to join an egg as part of the monster's breakfast. Another demon rides a naked woman like a horse. Other sinners are being shod by a demon blacksmith. The torments seem endless for everyone except for a man being led off the edge of the painting by an angel. As they make their escape from Purgatory, they are pursued by a demon armed with a crossbow.

The rest of the office seemed less mesmerizing, yet it was arranged to impress visitors with the sense of the power that lived there.

To Gerald, Cardinal Grosetti's desk was as oversized as the man himself. Easily eight feet long, it looked more like a showpiece table awaiting rescue from an antique shop that catered to the rich and famous. Oak legs carved in the shape of tree trunks entwined by vines supported a white marble top. Beneath the top, the lower part of the cardinal's red robe was plainly visible, creating an illusion of a man whose size was even greater than it was. Nothing sat in the center between the two men. The laptop computer had been pushed to the cardinal's left, along with his cell phone. A red leatherette file folder seemed dwarfed at Grosetti's right. It looked as though it had been carefully placed just behind a massive four-inch-thick Bible. Bound in brown leather, the book bore the wording "Holy Bible" in gold lettering on the cover and the spine. A gold fastener with a small lock kept its gilt-edged pages from being browsed by anyone without the key. It was the sort of book that would have been at home on a coffee table, to be admired but never read.

The walls were paneled with heavy dark oak, some of it carved, contrasting sharply with the bright ceiling and marble floor. Halfway up the wall to the left, oak bookcases were filled with old books, most of them bound in leather and protected by glass doors. If anyone looked closely, they would have seen that most of the titles were in Latin. A gold clock that Gerald guessed probably was from the French Enlightenment period was set on top of the center bookcase. It still worked. A large cross with the figure of Christ dominated the opposite wall, which included another door to a smaller room, in turn leading to the cardinal's private bathroom. The fittings on both doors were gold. On the floor between the second door and the far right corner, a brass pole held the Vatican flag, hanging limply so that its white and yellow fields with their crossed keys seemed to be playing hide-and-seek with anyone looking at them. The only other furniture in the room was a small cabinet to the cardinal's right. On top were an ersatz 19th Century telephone with touch-tone dialing, a large round antique glass ashtray and an oak cigar box, also with gold fittings. Most of the light came from a huge Italianate glass chandelier, whose weight seemed to threaten the stability of the ceiling. Other light came from above the bookcases via a pair of wall lamps that matched the chandeliers. A third wall lamp hung above Bosch's Purgatory but its only function was to illuminate the painted warning to what awaited sinners.

"Can I offer you a cigar?" Grosetti asked, reaching for the box. "They're from Havana."

"No thank you, your eminence," Brother Gerald replied. "I don't smoke."

"Then I'll pass, too." He said the words with a slight trace of disappointment, then added a lie. "It's a bad habit, but I make it a personal rule never to smoke alone."

The cardinal then offered the monk a brandy, which he kept along with other expensive beverages inside the lower part of the cabinet. Gerald politely declined. Again, Grosetti feigned mild disappointment, this time with an almost silent sigh. Gerald wondered if Grosetti was trying to soften him up. First the carrot, then the stick.

Cardinal Grosetti did not give his visitor much time to make up his mind. He reached for the red folder, opened it and pretended to read from the top sheet, tapping the desk with a pudgy forefinger. He flipped the sheet, glanced at the next piece of paper, then closed the folder. It all took less than a minute, convincing Brother Gerald that it had been part of an act, that the cardinal already was familiar with its contents. It had been a poorly acted scene by an otherwise skilled actor.

"Very interesting," Grosetti said. He shoved the folder aside, behind the Bible, folded his hands in front of him, and looked the monk straight in the eyes.

It was time to get down to business.

# CHAPTER 3

One of Rome's best views was from the small stone pavilion at the top of the Parco Gianicolense, the city's sprawling botanical gardens. It also was an oasis of peace, especially near the turn of the summer, when the green foliage was lush and flowers dormant in the cooler months were in full bloom. There were no cafes, shops or street vendors, a sharp contrast to the bustle of the larger piazzas below where tourists filing into them from the confusing maze of connecting streets often appeared to vie with locals to see who could make the most noise.

Father William and Brother Gerald sat on a bench outside the pavilion, taking in the view between pauses in what mostly was a one-way conversation. The densely packed buildings below shielded the Tiber River from searching eyes. But much of the rest of the city on the other side was spread out in a sweeping panorama of tiled red and orange rooftops, and the stone towers of historic churches, some of which could lay claim to having hosted miracles.

"That tower on the left is Sant Andrea della Valle," Father William said. "It was built in the Seventeenth Century. Only St. Peter's Basilica has a higher dome. Then, going across to the right, you come to the Gesu, which was built by the Jesuits in the Sixteenth Century. Next is Santa Maria Maggiore. It goes way back to the Fifth Century. The story goes that the Virgin Mary appeared to Pope Liberius and told him where to build the church. He never saw as much as the ground broken. It wasn't until nearly a hundred years later that Sixtus III was able to start construction. The last one on the right is San Carlo ai Catinari, also built in the Seventeenth Century."

"You almost sound like an experienced tourist guide. I suppose you've been to all of them," Gerald said.

"Only Santa Maria Maggiore. There are so many churches in this city, it hasn't been possible to see all of them in the four months we've been in Rome. It's a lot easier to get to see the priests at the smaller local churches that you can't identify from here."

Brother Gerald sat bent forward, elbows propped up on his knees. His heavily knuckled hands were tightly wrapped into fists that supported his chin. His dull brown eyes gazed straight ahead at the panorama under heavy lids that always looked like they were ready to close. He had hardly moved since sitting down.

"Am I boring you?" Father William asked.

"Father, I appreciate the history lesson and the view," Gerald replied. "But I didn't think we were coming all the way up here to study the skyline." He glanced at his wristwatch. "We've been sitting here for nearly ten minutes."

"So, you're still Brother Time," William said. You should get rid of that watch and those monk's garments and sandals, and stop referring to yourself as 'Brother.' You're not in a monastery anymore. Sometimes I think you regret being born too late to have been a nineteen-sixties hippie, even though you look pathetic enough to be one. It's about time you left the past behind you and became a civilized priest."

"I'm a creature of habit."

"Now, if you were a nun that would be funny."

"I don't see anything to laugh about."

"If I stop seeing humor in most things I might as well let my brain surrender and feel at home with the rest of what's left of my creaking old body. It wasn't easy for me walking all the way to the top of this place."

"We could have talked somewhere else."

"Probably. But as much as I've come to love Rome, what I've been

*EARTHLY SPIRITS*

hearing in some of the places I've been has made me a little paranoid. No one can hear us up here because hardly anyone ever comes all the way to this spot. Besides, these gardens have a peace that you can't find anywhere else in Rome, not even at the Vatican. Well, except maybe for the Vatican Gardens, but I'm still trying to find a good enough excuse to get me admitted there."

"What's there to hear? I still don't know anything more about what I'm supposed to be doing than I did since before my meeting with Cardinal Grosetti. That was three days ago and I still feel like I'm fumbling around in the dark."

"I may be able to shed a little light in your darkness."

"More gossip from the Vatican grapevine?"

"Did you do any better with Cardinal Grosetti?"

"You've got me there. It was more like a fishing expedition than an interview and I was the fish."

"What sort of questions did he ask?"

"That's just it. They were all vague. He didn't say anything that even remotely indicated he knew more than I did. That is, he knows what my assignment is and that it came from someone pretty high up, but apparently nothing more. He wanted to know about my personal history, how I liked Rome, was I comfortable at the Vatican, whether I was getting enough help, when would I have a rough draft outline ready. None of it seemed very specific. Oh, he knows what we're supposed to be doing here, but he doesn't know why. I think he's surprised that I was chosen for this assignment considering my rather bleak background. He wanted to know what you were doing, too. Naturally, I told him. He had a fancy folder with some papers in it, but hardly looked at them while I was there. Half the time he talked about the difficulties of old age and his ailments. It was more like he was just trying to make conversation and hoping I'd somehow I'd slip or respond with something that might interest him. I think he was more disappointed than me."

"What kind of papers?"

"I don't know. He never took them out of the folder."

"What did you tell him?"

"Everything, except for that night at the abbey. You know, when the dying ended. But I don't think anything I said was new to him."

"He must have given you some sort of guidance."

"I suggested it, but his response was that I should be patient and something about the wheels of Vatican bureaucracy turning slowly. I was there for nearly ninety minutes and the only thing I know more than I did before is that he probably knows even less than me. Unless that's what he wants me to think."

"Look, I'm just as surprised as you. I thought for sure you'd come back from your meeting with Cardinal Grosetti just bursting with information. I'd think he'd be right on top of it considering his position and the influence that comes with it. You're not holding out on me, are you?"

"How can you even suggest that? You know me better, especially after all we've been through."

"I was just speaking rhetorically."

"All right, what's the gossip buzzing along your grapevine?"

"Same as usual. No one really knows why we came to Rome, except to do 'important' research. But I still can't get over what you've said about Cardinal Grosetti not knowing much more. Everyone I talk to believes he's one of the two or three most powerful men in the Vatican, after the pope. If he does know more than he's letting on, he's playing his cards very close to the vest. Anyone who's doing any sort of research here has met him at least once and has to keep in touch with a couple of people in that bureaucracy he runs. You're the exception. Even word about the most sensitive issues leaks out. But we've been here four months and we don't even know who you're supposed to report to. They just rolled out the red carpet for our arrival, then left us alone. Have you noticed the way people look at us inside the Vatican? Like we're freaks in a circus sideshow."

"You haven't told anyone about why we're here."

"Of course not. Hints are dropped but no one asks anything direct. They're probably just being polite or have been conditioned to mind their own business. The longer I stay here and the more I hear, the more I can't help but feel that the Vatican has become nothing more than a vast conspiracy designed to keep what true believers are left happy. The written instructions Cardinal Sforza left for you were very explicit. More like a set of confidential orders. Obviously he knows. He's the only one who may somehow be linked to Nicholas."

The mention of the name sent a shiver through Brother Gerald. Nicholas, the man with no past who had come to Gerald in a dream to confess that he was the killer of four monks at Blessed Skyline Abbey. The man with an encircled letter 'N' tattooed in red on his left arm. The tattoo that should have been there, but was gone as though it never had been there after they found his body near a footpath in the Blue Ridge Mountains. The man whose death gave the police a convenient excuse to close the case of the deaths at the abbey. The man who claimed in the dream to be Lucifer. The man whose name he never wanted to hear again.

"Sorry, Gerald," Father William said. "I didn't mean to mention that name. I'll try not to let it happen again."

"It's all right, Father," Gerald said. "Maybe it's better if I hear it once in a while. I'm going to have to get over it eventually. If I don't, what am I going to do when Christmas comes, forget about Saint Nicholas?"

"Now that's the way to start thinking. Incidentally, I didn't mean to imply that Cardinal Sforza had any direct connection to you-know-who. It could be any of the cardinals, priests or even laymen who have influence at the Vatican. Everybody seems to have advisers. Sforza and Grosetti may have the ear of the pope, but so do a lot of others. Somebody is always advising somebody in that giant inner sanctum."

"Well, Sforza's the one who signed the letter that practically ordered me to Rome. Maybe he also was the one who assigned Father Shane to investigate demonic possession back in Virginia. Shane certainly doesn't seem to want to talk about it anymore and that's almost a total reversal of how he was when the Vatican sent him to snoop around Blessed Skyline."

"You might be right. But from what I've been led to understand, Cardinal Grosetti probably was involved in that. They say you can't trace anything that could be embarrassing to the Church back to him. If it's true, he's probably going to take a lot of secrets to the grave."

"Christ, what have we gotten ourselves into?"

"Pretty cushy jobs, I'd say. Except for maybe the career men or the truest of believers, I can't imagine not being the envy of any priest who knew what we were doing."

"You mean nothing."

"No. You're going to rewrite theological history."

"A politically correct history."

"Absolutely. You can't glamorize the devil. It may not land you in the dungeon anymore, but if you don't get it theologically correct, you could be consigned to clerical oblivion."

"That wouldn't be all that bad."

"Maybe not in Rome, but the Church has plenty of wilds where it sends priests who it considers to be non-clerics. By the way, have you thought about the suggestion I made at dinner the other night?"

"No, but as of now, I'm about ready to take you up on it. You may be right about me spending too much time digging through old papers. It's starting to wear on me. I probably could use a little fresh air."

"So, this park has had an effect on you, after all."

"No, Cardinal Grosetti, Cardinal Verano and the elusive Cardinal Sforza have."

"Then, they've done you more good than you realize. How about startiing on a new schedule next week? You can spend some time researching the devil in the Secret Archives and a couple of days looking for him in local parishes. And, maybe in a café or museum, too."

"I'm not going to run from one place to another."

"Definitely not. I've been limping ever since I suffered that stroke years ago. Let me tell you, though. Being here has had some sort of restorative effect on me. I move a little faster than I did even after I retired as abbot to that cabin in the Virginia woods. Now that the abbey's been sold and the brothers scattered to the four winds, I wonder if the Boudreau family sold the cabin."

The corners of the old priest's eyes caught something. He smiled and nodded to his left.

"Not as fast as that woman, of course," he said.

The two men watched her walk uphill along a path that curved between poplar and pine trees. They could not notice that she was breathing heavily, but even if they had, there were other signs that she was in a hurry to get to her destination, which seemed to be where they were sitting. Her swiftly moving legs battered the lower folds of her flower-patterned blue dress so that it fluttered like a flag in the wind. Her long auburn hair bounced in lively animation on her softly molded shoulders with each stride. Her blue handbag swung from its strap in her right hand like an erratic pendulum. She was heading straight for them in double time, something most Italian young women had little trouble making in high-heeled shoes, even along old cobbled streets.

When she reached the top of the hill, she quickened her pace and passed right in front of the two without acknowledging them. William and Gerald turned their heads to see why she was in such a hurry.

"She's going to be disappointed," Father William said.

The woman stopped about twenty feet past them at the Porta San Pacrazio, the gate where the Via Garibaldi meets the Passeggiata di Gianicolo at the Piazza le Aurelio, one of the highest points in Rome. A man in a dark gray business suit was waiting on the other side of the iron fence. Both tried to open the gate but it would not budge.

"There's one lunchtime assignation that's going to be delayed," William said. "That gate always is locked this time of day."

After exchanging a long handclasp and some words through the gate, the man turned and started downhill outside the park. The woman also turned, again passed the two priests as though they were not there and began retracing her steps in the long descent downhill at the same speed at which she had climbed it."

"We should be going, too," Father William said. "I'm getting hungry. Giorgio's place is only a couple of blocks from the park and should be open for lunch by the time we get there."

"That sounds good to me," Gerald replied.

"Even if my legs could make it, I still wouldn't go as fast as those two lovers."

"Me neither."

"Maybe there's hope for you, after all."

They rose from the bench and started along the path. Just before it curved downward, a dark-haired young man wearing blue jeans and a white T-shirt gave them a nod, passed them and continued downhill through the park. He was moving about as fast as the woman who had preceded him.

"If I hadn't seen it with my own eyes, I wouldn't have believed it," Father William said.

"Seen what?" Brother Gerald asked.

"Two miracles in less than a week."

"What is it this time?"

"You can be a dunce. It's that young fellow who's outdistancing us."

"What about him?"

"That fence is six feet high and the only way he could have gotten inside the park up here is through the gate, and it was locked."

# CHAPTER 4

Cardinal Grosetti had a sixth sense that was fed by three qualities. Two were suspicion and secrecy. For more than a week, his extra sense had been telling him that something important was happening. It had to be something very important if he knew nothing about it. So important that no more than two or three others at the Vatican might know anything. Cardinal Sforza could be one of them. Perhaps someone close to Sforza was another. He did not consider the Holy Father. There was no need for anyone to distract him now. The pope would know only when whoever else knew also felt that he was ready to be told.

Grosetti's third quality was intrigue and no one in the Vatican was more skilled at it. He had developed that natural talent under a master, the late Cardinal Brazzo, his predecessor at the Congregation for the Doctrine of the Faith. Long before he died, Brazzo had earned the nickname of Cardinal Machiavelli, which his contemporaries rarely spoke above a whisper. Grosetti rightly believed that he had surpassed his tutor some time ago. He had been head of the Congregation for nearly twenty years, plenty of time to sharply hone the skills that he had brought with him to the post. Now pushing seventy-five years of age in a body that sometimes felt like a century old, he still could play at intrigue with the enthusiasm of a young man. He would not have objected to being called Cardinal Machiavelli.

Though he was not sure that Brother Gerald was part of whatever secret was being kept from him, the monk became the cardinal's logical starting point. After all, the monk had not told him anything more than he already knew about why Gerald had been summoned from what the cardinal felt was an earned obscurity to Rome. But it seemed obvious that the Benedictine's research into the history of the devil must have something to do with the events that preceded the closing of Blessed Skyline Abbey in Virginia. Four monks dead, the abbey sold to a vacation resort developer. No, it could not be simple coincidence. There was something more.

Brother Gerald's personnel file, his personal history, his seeming innocence that bordered on evasiveness was only the skin of the man. Grosetti wanted the flesh and bones that he felt was being hidden beneath it. It was bad enough that Vatican insiders were keeping something from him, but the monk had some nerve not sharing whatever secrets he knew. If he was doing research, eventually he would have to put it in writing. Surely, he was aware that, except for personal correspondence and notes, anything that any priest wrote would go to the Congregation. Cardinal Grosetti would not be kept in the dark any longer. But he could not be detected sniffing around. That left him with two resources that could do the dirty work while he kept his hands clean and let his reputation insulate him from potential repercussions.

One was Father Monahan. Years earlier, Monahan had been recruited by Cardinal Grosetti after being summoned to Rome during an investigation of doctrinal irregularities that a few of the priest's parishioners had brought to the attention of diocesan superiors. The summons to Rome was unusual for someone who was only a parish priest. But Grosetti had seen an opportunity he had long wanted to grasp. Monahan was pliable enough to agree to recant from the pulpit of his church. As his reward, the priest was allowed more than the usual flexibility in running what had become a very prosperous parish in a rural area of Virginia, where Catholics were a minority of the Christian population. But, like so many others, the reward came with a price. The priest became the cardinal's most trusted set of eyes and ears in the eastern United States.

*EARTHLY SPIRITS*

It was Monahan who had provided the cardinal with periodic information on Blessed Skyline Abbey and anything else that he was asked to look into at the parishes nearby. He even had made contacts at the diocesan office. At first, there was little to report on the abbey. After Father William retired and was succeeded as abbot by Father Dennis, Monahan's reporting activity increased. When the monks started dying in numbers, he would pass on information to Cardinal Grosetti two and three times a week, at first by mail, later by courier and even telephone.

After the abbey was closed, that information flow abruptly ended. Father Monahan could add nothing about what happened to the Benedictine monks who were dispersed after the monastery gates were shut for the last time. He did not even know that Brother Gerald and Father William had gone to Rome. He never had been given the opportunity to uncover the personalities under the monastic robes of the two men and the other brothers. That would be his next assignment. In particular, Cardinal Grosetti wanted to know everything there was to be known about Brother Gerald that was not in the monk's personnel file.

Three brothers were in easy reach of Father Monahan. During the last days of the abbey, Brothers Albert and James retreated to the comfort of the parishes that had been in their charge for several years. There, they worked side-by-side on bingo nights, each getting a piece of the action. Brother Robert had moved down the road from Blessed Skyline and now was a clerk in the diocesan office. Monahan could visit each of them, making courtesy calls under the guise of wanting to talk over old times. Since all three priests had known Brother Gerald for several years, he also might be able to uncover a few clues that Grosetti could use to piece together the puzzle that nagged at him. Monahan could wrap it all up in a week.

A fourth priest who had served briefly at the abbey also was easily in Monahan's reach, but the cardinal felt it best to bypass him for now. Father Dennis no longer was a scheming abbot. He had been reduced to the status of pastor of a small church that had been losing attendance and money. It was an obscure post chosen to keep him in obscurity. But, the resourceful Dennis had unexpectedly increased attendance and revenue. At the same time he was starting to churn up a new set of waves that was making his diocesan superiors nervous. No, Father Dennis probably did not know much about Brother Gerald. Besides, he could be shrewd enough to see through Father Monahan and that could start people wondering why someone should be interested in a faceless monk. What little Dennis might know was not worth the risk. At least, not yet.

Another source of information was at Cardinal Grosetti's beck and call.

Once a shining star of the Vatican, Father George Shane seemed to be slowly sliding into oblivion since his return from Virginia, where he had been sent to investigate the deaths of the monks at Blessed Skyline Abbey. The young American priest still had access to the Vatican Secret Archives, though now he had to request it rather than come and go as he once pleased. He still was the Vatican's leading authority on demonic possession. But requests for his lectures and consultations on the subject had become rare. Father Shane suspected that it was because his report did not live up to Vatican expectations.

Despite his fall from grace, Father Shane's loyalties had not been shaken. He had an occasional doubt about his calling, but his faith never wavered. His faith was as much of a strength as his desire to learn everything there was to know about demonic possession. He did have one weakness—a lack of Vatican political acumen. That could be fatal to the career of a priest hoping to climb the rungs of the clerical ladder. To an academic priest like Shane, it was something that allowed the politically savvy to use him as a carpenter would a hammer.

Today, Cardinal Grosetti would discard the hammer and offer Father Shane the opportunity to reach for the brass ring that the priest felt had been eluding him ever since his return from Blessed Skyline Abbey to the Vatican seven months ago.

Except for their greeting at the main entrance to the Vatican Gardens and the exchange of simple pleasantries about the fine weather, the two men walked in silence along the path, nodding informally to a passing cardinal. Surely the priest had to be curious as to why he had been summoned. Grosetti would let him ponder in silence until they had reached the destination he had chosen.

When they neared the walls of the Campo Santo Teutonico, Grosetti broke the silence.

*EARTHLY SPIRITS*

"Back to where we first met last fall," he said. "But you must have known we were coming here."

"I hoped we were, your eminence," Shane replied.

They walked through the opening in the wall. Inside, it was just as Father Shane had remembered it. Blooming oleander added just the right touch of bright color to the dominating green of broad-leafed Canary Island palm, cedar of Lebanon and bay laurel trees, all groomed by expert gardeners. Nuns were busy tending the cemetery, where graves had risen to four levels above ground by the demand of burial space for Roman Catholics from the old German states of Charlemagne who died in Rome.

Grosetti led the way to the empty stone bench that the two men had occupied on their only other visit to the cemetery garden. As he always did, the cardinal took nearly a minute, fighting the pains and stiffness in his joints, to seat his large aging body in relative comfort. Once seated, he motioned for Father Shane to join him. Suddenly, the cardinal was jovial, poking fun at the excesses of youth that had contributed to the ongoing collapse of his physical self. Shane had heard it all before, but pretended it was all new to him. Grosetti smiled at the priest, not malevolently, but with a deliberate touch of benign disbelief so that the younger man would know that his polite discretion did not fool the cardinal.

The smile had its intended effect. Shane had innocently sought to make the old man feel as though he was passing down words of aged wisdom. Like so many words passed down to much younger ears, the wisdom that came with them was as dubious as their originality. The only guarantee they came with was repetition. The young priest should have known better from his first experience with Grosetti. Had Shane never been given that assignment, which he could not have rejected, he might still be doing what he enjoyed most, what had caught the eye of someone at the Vatican even while he still had been a student at the seminary. Instead, now he worked in the shadows and would grasp at almost any straw that would help pull him back into the light. Perhaps the cardinal was going to offer that straw. If he did, Shane knew it would not be for free. The cardinal must want something. Why else had he arranged this meeting? Shane would be careful, but not weak. He had learned that every word Cardinal Grosetti's spoke seemed to hint as though it should be kept secret.

The silence that passed between the two men lasted fewer than thirty seconds. Like all such silences, its effect was one-sided. Father Shane suspected it was intentional and that Grosetti would decide when to make the first move of whatever game he was playing. Finally, the cardinal nodded his head toward the center of the garden where nuns were busy tending to the final resting places of the dead.

"They do take their work seriously," he said. "Look, not only do they carefully lay flowers at the graves, they even pull the smallest weeds from the soil. What do you think of that?"

"They must have a deep devotion to perfection," Shane replied.

"It certainly seems so. Do you know who they are?"

"The Sisters of Christian Chartity."

"Very good. I doubt that every cardinal knows that."

"And they all come from Paderborn, Germany."

"Now that's something most cardinals probably don't know. Then you haven't forgotten our first meeting last fall?"

"How could I forget it, your eminence?"

Father Shane's choice of words surprised the cardinal. Their meaning seemed to signal impertinence, but he detected none in the priest's tone. He paused only for a few seconds, convincing himself that the priest's words had no meaning beyond face value. Meanwhile, Shane began to feel relaxed. He had made a a deliberate move of his own with superb subtlety and guessed that Cardinal Grosetti was trying to figure out how to counter it.

"Enough about the sisters," Grosetti said. He had lowered his voice, though there was no one within hearing distance. "I felt it was time to have a talk about the report you did on your investigation of what happened at Blessed Skyline Abbey. You must have been wondering why it's taken so long for you to hear anything about it since it's been almost six months since you turned it in."

"Yes, I have."

"Well, things don't always move as fast as we want them to. I'm sure you've heard stories about the Vatican bureaucracy."

*EARTHLY SPIRITS*

"I don't pay much attention to gossip, your eminence. But I do know that the Church has to carefully consider every possible implication of any event before reaching a conclusion."

"That's right, my son. And, not everyone reaches the same conclusion. Some people even differ on the implications. Such is the nature of the clerical calling. Everyone seems to have his own interpretation of every phrase."

"Has that been a problem with what I submitted?"

"Not at all. You did a fine piece of work considering that you were bound by the constraints of time. If I'd had my way, I wouldn't have waited until the third brother died to send you to Blessed Skyline. You would have been there after the second death."

"More time certainly would have helped."

"Still, there has been some debate over your conclusions."

In the end, Father Shane had played it safe. He went with the official police version, which was multiple homicide. The murders of four Benedictine monks were blamed on an amnesiac drifter who had been given the name Nicholas. His body was found alongside a trail in the Blue Ridge Mountains a few days after a fourth monk died in a fire at the abbey. Nicholas had died of liver failure. The police, whose investigation was lax, concluded that he had faked his amnesia in order to be sheltered at the abbey. His true identity never was known. He never had been interrogated. There was no arrest. There was no trial. No one could explain how the murders had been committed. No motive ever was established. It all seemed too convenient even though the dying ended with his death.

The unexpected ending to the mystery left Father Shane with little choice. He had not found any evidence of the demonic possession that he believed he had been sent to Virginia to unmask. He often had wondered since his return to Rome whether his report's omission of its possibility was a mistake. No one questioned his continuing research into demonic possession. But, few seemed interested in listening to him lecture about it since then. Until now. And it was no one less than the powerful head of the Congregation for the Doctrine of the Faith, and he was raising the subject with overtones of disappointment. Rather than wait for Cardinal

Grosetti to explain what he meant by the "debate" that his report had stirred, he went straight to the heart of the matter. His directness caught the old cardinal off guard.

"By their very nature all conclusions trigger debate, your eminence," he said. "I'd appreciate knowing as much as you can tell me."

"No one truly disagrees with your findings," Grosetti replied. "But a few questions have been raised."

"What questions?"

"There have been suggestions that the background summaries of the monks that were in your report could be more detailed."

"I tried to include what I thought was pertinent."

"I understand, Father. As far as I'm concerned, no one could have done better considering the limitations on your time and the sudden end to the affair. I'm perfectly content with the way you handled everything."

"Then, someone else wants more."

It was just the answer Cardinal Grosetti wanted to hear. He had thrown out the bait and Shane had lunged for it. This young American priest either lacked political skill or was eager to regain his status as the boy wonder of the Vatican. Perhaps both. Closing the trap would be easy.

"Yes," the cardinal said. It's been suggested that you expand the biographies of the brothers. You can do that, I suppose."

"Is that all? That shouldn't be much of a problem'" Shane said. "But it would be helpful to know just what I missed."

"Don't be too hard on yourself, my son. You touched on everything. But there's a desire to know more about the brothers. From a technical standpoint their backgrounds as men of the cloth were well detailed. But there's a desire to know a little more about their human side."

"I included everything in their personnel records and what little I learned from my conversations with them."

"I'm sure you kept your notes."

"Yes."

"Perhaps you should go back to them. You might find small details that didn't seem important at the time might have some significance now. There's a good chance they might even jog your memory so that you

*EARTHLY SPIRITS*

remember something they told you, perhaps only in passing. Something that will help fill in the gaps."

"You mean their habits, their acquaintances outside the Church, the kind of books they may have read?"

"Exactly. Their wishes, their fears, their goals. Anything that might give their biographies souls."

"I probably can do some of that. It's a shame I don't have access to them anymore. Does this mean I'll be returning to America?"

"That won't be necessary this time. Your notes and recollections might be enough, but there are other human resources available to you here."

"Father William and Brother Gerald?"

"Exactly. Both served with all of the brothers for as long as they were at Blessed Skyline Abbey. Brother Gerald could be particularly helpful since he was there during the terrible events of last fall. You probably know him better than you do Father William."

"We did become fairly close while I was there."

"See, your rewrite won't be as difficult as you may have thought."

"When is it expected to be done?"

"You're not expected to rush it. Say, three weeks from now. Take them out to lunch or dinner a couple of times. I understand that Father William has found some interesting places to dine. And it's about time that Brother Gerald took a break or two from his research in the Secret Archives. He'd probably appreciate a little relaxation."

"He does keep close to himself."

"Well, then you'll be helping him, too."

"What if he asks me about my renewed interest in the brothers? He's not someone who's easily fooled. He's got a very logical mind and once he starts thinking about something can put together pieces that most people wouldn't recognize."

"Tell him the truth. That you need a little more information for your report. That kind of candor should make him open up. We don't want to make him suspicious when there's nothing to suspect. And, while you're at it, try getting him to tell you something about himself. And Father William, too. Father William probably will be eager to tell you a lot. From what I've been told, he enjoys conversation."

"Then discretion isn't that important this time."

"Discretion is always important. As usual, our conversation should be kept between the two of us."

Father Shane knew how to interpret Cardinal Grosetti's words. Discretion was more important than the cardinal would admit. Grosetti only had pretended to be candid. What he wanted was for Shane to be a player in a game of political espionage. But why? It certainly was not to pad the biographies of the monks with useless information. Unless someone at the Vatican suspected that one of the monks had murdered the four Benedictines and wanted to build a profile. Did the Vatican even have a profiler?

When the cardinal declared their conversation over, Shane rose from the bench, kissed the old man's ring of office and left through the arch in the garden wall.

Cardinal Grosetti sat there for another hour, continuing to wrestle with the new mystery that had been tantalizing him. Brother Gerald had to be the key to unlocking the door to the puzzle. The monk's assignment, writing a new history of the devil, may not make any sense, but neither did anything else. Until he arrived at the Vatican, he had been a Benedictine monk with no ambition and not much of a future in the Church. Why him? He had spent his entire clerical career at Blessed Skyline Abbey; more than twenty-five years. What could he know about evil or even sin, unless there was more than the usual priestly share of it going on inside the abbey walls? There must be some secret that Gerald was reluctant to share. It all had to be connected: Brother Gerald, his Vatican assignment, the death of the monks, the abbey itself. Whatever it was, Grosetti already had discounted the demonic possession that had been suggested as a possible cause of the deaths of the monks in Virginia. Demonic possession indeed. The cardinal never had believed in it. If a competent psychiatrist could not banish demonic nonsense, no exorcist could help the afflicted. Perhaps someone at the Vatican had gone mad or was trying to resurrect the Middle Ages.

As for Father Shane's report, Grosetti wondered whatever had happened to it.

# CHAPTER 5

"The Italians say that if you sit here long enough, sooner or later you'll meet everyone you've ever known," Father William said.

"New Yorkers say the same thing about Times Square," Brother Gerald replied.

"What do they know? Besides, where would you rather be? Times Square or the Piazza Navona?"

"All right. Chalk another one up for you, Father. The Piazza Navona wins on points."

"And what about you, Father?" William had turned to Father Shane, who had said little during the half-hour at the café table where the three men had been enjoying late afternoon glasses of wine. "You've been pretty quiet."

"I've been enjoying your verbal sparring match," Shane answered.

"Well, how would you vote?"

"I call it a draw."

"A draw? You can't be serious. Times Square is popular flash. The Piazza Navona is cultural class."

"I wasn't referring to the two places."

"He means us," Brother Gerald said. "Our discussion about Times Square and this place. And probably everything else you've been picking at."

"Do the two of you always go on this way?"

"No. Just most of the time. Today's been especially tiring. Father William's walked me from one end of Rome to another."

"All he does is complain," the old priest said. "That's what years of sitting on your rear can do to you. We've only walked a couple of dozen blocks or so and I've got a gimpy leg. Imagine what he's going be like when we leave here and walk back to the Vatican."

"That won't bother me as much as tomorrow will."

"What's the big deal about tomorrow? You'll be sitting fattening your rear again on a seat in the Secret Archives."

"My rear will be okay. But I'm sure the rest of my body is going to ache in places I didn't know I had."

"Well, I've got just the cure for whatever might be aching you now. And since Father Shane is paying, I'm ordering one more round for the road."

Father William signaled for the waiter.

"Let's just enjoy the floor show," he added when the wine arrived. "Or, as they used to say in ancient times, 'let the games begin'."

The games had started centuries earlier at the Piazza Navona. Originally, it was an oblong athletic stadium built late in the First Century AD by Emperor Domitian. Called "Circus Agonalis," it held nearly 30,000 spectators. As the centuries passed, the area's name changed along with its use. Inevitably, the public shortened the name Circus Agonalis to the slang "n'Agona." By the time it took on the shape of a piazza, it got the name that it's called today.

When the public lost interest in athletic competitions, the area became a market for city vendors selling all sorts of goods from fresh food grown outside Rome to animals slaughtered on the spot for the kitchen stove to household items to clothing to crafts. It also became a site for theatrical spectacles and sometimes would be flooded with water to entertain the public with mock naval battles.

In the Seventeenth Century, Piazza Navona was given the ornate Baroque facade it still wears today. Pope Innocent X ordered the new look to honor his family, the Pamphili, which had a palace on one side of the piazza. It was the first building to be renovated. At the same time, he

*EARTHLY SPIRITS*

commissioned the remodeling of the piazza's church of Sant' Agnese in Agone. This project was especially popular with the faithful because Catholic legend says the church is built on the site of a house of prostitution where Saint Agnes was rescued from dishonor by a miracle—her hair suddenly grew long. The event is to have so stunned the proprietors and clientele that they believed divine intervention had sent them a 'hands off' warning. The Pope had the modest shrine to Agnes enlarged. Nothing was recorded about what happened to the other women.

Obviously aware that man does not live by prayer alone, Pope Innocent added a touch of passive recreation to the site. He also commissioned the great sculptor Bernini to build a monumental fountain in the center of the piazza. Called the Fontana dei Quattro Fiumi, a lion and sea monster rise in marble from its waters while four men representing the major rivers of four continents cling to rocks. An obelisk taken from the Maxentius circus towers above the figures in the center. While hieroglyphics on the obelisk tell the tale of Domitian's ascent to power, the pope was not about to let posterity give the emperor the credit for the creation of the monument. So, Innocent had his family crest sculpted at the top of the obelisk and at several points around the fountain. He also restored the two Sixteenth Century fountains at the ends of the piazza, but they kept their relatively simple look until the Nineteenth Century.

Now, like most days when the weather was pleasant, the Piazza Navona was a non-stop festival where street entertainers competed with artists for the attention and money of pedestrians. A café seat guaranteed spectators the best view of the pedestrian zone that had become the most popular meeting place for the city's residents.

"Now there's the best street act I've ever seen," Father William said.

"Who?" Brother Gerald asked. "The juggler, the accordion player, the mime?"

"None of the above. Least of all the mime. I know it's not the Christian thing to say or even think, but every time I see a mime, I'm tempted to push him over."

"I'm tempted to agree with you," Father Shane said.

45

Brother Gerald looked from the young priest to the old, shook his head and said:

"Will wonders never cease? Father William has finally found someone who agrees with him. That's a miracle equal to any in the Bible. And it bridges the generation gap at the same time."

"At least one of you has an eye for the finer forms of entertainment," Father William said.

"Which act were you referring to, Father?" Shane asked.

"The fellow over there on the right, near the fountain in front of Sant' Agnese in Agone Church."

"The man with the bottles on the table?"

"Yes, I've been watching him ever since he set up about half-an-hour ago."

"I don't understand what he's doing."

"Watch him. Both of you."

"Is he drinking wine?" Brother Gerald asked.

"How observant," Father William replied. "When people walk in front of his table, he pours a little wine into a small glass and drinks it. That's an original act."

"Like he's doing now?"

"Yes. And look, a woman is actually dropping a coin or two into the hat on the table."

"She has to be a tourist. I can't believe anyone who lives here is paying him to drink wine. My God, he's going be drunk before it gets dark."

"I doubt it. I've been watching him carefully. He drinks only a very small amount each time, probably less than a teaspoon's worth. And not for everyone. He waits until at least three or four people are passing by. He probably drinks the equivalent of two, maybe three, glasses in a couple of hours."

"He can't do this every day."

"He sure can."

"How much you think he collects?"

"At least enough to keep him in wine," Father Shane quipped. "Speaking of getting drunk, that big man staggering in our direction across the piazza looks like he's been there and done it."

46

*EARTHLY SPIRITS*

At almost the moment Shane's two companions turned their eyes in the direction he had indicated, a tall, heavy-set man wearing a dirty gray T-shirt with faded lettering and rumpled tan pants picked up one of the metal cans set around the piazza to encourage people not to litter. He held it over his head for a few seconds and shouted something in Italian. Passersby gave him a wide berth just before he tossed the can onto the ground in front of him. Plastic cups, food wrappers, newspapers and other litter spilled out. Then, he quietly sat down on a nearby bench that had been hastily evacuated by a mother, father and young daughter.

The man sat there quietly, his wild black hair slipping across his forehead as his head slumped toward his chest. After a few minutes, strollers who either had regained their courage or were unaware as to what had happened, no longer gave the bench wide berth. Even the three priests lost interest. Still, no one had enough courage to claim part of the seat for themselves.

Then, suddenly, the man sat up straight, stretched his arms out from his sides and rose to his feet. He stood in front of the bench for a moment, then began staggering in his original direction. He began to shout, again scattering people from his path. He reached the edge of the interior of the piazza, where a narrow paved road for bicycles and scooters circled the giant oval. He reached for a red scooter parked about thirty feet in front of the café table where Fathers William, Shane and Brother Gerald were sitting. He climbed onto the seat, started the machine and took off.

"He's going to hurt himself and some poor pedestrian, too," Father William said.

"I don't think so," Brother Gerald said. "Look, he made the turn in front of the church with no problem."

"Gerald may be right," Father Shane said. "He seems to be going at a good clip and doesn't seem to be wobbling at all. In fact, he's driving almost perfectly straight."

"Everyone's giving him a clear path."

"Not everyone," Father William said. "That young fellow down there running across the piazza after him doesn't seem too happy. It must be his scooter."

They watched the young man in a yellow shirt vainly pursuing the big man. When he realized he was not going to catch him, he stopped, waved his arms wildly, and shouted. Then, he saw the scooter make the turn at the opposite end of the oval and come back toward where he had started. The scooter's owner turned and ran back in the opposite direction where a police officer already was waiting in the middle of the circling road. The big man put on the brakes and stopped a few feet in front of the uniformed officer. He climbed off, bowed to the crowd sitting at the tables at the outdoor café where the priests were finishing their wine and walked up to the policeman. They talked for a few minutes, then the man turned and lumbered away to the left.

"We ought to be going, too," Father William said. "I don't think any act is going to top that one. Besides, I'd like to stop at that bakery in the little street that connects the :Piazza Navona with that other piazza where they sell the flowers, fruits and vegetales."

"Don't tell me you've also developed a sweet tooth since moving here," Brother Gerald said.

"No, but they make the most wonderful Italian cookies at that bakery. Did you know it's open twenty-four hours a day? And I don't go to bed as early as I did during my monastery days."

"Cookies for a late night snack? With milk or wine?"

"Tea."

The three clerics finally rose, walked down the half-dozen short, gray stone steps from their table to the piazza's ground level and began walking toward the cobbled street that was home to the bakery that never closed. Halfway there, just ahead of them, a hulking figure stood almost motionless in the shadows of an arched entrance to an alley that led off the piazza to the left, connecting to another street. It was one of those routes guaranteed to befuddle the most experienced map reader. Brother Gerald was the first to notice him. It was the big man in the dirty gray T-shirt who had dumped the trash and taken the scooter for a joy ride around the Piazza Navona.

As they neared the man, his face emerged from the shadows. He wore the barest trace of a smile on lips that were surrounded by the graying of beard stubble in need of a shave. Most striking were his eyes. They seemed alive, even brilliant; certainly not the eyes of someone who had drunk too much alcohol. The face looked almost like a portrait whose eyes had been carefully cut away to allow someone unseen behind a wall to watch the movements of guests arriving for a dinner party at a haunted house. Gerald felt the man's eyes were looking directly at him. Then, as he and his companions began to walk past him, the man spoke.

"Brother, could I please have a word with you?"

The voice was surprisingly soft and sober. Less than thirty minutes earlier, he had been shouting aggressively and drunkenly. His words seemed so out of character that none of the three clerics immediately thought it odd that the words all were uttered in English, without the slightest hint of an Italian accent.

Though he wanted to keep walking, Brother Gerald could not help but stop, just a few feet from the man. Fathers William and Shane paced off another dozen steps before noticing the Gerald no longer was with them. They both turned and watched the monk talking with what looked like the shadow of a giant. The conversation was brief and less than a minute later, Gerald rejoined the two priests. The three priests talked without moving, almost as though they were fixed to the cobbled pavement.

"Thanks for waiting for me," Gerald said.

"What was that all about?" Father William asked.

"You might not believe me… and I'm not sure I believe it myself." Gerald seemed almost dazed and had spoken the words just short of stammering.

"Try us."

"He wants me to meet him tomorrow at noon, at the entrance to the Coliseum."

"Why?"

"He didn't say, other than that it was important and urgent."

"That's it?"

"Yes."

"What did you tell him?" Father Shane asked.

"Nothing," Gerald said. "He did all the talking."

"You're not going, are you?" Father William asked.

"I don't know. I think maybe I should. I probably will."

"Why would you do that?"

"A couple of reasons. The way he talked, for one."

"My God, I don't know why I didn't pick up on that. I must be getting senile. He spoke in English, didn't he?."

"I meant the tone of his voice. There was something else, too, that only I saw. Or, at least I think I saw. It was like he was both new and familiar at the same time. He reminded me of someone."

"Who?"

"I'm not sure, so maybe I shouldn't say. I know it sounds ridiculous but I can't help but feel that if I say who I think it was, he's going to involve me in something that I'd rather avoid."

"Like what?"

"I don't know."

"You're can't leave us with a riddle."

"If you think that's a riddle, try this on for size: he had a red letter 'N' tattooed in script in a red circle on his left forearm."

# CHAPTER 6

Three days after their talk in the Campo Santo Teutonico in the Vatican Gardens, Cardinal Grosetti and Father Shane were meeting again. This time it was at the cardinal's intimidating office at the Congregation for the Doctrine of the Faith. Shane had been there once before, late in the previous autumn when he gave Grosetti his report on the events at Blessed Skyline Abbey.

"You must think this is highly unusual," Cardinal Grosetti said from across his long desk under the oversized copy of the terrible and mesmerizing, yet darkly humorous vision of Hieronymus Bosch's painting, the Last Judgment.

The American priest knew what the cardinal meant, but kept silent.

"Beyond certain people on my staff, I rarely see anyone twice in a few days," Grosetti continued. "Except for the occasional cardinal or if the Holy Father requires my presence, of course."

Under other circumstances, Shane would have welcomed this meeting. But, today he would have preferred being at the Coliseum, where he was certain both Brother Gerald and Father William were going. So he replied with an answer that straddled the line between truth and falsehood:

"I'm honored, your eminence."

Grosetti was not sure whether Shane was wearing a mask of his own. Was he being humble or sarcastic? He felt more comfortable thinking that the priest simply felt that he had to say something. Because unexpected news had added urgency to what Grosetti wanted, he decided that it was best to don a different mask of his own. He would be as informal as possible. He doubted that he could gain anything by making his visitor feel uncomfortable. So, he continued in the most polite manner he could imitate. It was not as polished as his other faces.

"I regret that my time is limited today. I would have preferred a walk and chat in the gardens, but duties keep me here. I was hoping you could give me a brief update on what we discussed the other day."

"I don't know if what I can add is important or even interesting," Shane replied.

"Have you talked with Brother Gerald or Father William yet?"

"Both of them. We had a late lunch yesterday and later spent some time relaxing at a café at the Piazza Navona."

"Sharing some wine with Father William?"

Shane wanted to ask how Grosetti knew that, but the smiling cardinal quickly answered his own question.

"Father William has been earning a reputation as a connoisseur of food and drink ever since he arrived in Rome. He talks incessantly to everyone about it. It might be socially and culturally rewarding to have him drop by for a conversation. Did you have an enjoyable time?"

"Yes."

"Very good. I wish I had more time to spend at the Piazza Navona."

"I took your advice, your eminence, and told them about the need to fill in a few personal details in my report."

"How did they react?"

"They were surprisingly open."

"That's encouraging. I've always believed that honest openness is a virtue that can bring people closer together."

If Father Shane ever needed confirmation that Grosetti was playing some sort of Vatican political game, the cardinal's words sealed it. As the priest had become more ignored over the past few months, he began developing a healthy suspicion that he had been used by being sent to

*EARTHLY SPIRITS*

Virginia to learn what was killing the monks at Blessed Skyline Abbey. Rarely did anything move swiftly in the Vatican bureaucracy. All right, maybe the safe conclusions he had gone with in his report did not please everyone. But four monks had died under circumstances that bordered on the occult. He should not have been kept in the dark about his report for more than six months. And now that the light finally had been turned on, it was not so dim to prevent him seeing a glow of revelation. Background material on the Blessed Skyline brothers? And, a sudden need to know something more only three days after he had been given three weeks? No, there had to be something else. If anything, Grosetti was not being honest or open. He was using Shane as a spy and the young priest resented it. Even more, he resented a new truth that he had learned in Rome—how to lie.

"So, what can you tell me?" Grosetti asked.

"Both of them seem to have strong personalities," Shane said.

"You mean Father William and Brother Gerald?"

"Yes. They differ on a lot of things."

"Do they argue?"

"I wouldn't call it that. It's more like what we Americans would call needling."

"I recognize the word. Could you be more specific?"

"It's never anything serious and never about clerical issues or doctrine. It's friendly. If Brother Gerald likes a certain food, Father William will tell him he has no taste. Yesterday they disagreed over how far they had walked and whether the Piazza Navona or Times Square in New York was the better place. Things like that."

"That sounds like something you'd expect out of a long friendship between a superior and a subordinate. And it's probably been heightened by a reversal of their roles. You do know why they're here."

"Sort of, your eminence. But only that Brother Gerald is researching the history of Lucifer and that Father William is helping him."

"You say 'sort of.' Is there any reason for you to think they're here for another purpose?"

"No, not at all. I only meant that I don't really know any of the details of their work."

53

"Have they mentioned how they're progressing?"

"I asked, but Brother Gerald only indicated that it was tedious. Father William complained about having to do the legwork. What I mean is he said he visits neighborhood churches talking to local priests while Brother Gerald spends most of his time in the Secret Archives."

"Yes, I know that. What about Brother Gerald? Did he say anything about his past, before and after he joined the brotherhood."

"Not much. The other monks used to call him 'Brother Time'. I didn't note that in my report because it didn't seem important."

"A strange nickname."

"He told me a little about it. When he was a boy, his father collected timepieces and taught him how to repair them. Apparently he became very good at it. One of his duties at Blessed Skyline Abbey was to keep the clocks working. Some of the brothers used to joke that the clocks there kept better time than the clocks in the Vatican. I don't see where it's significant."

"It probably isn't. But, just the same, it's an interesting insight into the man."

"Originally, he was studying to be an engineer or an architect. But when his parents separated, he left college during his sophomore year and entered a seminary to study for the priesthood. He spent his entire career in the Church at Blessed Skyline Abbey."

"Yes, an unusual choice in this day and age. His personnel record indicates that he resisted efforts to have his own parish. A shame. Intelligence without ambition."

"I think it's more a matter of contentment."

"Contentment is all well and good. But it also can be the enemy of progress. What did the other brothers think of him."

"They respected him. Some of them almost revered him as saintly. But he didn't have many of what you'd call close friends. Father William obviously was one. But he stuck pretty much to himself. He's a no-nonsense person."

"Is that all?"

"There's one other thing that I know. Brother Gerald is a historian. Not a professional historian, of course, but enough of a self-educated

*EARTHLY SPIRITS*

amateur to be an authority in certain areas. Apparently, he's read several hundred books on history. Everything from ancient times to World War II."

"Religious history, too?"

"I don't know, but probably. He certainly knows something about the saints, especially the saints whose names matched those of the four brothers who died in Virginia. But that's really nothing new. Even the press eventually learned about that. I can't think of anything else that you don't already know about Brother Gerald."

"That's more than I expected on such short notice. What about Father William?"

"Since he'd been retired from Blessed Skyline Abbey when I got there, I had very little contact with him. Except for a slight limp, he exhibits no visible signs of the stroke he suffered years ago. He's very outgoing and has a very sharp mind. He also seems very opinionated on almost every subject."

"That, my son, is one of the blessings of old age. It allows you to express all the opinions you've stored up over the years. People either respect you for acquiring wisdom or ignore your complaints as a symptom of aging. You can even get away with being eccentric."

"I'll try to remember that for later on in life, your eminence."

"Did you learn anything about the other brothers?"

"Not much. Father William wondered what had happened to some of the novices after the abbey closed, but neither he nor Brother Gerald knew. Father William made a few remarks about Brother Martin. It was the one subject that he and Brother Gerald agreed upon."

"The abbey cook?"

"Yes, but the talk was only about how bad Brother Martin's cooking was."

Cardinal Grosetti smiled. It was as genuine as the laugh that followed.

"Their palates obviously have been awakened since coming to Rome. Though, I do believe that this Nicholas fellow, the one who's supposed to have so cleverly killed the four brothers, was something of a miracle worker in the kitchen. Did his name come up in your conversations?"

"It was never mentioned."

"Well, you've done some excellent work in so short a time. Be sure to put all of it in the biographical section of your report. And, talk with them some more. You never know what you might learn that could be helpful."

"I'll try, your eminence."

"I've got a busy afternoon ahead of me and I'm sure you've got work to do. We should get together at least once more before you finish updating your report. I'll try to fit you into my schedule for sometime next week. I'll get a message to you on when."

Father Shane rose and took a step forward.

"No, that's not necessary, my son," Grosetti said. I'm not one of those people who stands on every formality. You kissed my ring when you arrived. You don't have to do it again."

Walking along the corridor on his way out, the priest felt that he was heading for a career crossroads. Cardinal Grosetti wanted him to continue spying. But why? Did the cardinal or someone else near the top of the Vatican food chain believe that demonic possession was responsible for the deaths at Blessed Skyline Abbey? Even if that were so, how could Brother Gerald's youthful past, Father William's age and Brother Martin's cooking have anything to do with it? Shane once believed demonic possession could have been the cause. But he knew that almost was wishful thinking because the history of demonic possession was his specialty. Now he did not know what to believe except that he felt like a pawn being prodded by bishops. And none of them were talking openly. He might no longer have the access that he once enjoyed, but he was not blind. So much whispering was going on in the Vatican lately that he expected it to erupt any day into the most outrageous rumors. Grosetti must be involved. Shane would continue to do the dirty work that had been assigned to him, but not for the cardinal alone. He would do it for himself, too, even if it meant taking the wrong turn at a career crossroads and ending up as a small town parish priest. It was a risk he felt he had to take. He was starting to learn how to play the game of Vatican politics. That was why he decided not to mention the unexpected meeting between Brother Gerald and the hulking man. Not until he learned more about it.

Cardinal Grosetti, meanwhile, had even more to deal with than Father

*EARTHLY SPIRITS*

Shane. Just moments after the American priest's departure from his office, the cardinal placed an overseas telephone call to Father Monahan in Virginia. Monahan had called Grosetti the night before and now the cardinal was hoping his clerical spy in the United States could tell him more. Something was happening at the archdiocesan level, Monahan had reported. Something as unusual as it seemed important. Something that would had to be of special interest to Grosetti.

Monahan did not know why, but the archdiocese had summoned Father Dennis, whose brief tenure as abbot at Blessed Skyline Abbey once seemed to have all but ended his hopes for a bright future in the Church. No, Monahan did not believe that Dennis was going to be resurrected from the rural parish career grave to which he had been consigned. He did not believe it because Dennis was not the only one summoned.

The archdiocese also had issued to orders to appear at its headquarters to all of the monks still wearing the cloth who had served at Blessed Skyline Abbey. They were not being asked to make social calls on the archdiocese. Something obviously important was in the wind. It must be connected to everything that had happened at the abbey. Curiously, the summons did not extend to Father William and Brother Gerald.

Monahan did not know why those two had been exempt. But he would eventually learn the reason: the archdiocese did now know where the two priests were.

# CHAPTER 7

The cats started emerging from their hiding places about fifteen minutes before noon.

A solid gray male clad in short hair was the first to appear. Except for sharply nicked left ear, he could have been mistaken for a pampered house pet. So could most of the others that followed. The orange tabby, the two whites, the black-and-white and the tortoiseshell with its mottled pattern long hair all could have used a good brushing by a pet groomer. But they otherwise looked well kept and well fed.

Three things distinguished the six felines from cats that lived their lives as house pets. The first was their number. Unless they're from the same household, pet cats rarely meet peacefully in groups of more than two or three and then only if they're on the best of unlikely good terms with each other. The second was where they had gathered, under a shadowed stone archway behind the bars of a rusting iron gate near the entrance to the Coliseum. It was one of the gathering places at the ancient amphitheater that would have been recognized by most residents of Rome. Anyone still not convinced could get the final clue by trying to pet one. Then, either the cats all would scurry away, or one or two might lash out with its claws. These six cats were feral.

"Don't even think of touching them," Father William said. He and

*EARTHLY SPIRITS*

Brother Gerald were standing a few feet from the barred tunnel where the cats were gathered. Four were sitting, the gray had stretched into a lying position and the tortoiseshell was carefully licking a front paw, which it then used to brush away in a vain attempt to loosen a patch of matted fur on its side.

"I wasn't," Brother Gerald answered. "I was just fascinated how they seemed to come out of the ground. One minute the only thing there was dirt, the next it was filled with cats."

"They live in the Coliseum. But this is your first time here so you wouldn't have known that."

"Like those cats who live in what's left of the sunken Roman villa we passed on our way here?"

"Just like them. You'll find them all over Rome. People toss food to them, even towels and old clothing so that the cats will have something comfortable to sleep on. Taking care of stray cats is an old tradition here. It started in ancient times when the city was infested with rats. People brought the cats in to take care of the rats and centuries later they're taking care of the cats."

"Then, they're all homeless."

"I wouldn't call them that. Homeless people should have it so good. These cats get food, water and old rags for comfortable bedding. They have plenty of nooks and crannies for shelter where they can curl up when the weather's bad. Cats know how to make themselves comfortable. They can even build something you'd swear was a large nest. They don't have to earn their living by wearing silly ribbons and bows entertaining people by rolling around a floor with a ball of yarn. They'll lay around all day here in the sun until it moves off, then tonight if they want a change of diet, they'll catch mice and rats. They don't have to worry about losing their reproductive organs to the veterinarian's knife. They're as independent as cats were meant to be."

"There's something I don't get. If they're as independent as you say and as wild as I think, why are these six cats here? I mean, look at all these people strolling around or waiting to get into the Coliseum. I'd think they'd want to stay as far away from people as possible."

"For one thing, they're not all here. There probably are forty or fifty more inside. For another, like us, they're waiting."

"Waiting for what?"

"You'll see soon enough."

"Speaking of waiting, it might have been a mistake to let you come with me. The man in the Piazza Navona asked me to be here. He didn't say anything about bringing someone else. Maybe he's already seen us and decided we're one person too many."

"He didn't say to come alone, did he?"

"No, but…"

"Trust me. If it was so important for you to be here, so will he. Either he's going to be late or he never had intention of showing. It's not quite noon, anyway, and based on what you told me last night, if he's anything near what I think he might be, he'll be right on time. All right, maybe even fashionably late by a minute or two."

"If you think he's what you believe he is, how can you be so calm? Just the memory of that dream I had always makes me nervous."

"At my age do you think anything can seriously frighten me? Besides, there's only thing that might cause me to miss this."

"What's that?"

"The Second Coming."

"On the one hand, I hope you're not going to be disappointed and on the other, I hope you are. I'm not sure I can handle a face-to-face meeting with something that I wish had stayed a dream and, for all I really know, may have."

"You're slipping into denial again."

"It helps me to keep my sanity."

"Whatever, I don't expect to be disappointed. Look at who's coming to dinner. Or should I say lunch?"

Brother Gerald scanned the Via di San Gregorio where hundreds of men, women and children were walking from the ancient Circo Massimo chariot racing grounds toward them. As they neared, almost all veered slightly off course to pass under the massive Arch of Constantine, as though it had been built just for them. The last great ancient monument built in Rome, the arch commemorated the Emperor Constantine's

*EARTHLY SPIRITS*

victory over Maxentius. Most of the arch's statues and other sculptures were taken from other monuments and stone faces were reworked to give them the likeness of Constantine. No one knew whether it was an order of royal vanity or if the sculptors were trying to curry favor with the emperor. Constantine may have been pleased, but the sculptors, masons and other craftsmen eventually were not. Monumental arch notwithstanding, Constantine moved the seat of the empire to Constantinople in what later became Turkey. A lot of workers fell on hard times in Rome because most Imperial commissions then went to other artisans in the new capital.

"Where?" Gerald asked. "I don't see him."

"That's because he isn't there," Father William said.

"Then who do you mean?"

"The cat lady."

"Who's the cat lady?"

"You'll see."

Moments later, a gray-haired woman walked up to the iron gate that barred the people of the outside world from getting too close to the cats. Bright pink cheeks, a light trace of gray facial hair under her nose and bright red lips gave her face the look of a caricature that had been painted by a street artist with a sense of humor. She wore a short-sleeved yellow dress with blue polka dots that could not hide the defects of a lumpy body. She set a brown paper bag and a black handbag on the ground at her feet, then bent her round body slowly forward as though she was going to make a futile effort to touch the toes of the black shoes that tightly encased her bulging feet. She began talking to what seemed to Brother Gerald to be no one in particular until he saw the cats hurry to the inside edge of the gate. He could not hear the words, but realized that the woman was talking to the flock of felines.

"Watch and listen carefully," Father William whispered. "Even you're going to enjoy this."

The woman took a can of cat food from the paper bag, pulled off its pop-top and set it on the ground at her feet before dropping the lid into the bag. She repeated the exercise with two more cans. When she was finished, she opened her handbag, reached inside with a pudgy, wrinkled hand and retrieved a sugar spoon.

"Just be patient, my little ones," she said.

Four of the cats sat quietly, obeying. The orange tabby paced from left to right and back again, while the gray male tried to nudge in front of the tortoiseshell.

"Now be a gentleman and wait your turn," she said, with a disapproving look at the gray. Surprisingly, it obeyed. Then, slowly she began spooning cat food out of the cans and, one-by-one, fed each of them with the utensil. Five of the cats licked their portions slowly off the spoon. The gray male seized the bowl of the spoon in his mouth and emptied its contents in one gulp. All the time, she chatted away happily in sing-song Italian fashion, almost as though the cats could understand her.

"Eat... enjoy yourselves... it's good for you... you're a hungry one today..." Once she even broke into French with a cheerful "bon appetit."

When the cans had been emptied, she reached into her handbag, this time for a cellophane bag filled with small flavored cat treats.

"You didn't think I'd forgotten your dessert," she said. She tore open the package, pulled out several treats and stuck the open palm of her right hand between two of the bars in the gate. Instead of lunging at her hand, one-by-one the Coliseum felines each took one of the treats. She then dumped the few that still remained in her hand on the ground behind the gate.

"We musn't stuff ourselves," she said, laughingly. "Tomorrow is another day."

The woman reached into the brown paper bag again, this time for a small bottle of water and a cheap plastic bowl. She uncapped the bottle, poured most of the water into the bowl and shoved it through the bars. What little water was left was poured onto the spoon, which she then wiped clean and dry with a paper napkin from the paper bag. She put the spoon back into her handbag along with the treats. The napkin then went into the paper bag, followed by the empty bottle and empty cat food cans. She then grabbed her handbag by its strap with one hand and the paper bag with the other. She took a few steps to a nearby trash receptacle and tossed the paper bag with its contents into it.

*EARTHLY SPIRITS*

"Apparently, she does this twice every day," Father William said. "I've only seen her the four or five times I've been here, but one of the Coliseum attendants told me she lives in the neighborhood and has been a regular for almost five years and is almost on time. The cats have become so used to her that they must set their biological clocks to alert them when she's going to arrive."

"Four or five times?" Gerald asked. "Is that what you're doing with your time?"

"Now, boss, don't get upset," Father William said. "I come here only on my free time or after I've visited one of the nearby neighborhood churches. Though I have to confess I had a date here. With a nun."

"Aren't you a little too old for that kind of recreation?"

"You're not suggesting I chase altar boys instead."

"Father, I learned long ago never to suggest anything to you."

"Anyway, she was from a convent a few blocks behind the Coliseum. One of the priests at a church said she had an interesting story to tell about one of the nuns who'd experienced a mental wrestling match with the devil."

"Not demonic possession again?"

"Turned out the poor girl had been suffering from sexual repression. The mother superior wanted an exorcist to drive out the demon, but a psychiatrist concluded that her hormones were acting up. She was only in her early twenties. So, against the mother superior's wishes, she was released from her vows."

"I suppose you put the details in the notebook you've been keeping."

"It's all there for whenever you're ready to read it. But at least the day wasn't a total waste of time."

"The nun you met?"

"None other. We took a stroll along the Via dei Fori Imperiali, the wide street that leads up to here. On Sundays they close that street to vehicles and it's filled with people and vendor stalls. On one side you've got the ruins of the old Roman Forum and on the other that little park with marble busts of some of the better known ancient emperors. And, guess what?"

"Even if I won't, you're going to tell me anyway."

"Mussolini built that street back in the nineteen-thirties. He wanted a grand route to the Coliseum. But in the process, the builders, with Mussolini's approval, plowed a lot of Roman ruins into the ground. They're still there. Archaeologists would love to dig for them. The national and city government have been arguing what to do about it since the end of World War II."

Brother Gerald looked at his watch, then slowly turned to look around him. Like before, he saw plenty of faces, but none of them looked familiar.

"Well, it's twenty minutes past twelve," he said. "At least your cat lady was on time."

"I don't understand it," Father William said. "I was sure he'd be here. Maybe we should give him another ten minutes."

"Why? If he was who he seemed to be pretending who he was, he would've been here by now."

"Let's give him the extra time. Then, if he doesn't show, we can go into the Coliseum. Frankly, I don't understand how you could have stayed away from it all the time we've been here, what with your keen interest in history. Even if he does show, let's still go inside afterwards. It's quite an impressive oval, more than two football fields from the longest end to the other. You can almost imagine the spectacles that were held there. Gladiators, cheering crowds, maybe even an appearance by the emperor, himself."

"Okay, but just ten more minutes. Not a second later. I'll even take a look at the Coliseum with you."

"We all were on time," the voice said.

Father William and Brother Gerald looked at each other, then quickly glanced around. They saw only what looked like it could have been the same featureless crowd, most of them tourists wearing faces that looked pretty much the same as those they had been looking at earlier. They could have been the faces of crowds gathered at the ruins of the ancient Roman Forum or of people at Piazza San Pietro on a Sunday hoping for a glimpse of the pope giving his weekly blessing to the multitude from the window of his Vatican apartment.

"Not very observant, as usual, brother," the voice said again. It was not

*EARTHLY SPIRITS*

the voice Brother Gerald had expected to hear, but it had the faint familiarity of a voice that not only had he never expected to hear again, but firmly hoped that he never would. Now he heard it clearly and so did Father William. But, where was the speaker?

"Cat got your tongue, brother? And of all people, Father William, I'm surprised it has yours, too."

They turned their heads again and again, then finally both sets of priestly eyes became fixed on the same person. She turned toward them with a smile. It was the woman in her early sixties with a caricature of a face and wearing a yellow dress with the blue polka dots that could not hide the defects of her lumpy body.

"I'm never late…," she said, "… for any important date."

# CHAPTER 8

Ewan Sinclair had not seen anyone along the path.

No one had followed him from the village, which he had left twenty minutes earlier. Not that anyone would have had reason for following. Neither had anyone approached him from the direction in which he was headed. The fields that bordered the dirt footpath path also were empty except for an occasional bird or butterfly skimming along the top of the tall grass and blooming yellow wildflowers. All of nature's beauty was being awakened by the warming nourishment of the late spring light. Even the night was beginning to fall under the spell of the sun. Minute-by-minute it was being turned away until the days had been built with more hours of sunlight than darkness. The imbalance would reach its peak in a few more days. Today, though in nightly retreat well to the west behind Sinclair, the giant yellow orb continued to fill the sky with so much blue that there seemed to be little space for even the scattered wisps of white clouds. The first stars of night would not be able to glisten for at least another two hours.

Sinclair could have taken a shorter route. He could have walked uphill through the winding streets of the expanding residential section where new homes and the demands of their inhabitants for services were transforming the village into a town. Or, he could have driven that route in a few minutes.

*EARTHLY SPIRITS*

Today he had felt the need to escape from the confines of his law office where lately he had spent too much time past closing listening to women ready to divorce their husbands, and to couples seeking advice on buying and selling real estate. So few of his days found him in court where, as a law school student, he had expected to pursue his future career. Still, he had to concede that he had no serious complaints. He owed his profession and the financial rewards that came with it to the society. It had helped pay for his education and made certain that he would have a solid practice after graduation. The society had taken care of him and now he was repaying it in kind, taking care of what it occasionally asked. If it had not been for the society, he might be only a name chiseled into a stone memorial plaque on a wall.

The footpath was his escape route from reality, if only temporary. As Sinclair felt the ground begin its gentle rise toward the cliff, he knew that he could feel free for another fifteen minutes or so. Almost as free as the seagulls gracefully riding the high wind currents above and beyond the cliff. There was no need to rush. He could have made the walk in less time at a faster pace. But what was the point? Whatever was waiting for him could wait just a little longer. He had been told that it was important, not urgent. What was it this time? Someone trying to gracefully cut a relative out of an inheritance in favor of the local parish church? Another family property dispute? He would know soon enough, so he banished the thoughts and returned to the pleasures of the solitary stroll that he had taken often as a child but rarely as an adult. He took in every breath with relaxed enjoyment, savoring the mild salty taste of the gentle air blowing in off the Atlantic Ocean. He loosened the knot in his necktie, removed his jacket and flipped it casually back over his right shoulder. He would restore his professional look when he got to where he was going. His only regret was that he had left his comfortable walking shoes at his office. He was sure his feet would hurt before he reached the top of the rise.

Halfway up the slope, the turret of the crenellated stone tower appeared. As a child he always had imagined it to be the tower of a castle, rising out of nowhere, an illusion stimulated by the far-reaching landscape. Now, years later, the Norman-style monument still had the same effect on him. Bit by bit, the castle vanished as he neared the top of the rise. The rest of the building was slowly emerging.

St. Andrew's Church stood alone near the edge of the cliff on the far side of the hill. Though the castle had now been exposed as an illusion, the stone building remained almost was as impressive as its tower. In the nearly three-hundred years that it had been there, crumbling cliffs had moved the edifice nearer to the edge so that, at first glance from the top of the rise, it looked perilously close to plunging into the wave-battered rocky shore below. But that, too, was an illusion. Enough land separated it from the precipice to maintain its prestigious position for at least another century. By then, future technology might find a way to lengthen the building's life even more. No matter whether the church was approached by footpath or paved road, it presented a memorable sight on a clear day, even to those who had seen it week after week and year after year. Set against the backdrop of Atlantic waters that merged into a blue-sky horizon that seemed to stretch into infinity, the scene was a picture postcard view of a romantic's notion of an idyllic Nova Scotia seascape.

A church had been on the site almost back to the beginning of the written record of the area. The first house of worship was a small wooden chapel, built by the first settlers. Worship was only one of its early uses. It also served as a post from which mostly bored volunteer sentries could keep watch for other voyagers who might dare to venture across the Atlantic. But none followed them. History had overlooked those original adventurers, who arrived in the New World nearly a century before the first voyage of Columbus. Late in the Sixteenth Century, the chapel was replaced with a bonafide church, built with wood on a stone foundation. The foundation was all that survived when the church experienced its third incarnation early in the Eighteenth Century. The new church was built partly because of the need to accommodate the growing population of the devout and partly as a testament to the heritage of the faithful that had founded the community.

Though fashions in architectural style had changed by the Eighteenth Century, there was almost no debate on the shape the new church would take. It would be Norman, an almost miniature version of the great medieval cathedrals of Europe. The community could afford it, having prospered on the fishing and fur trades. Buttresses were needed to reinforce the stone walls because of the many lancet windows of stained glass. Another stained glass window, this one circular, had been set under the peaked roof entrance, which was crowned by a large cross. Below the window, an oak door at the top of a porch with nine steps led to the interior. Worshipers would enter a church whose walls were painted with frescoes in vivid colors. The frescoes and stained glass windows were an art gallery of Biblical characters acting out their stories and of saints delighting in the imaginary ecstasy of martyrdom. Thirteen steps led to the chancel where the sun rising out of the Atlantic Ocean in the east blazed through three stained glass windows hovering above the high altar. The center window depicted Christ ascending into heaven, flanked by two smaller windows with images of medieval knights. Norman arches and columns lined the nave, where seats were placed for the faithful. The tower was entered by a door near the pulpit. Stairs zig-zagged from the base of the tower to the belfry. From there, a ladder led to the crenellated rooftop, which in an earlier European era, could also have seen service as a battlement.

Perhaps the most important area of the church was one rarely seen except by the pastor, church officials and a handful of very special persons in the parish. Most people in the village knew of the dirt floor passage under the church that sometimes was used on special holy days when the priest would lead his flock from a small secondary door along what was considered consecrated ground into the nave. But, while many had heard rumors, only a few knew of a locked room off a small, narrow corridor that connected to the holy passage. According to the stories, the chamber was a repository for sacred relics brought to Nova Scotia by its settlers in 1398.

So much legend had surrounded the relics that most residents of the area either considered them fable or had accepted their existence as part of a belief system. They were reputed to include everything from the Holy Grail to the Lost Ark of the Covenant. Many of the residents who could trace their village roots back no more than a generation or two had no opinion. Only a handful of the living knew the truth.

Little legend diluted the local version of the history of the settlement.

Nearly everyone believed that the village had been settled by fugitives from the Holy Roman Inquisition, which in the Fourteenth Century was determined to eradicate the Knights Templar. The tale was written in detail in the local history and displayed with colorful drawings at the local museum. The tourist brochures included an abridged version.

Founded in 1119 by Hugh des Payens and Geoffrey de St. Omer who took vows at the Temple of Solomon in the Holy Land, the Knights Templar gained official recognition throughout Europe nine years later from the Council of Troyes under Pope Honorius. The new order of knights greatly influenced France for nearly two centuries. They promoted Christian devotion, chivalry and education, including the creation of the University of Paris. However, when King Philip IV ascended the throne of France in 1285, it marked the beginning of the end for the Templars in Europe. First, the king exiled the Jews and Lombards, confiscating their wealth, which he added to the royal treasury. Not content with being merely wealthy, the king then taxed the Church and its clergymen. By 1300, professors at the University of Paris were placing their theological authority above that of the Vatican. Three years later, the patience of Pope Boniface VII was exhausted and he was ready to excommunicate Philip. But before he could act, William de Nogaret, one of the king's advisers, led a contingent of two-thousand mercenaries in an attack on the papal palace at Anagni and captured the pope. After the pontiff's death, Pope Benedict excommunicated William only to be poisoned a month later. In 1309, Philip used his political and financial power to elect Clement V as pope. Clement was French and the papal seat was moved from Rome to Avignon, France.

Fearing a threat to his rule from the highly religious Knights Templars, the king ordered their arrest in 1310. Their property was seized, they were dragged to the dungeons and tortured on charges of treason and heresy. Though a special court hesitated when it came to finding them guilty, King Phillip had no problem reaching a verdict on his own. Fifty-four of them were burned at the stake and the order was officially abolished. More persecution followed. Anyone believed associated with the Knights Templar lived in fear. In time, even the new Avignon papacy was convinced to hunt down the heretics. Those Knights Templars who

*EARTHLY SPIRITS*

survived the king's wrath also became the perfect political target along with their supporters, being blamed for the famine that soon was to ravage France's population and prosperity.

What was left of the Knights Templars sought refuge in Scotland, where the survivors were welcomed by the powerful Saint Clair family. They had fled continental Europe just ahead of the arrival there of the Black Death. Naturally, some blamed the plague on the Templars. Though the order was comfortable in Scotland, it yearned for a home of its own. So, it took its quest to the seas. One of its voyages found Nova Scotia.

Though Columbus later got history's credit for being the first European to sail to the New World, the Templars and their early descendants never were eager to challenge the primacy of the 1492 accomplishment. They had good reason. The Inquisition had moved to Spain, the point of the departure of Columbus. Even after the Inquisition had been shorn of its power to intimidate with terror, the settlers preferred to remain in the wings of discovery. By the middle of the Twentieth Century, the whole matter of discovery was complicated even further by a growing belief that the Vikings had beaten everyone to North America except, of course, what were then its native inhabitants.

The bloodline descendants of the Knights Templars knew better. They had been told the tales of the Arab mysteries of sacred geometry and its relationship to natural forces. Even centuries later, few of them doubted the age-old belief that the ancient Greeks, Phoenicians and even Mesopotamians had sailed the world searching for precious metals and jewels, and even to trade with native cultures. They must have kept records of their voyages, including maps. These had become the lore of the community, maps found and guarded over generations by a select few of the Knights Templar. Maps that had enabled them to find Nova Scotia and even make voyages between there and Scotland in an era when most people believed that the world was flat.

Like many others descended from the original settlers, Ewan Sinclair had heard all the stories. He believed some, doubted others and reserved opinion on the rest. But he preferred leaving it to the historians to sift what facts they could find out of the dustbins of myth and legend.

Practical legal matters dominated what time he had for investigation and he was good at that. Yet, deep inside, he lately had been feeling an inexplicable craving for something. Because he had just turned forty years old, he chalked it up to mid-life crisis. So, he thought of buying a sports car.

Now, as he approached Saint Andrew's Church, he could see the headstones of the graves in the churchyard off to the north side of the building. The climate had been equally unkind to the stone markers of the dead as it had been to the stone exterior of the church. The names and dates on the older headstones had been erased by the elements years before Sinclair was born. The original light gray of the church's exterior walls now was dark. Both headstones and walls bore streaks and spots painted by the weather as though they had been brushed by an incompetent surrealist who also had added green with touches of moss.

Sinclair thought it odd that the only car parked outside the church was Father John Cameron's old black sedan. He had expected at least one other vehicle. Perhaps whoever was to be the recipient of whatever legal favor Sinclair had been summoned to confer had ridden with Father John from the village where the priest lived in an old fisherman's cottage that had been converted into a rectory. No one expected their pastor to live in exile on the lonely hilltop, where most nights and some days could be forbidding.

Old fishermen's cottages were a dominant feature of the side streets of the village. However, few of them still were occupied by fishermen and their families. Once the prosperous center of the region, the village economy had all but collapsed thirty years earlier when the locals were caught in a fisheries war between Canada, the United States and the old Soviet Union. Treaties eventually were signed, but by then the factory ships of corporate fishing fleets had gained dominance over the most productive waters. The rise of the factory ships forced the closing of the antiquated fish cannery. Now it sat ashore outside the village as a rusting reminder that nothing is permanent. Some local fishermen still could make a living with catches sold to restaurants and at outdoor markets, but for most the heyday of the independents was over.

Only the intervention of the modern-day Knights Templars was able

*EARTHLY SPIRITS*

to save the village from becoming a coastal slum. Reminded of how they had gotten to where they were, the more affluent members of the society were convinced to invest in the village's future, though in some cases it took a little arm-twisting to open the purse strings. The money went into historic restoration and resort development, both equipped with the sort of amenities and promotion sure to lure tourists in search of the quaint. Light industry took an interest. A private school was established. Seasonal festivals were launched. New housing was built. And, the old fishermen's cottages became the most sought after real estate. Prices of the tiny homes soared.

Of course, most of the people who sought membership in one of the Knights Templar lodges also claimed an ancestry that dated back to the families that were said to have settled the area in the late Fourteenth Century. Exchanging secret Masonic-like handshakes, pinning enameled society lapel buttons on their jackets, wearing rings with emblems that only they recognized, carrying society membership cards in their wallets and attending lodge functions made them feel like Templar descendants. For many, the ancestry link was slim, at best. But, what was the harm?

Sinclair had gone through all those motions, but none ever equaled what he felt whenever he entered Saint Andrew's Church. Now, as he once more pushed open the door in the south wall and let it close behind him, it was there just inside the small entrance passage, almost staring at him rather than the reverse. The stone plaque was only one of more than two-dozen special memorials inside the church. This was both a parish church and a fishermen's church, named after Andrew because he was the patron saint of fishermen. However, this memorial had special interest for Ewan Sinclair. Fitted to the wall at eye level, the square stone was etched with four names, one above the other in what seemed like no particular order::

"Joseph Scott, Roger McIntosh, George Deschamps, James Perth"
A date was etched below the names.

A fifth name should have been there. But, William Sinclair, his father, had sprained an ankle earlier on that October day twenty-seven years ago and could not join his mates on their scheduled outing. Their fishing boat was too far out to sea to make it back to port when the storm struck. The

73

boat never was found and neither were the four men. His father saw his ankle sprain as a sign from God. He sold his fishing gear, started a successful jack-of-all-trades business, steered his son away from a career at sea and never again set foot on a boat. He died of a heart attack sixteen years later at his old fisherman's cottage. The mother died a year later, quietly in bed, after a long illness that friends and neighbors said was the result of a broken heart. Ewan had no brothers, sisters, aunts, uncles or cousins. He was the last of the family line.

After pausing for a moment at the stone tablet, Sinclair stepped out of the entrance hall. He saw Father John sitting alone in the first row of chairs at the front of the nave. The priest turned his head and beckoned with his right hand as he called for Ewan to join him in a voice that echoed under the vaulted ceiling of the otherwise empty church. So did Sinclair's shoes as he walked along the worn tiles of the gray stone floor toward the priest. He shook hands with Father William, then sat down next to him.

"I heard the door close and guessed that it was you."

The priest's voice came from deep in his throat, a manner of speaking that had environmental, rather than natural, roots. He had been raised in a small village in Scotland, where everyone talked loudly in the local pub he had frequented in his younger days. That had been ideal voice training for someone destined to give Sunday sermons. Father John's vocal talents also gave him an advantage at the pub around the corner from his village cottage. Not only could he command audiences at the bar, someone else always was willing to pay for his drinks. If his booming voice was not enough to instill the fear of the Lord into the more devout, his look alone could do it. His face had the features of a prizefighter. Though he never had entered the formal ring, during his youthful days in Scotland he had earned a local reputation for accepting and issuing challenges for impromptu displays of fisticuffs, always after he and the other willing combatants were well into their third or fourth pints of local ale. Over the years, his younger pugilistic looks were united with the alcohol that had implanted itself firmly in the vessels that carried blood to and from his face. He made good use of his acquired attributes in the Sunday pulpit. Yet, his eyes betrayed a genuine interest in people. They looked like eyes that anyone could trust. Everyone believed that Father John would never hurt as much as a fly.

"Sorry that I'm a few minutes late, Father," Sinclair said quietly.

"You're never late, so I figured you must have walked here through the fields" Father John replied. "Now that you're here, I'm sure you did."

"How can you be sure?"

"You look like a rooster trying to be a hippie. That mop of red hair. You neglected to smooth it out. It's windblown."

Sinclair ran his right hand through his hair several times.

"I should have driven," he said.

"Nonsense, Ewan. Everyone needs to get away from it all every once in a while. Saint Anthony used to take sabbaticals into the wild just to think."

"Who are we waiting for?"

"No one. You look surprised."

"I thought you wanted me here to…"

"No, no. This isn't anything like the usual business. Something has come up. A very special something that requires a very special request of you. And it has nothing to do with your considerable legal skills, though they might come in handy. Certainly your unique ability to find things should."

"It sounds like you've tossed me a line and are waiting for me to take the bait."

"Intrigued, are you?"

"I wouldn't exactly call it that."

"Well, Ewan, I expect you will be. I certainly am."

"Okay, I'll bite."

"It's such a long and very old story that I almost don't know where to begin. Until I was told about it this morning, I didn't believe it was possible. But I was assured by sources that I trust that it comes down from the best of authorities."

"You could begin at the beginning."

"Now, before you think I'm a lunatic, are you still as convinced as you once were in the teachings and goals of the society? I ask you because this could be a validation of everything the true Knights Templars have believed in for so long."

There it was again. The society. The order. The fellowship. The secret organization that Sinclair was raised to believe had so much power that its members were just biding their time before the moment came when they could assume some mythically inherent position as rulers of the world. He was not alone. Over the centuries many people believed it. But King Phillip II of France and the papacy had convincingly dismissed that notion. What was it now? A small group of people claiming to be descendants of immigrants from Scotland who won the race against Columbus to the New World by almost a hundred years? A small group of mostly old men who met at the most secret of gatherings in the most secret of places. That also was their secret to the perception of power. Because they were so few in numbers and practiced whatever they did in secrecy, they must know something the masses did not. That alone had created a cultish belief system that had convinced ardent followers that they had power that really did not exist. Sinclair had grown past that belief, but he owed the society so much that the only thing he could think of saying was:

"Yes."

"Good," the priest said. "Then, I think it's about time you had a look at that room under the church that everyone talks about."

# CHAPTER 9

Everything seemed to finally be coming together and falling apart at the same time.

Brother Gerald could not make up his mind which way the pendulum was swinging. The Secret Archives, the furtive glances in the corridors of the Vatican, the meetings that concluded nothing, the secrecy that seemed to descend on every question he raised. Now it also was the resurrection of a man called Nicholas, who claimed to be the Devil and was dressed like an old woman who fed cats.

Maybe Father William had it right. The old abbot's wanderings through the back alleys and neighborhood piazzas of Rome had invigorated him. The old priest seemed to be getting younger while Gerald was aging. Gerald wondered how long it would be before Father William lost his limp.

But this was bizarre. Despite everything that had happened more than a half-year ago in Virginia, the monk had never accepted the claim of Nicholas, when he was a living, breathing and ordinary man, that he was actually Lucifer. Now this was supposed to be the same Nicholas, but this time he was a woman. It was all too confusing for Gerald's normally ordered mind. At best, he felt uncomfortable. On the other hand, Father William, who only had Gerald's version of the past events and believed them was just the opposite. The old priest should have been frightened out of his clerical collar. Instead, Father William seemed to be having the time of his life strolling through the grounds of the ruins of the ancient Roman Forum, chatting away with the cat lady, Nicholas, Lucifer or crazy old woman, whoever he, she or it was. Side by side, just two steps ahead of him, they could have been a couple of old friends out for a pleasant early afternoon stroll.

Even more bizarre was the topic of their conversation. Considering Father William's willingness to at least give the woman the benefit of the doubt as to her identity, Brother Gerald expected the old priest to ask about the Creation, the Fall of Lucifer from grace, Heaven and Hell, and everything biblical. From the moment of their surprise encounter outside the Coliseum, neither of the two uttered as much as a theological word.

Gerald, meanwhile, had remained almost dumbstruck as they walked from the centuries-old Roman amphitheater along the Via dei Fori Imperiali to the Forum. The two seemed to pay little heed to what little Gerald had said. He did not feel ignored but, rather, curiously relieved. So, he listened, picking up a word here, a phrase there. When not mentally reliving the nightmare of Blessed Skyline Abbey, his mind used its vigorous disbelief to keep fear at bay. Finally, the limping old man and the waddling woman stopped at a stone bench on one of the paths near the middle of the ruins and sat. The woman patted the empty space to her right for Gerald to also sit, leaving her between the two clerics. The monk hesitated, then noticed for the first time that the historic grounds were packed with visitors. It was as though he had come out of a sleep and realized that the three of them were not alone. There was safety in numbers.

He took the seat he was offered, taking care to leave enough space as he could between him and the cat lady without being in danger of falling off the edge. No sooner were all three seated than the conversation between Father William and the woman resumed.

"It doesn't look like much now," the woman said. Her voice was feminine but it had a slight masculine tone that reminded Gerald of someone he had tried to forget. She pointed to the nearby Palatine hill that was occupied by what was left of the Roman Imperial Palace.

*EARTHLY SPIRITS*

"Now that was really something in its day," she said. "It always brings back fond memories."

"The Domus Flavia," Father William said. "It was the official residence in Rome of the emperors until the Empire collapsed."

"Actually, until Constantine moved everything to Constantinople. I never agreed with that move. I always felt it watered down the majesty of the empire. Believe me, if I could have done anything to stop him, I would have. But, as I just told you, when I was assigned, or exiled, here with my small force of devils to try to keep your young race from tearing this world apart, my orders were not to interfere."

"We haven't done that poorly, have we?"

"I've seen worse. It's a shame the Romans didn't survive. They would've have known how to make things work. Just look at what'sw left of that palace. It was magnificent."

"Wasn't it the Emperor Domitian who built it?"

"Yes, but he died before it was completed. The rooms were sumptuous. The throne room, where the emperors held public audiences, was huge. The cards were stacked against visitors. Not only did they have to face an emperor who was officially called "Dominus et Deus," they were surrounded by giant colored marble statues placed in niches around the throne room."

"But the emperor didn't really live in the palace. I believe he had a private residence on the palace grounds."

"Yes. The Domus Augustana. It looked out onto the Circus Maximus, on the other side of the hill."

"I still believe that the forums were the single most important contribution Rome's leaders made to the public. Julius Caesar, especially. When he enlarged the old Forum, it gave the citizens a new outlook on life. It made him popular with the masses, which is why he did it."

"Sort of like urban redevelopment."

"Exactly like it. New public squares, shops, theaters, baths, temples to their gods, even housing."

"He may have started the expansion, but it was always a work in progress. Augustus, Vespasian, Nerva and Trajan built the rest of it."

"A city within a city. I can imagine it being filled with…"

Father William never got to finish what he was saying. Brother Gerald, who felt his conscious self begin to slip, managed to find the mental energy to shake himself wide awake. He moved forward as if to rise from the bench and, with a voice that seemed raised beyond his control, he uttered what sounded like a command:

"What the Hell is going on? I didn't come here to get a history lesson while listening to the two of you trying to politely upstage each other. I want to know who you are, Madam Cat Lady, who that was who told me last night to be here today and what this is all about. And unless I get some answers pretty quick, I'll be on my way and the two of you can spend the rest of the afternoon discussing what emperor lived where and how many Christians were fed to the lions."

"Actually, none were," the woman said.

Her remark was so swift and sounded so authoritative that it caught both priests by surprise. They looked over her head at each other. Gerald could think of only one thing to say:

"What?"

"I said none were," the cat lady replied. "It's a myth propagated by the early Christians. The more they could make everyone believe that they suffered, the more sympathy they believed they could earn for their cause. It also was used to try to unite the Christians. Back in those times, there were nearly two-hundred Christian sects. Some of their leaders understood the potential influence unity of numbers could have. Soon, everybody, including all the Christians believed the story."

"You're telling us the Romans didn't persecute Christians?" Father William said.

"Not at all," the woman replied. "All the atrocity stories have some truth in them. Except that they never threw anyone to the lions or the tigers or the leopards. Those poor beasts were left to the gladiators."

"Okay, let's say you're right," Gerald said. "I don't care. Just get on with what I asked. And don't give me that devil story, either. I've seen your arms. They don't have any tattoos."

"An oversight, brother. I had a bit of a problem this morning and was rushed to keep my appointment with you. But I'm Nicholas, all right. But why not just call me Nicole? It sort of fits my new character."

*EARTHLY SPIRITS*

"I prefer calling you a fraud. I've had enough. I'm leaving."

"All right. You also know that I don't do card tricks. If we had a bottle of wine I could change it into water, but then who'd want to drink it? All right, if you insist. Watch carefully. See, nothing in my hands and nothing up my sleeves, which anyway are too short to conceal anything.

The cat lady turned her left forearm to the outside so that both clerics could see it. She rubbed her arm with her right hand, then pulled the hand away.

"How's that?" she asked.

"As bad as the rest of your act," Gerald answered.

The woman looked at her arm. It was the same as before.

"Oh, I forgot to say the magic word," she said as Brother Gerald started to get up from the bench.

She repeated the rubbing of her arm with the left hand, adding one spoken word:

"Abracadabra."

When she withdrew her hand, there, halfway between her right elbow and wrist was a red tattoo; a large letter 'N' inside a circle.

Brother Gerald settled back onto the bench very slowly. He and Father William stared at the tattoo and even the old priest looked as though he could not believe his eyes. Then they looked at each other and, for the first time, both felt discomforting chills. William said nothing, but Gerald recovered quickly.

"Not bad, but I've seen better," he said. "There's a street magician in New York who actually levitates himself off the sidewalk."

"That's nothing," the woman said.

"Can you do it?" Father William asked, almost meekly.

"Sorry, Father. I don't have the kit. You can buy it at some magic and puzzle shops. There's a really good one in Paris, near the Sorbonne. I think the kit costs about forty dollars, American."

The cat lady had gone from casual to flippant. She was poking fun at the two clerics, and while William had eased enough from his shock to take it with a grain of salt and a bucket of awe, Gerald was annoyed. He started to rise again, as if to leave.

"Don't go so soon, brother," the woman said. "We've got to talk."

81

"If you're really who you're trying to make us think you are, you should be able to keep me from leaving," the monk said.

"Oh, Gerald, Gerald. You couldn't have forgotten so quickly, not with that organized catalogue of a mind you have. Certainly you remember what I told you about choice during our little chat in your cell the night I left the abbey."

"You mean about God giving men the right to choose, but penalizing them for it when they made the wrong choice."

"Good. You do remember. Then you also must remember me telling you that's one of the reasons I got the boot from Heaven. How, after I argued that with you-know-Who that such liberalism wouldn't work, He stuck me on Earth with my loyal legion, leaving me to make sure that it did. Actually, when thinking back, even I couldn't have come up with a more fitting punishment."

Gerald looked past the woman at William.

"I certainly say anything to him or to anyone else who could have told him about your previous encounter," the old priest said. "You should know that."

"Of course he should, Father," the woman said. "You should be ashamed, Gerald. Father William may have trouble keeping his mouth shut, but he'd never violate a confidence. I suppose you told him everything and in confidence, too."

"If you really are Luci... Luci..."

"Still can't say my name? I could do something about that if you want. If you keep going on like that you just might develop a stutter."

"I'd prefer to work it out on my own."

"Aha, choice. Very good. But, I didn't tell you everything that night about choice. Now, considering what's happened since then and why I wanted us to meet again, you are entitled to know a little more."

"What else is there to know?"

"I'm not going to bore you with the details. Besides, time might not be on our side. You see, choice is a right of the soul. Without a soul, your ability to choose would be pretty much limited to the basics of survival, like the animals. They can't make moral or ethical decisions which, when you consider what humans have done to the Earth, isn't such a bad limitation. You have a soul, an animal doesn't."

*EARTHLY SPIRITS*

"That's what the Church teaches us."

"At least it got that right. But there's more to it than that. Who do you think Adam and Eve were?"

"That depends on whether you believe the biblical story."

"It wasn't that far off. Adam and Eve really existed. But they weren't humans. They were monkeys. God gave souls to a pair of monkeys. Can you believe it? He called it creative evolution. I'll tell you, I wasn't the only one who warned him about doing that. Because I objected the most, I took the fall. That old forbidden fruit story, that was my idea. I wanted to show Him that one of the first things they would do was break the rules. What else could anyone expect? After all, they were only monkeys with a couple of inexperienced souls."

Father William's eyes had flashed with such eagerness while the cat lady was talking that he momentarily forgot that she was a woman. Whatever concern he had felt had been swept away by his fascination with what she had been saying. Before Gerald could respond, the old priest burst into the conversation.

"Was that you last night at the Piazza Navona?"

"The big drunk with the torn shirt. That was me."

"All right, then," Brother Gerald said. "If that was who you're claiming to be, why that body? Do you have a thing for alcoholics? And why are you this woman today?"

"I thought you'd never ask. Like Nicholas in Virginia, alcoholics don't live very long, so they're likely to provide the most available bodies that aren't maimed. But that one was really in bad shape. He'd been hit earlier in the day by a car and his back was broken. I needed a body fast to be able to get to meet with you, so I had to take what I could find. It took every bit of my energy to keep it going. I'm surprised I made it through the day. I even experienced a bit of pain. That's not a nice feeling. Just in case you don't believe me, you can check it out. Go back to the Piazza Navona and ask anyone who works there. They found the body in the same alleyway where we met."

"Why the big show last night?" Father William asked.

"I admit I did overdo it a bit. But I had to be sure you'd notice me. I can't go into the Vatican, it's off limits to me. And I couldn't be sure that

83

my connection there would be convincing enough for you. And, no it's not Cardinal Sforza or any other clergyman. I had to talk to Brother Gerald and I didn't want that Father Shane listening in. I knew Gerald isn't afraid of anything, so he'd stop when I called to him. Shane isn't a shrinking violet, but he doesn't have that kind of courage. If he had any idea who you'd be meeting today, he wouldn't have missed it. I can imagine what it would look like to everyone here with him trying to pray while he was sprinkling holy water over me. By the way, it wouldn't have done any good."

"And me?"

"I knew you wouldn't miss this for the world."

"Are you everywhere?" Father William asked. "How do you find these bodies so easily?"

"Of course I can't be everywhere. Contrary to what the Church teaches not even you-know-Who can do that. Finding a usable body isn't as easy as you might think. When I need one, I usually just go to a hospital. Your modern medicine manages to kill a lot of people every day in hospitals. I take whatever's available at the time, which means I've got to be ready just at the moment of death or, if I'm in a hurry, someone who's going to die in an hour or so, anyway."

"And the cat lady?"

"Heart attack. She died last night a few hours after being admitted to intensive care. Nice woman, Mrs. Tirenese. The cats will miss her. But don't worry, Father. The kitties won't go hungry. One of her neighbors will continue her charitable work at the Coliseum."

"How do you know?"

"It's refreshing to see that you've a soft spot in your heart for animals, Father, particularly cats. She had a dream."

"You mean a nightmare," Brother Gerald said.

"No. It was nothing at all like our nocturnal session back at your old abbey in Virginia, brother. She'll remember it as a pleasant vision suggesting that she should assume the responsibility now that poor Mrs. Tirenese is gone. In the end, her soul may even be rewarded. God loves animals, too, you know. Of course, I'm going to have to shed this body, too."

84

*EARTHLY SPIRITS*

"And how are you going to do that. You just can't fall down in an alley. The woman was in the hospital, probably with all sorts of tubes hooked up to her."

"I'll simply sneak back into the hospital morgue, lay down on a slab, cover myself with a sheet and vacate the body there. Sooner or later someone will figure out it's Mrs. Tirenese. They won't know how she got there. Don't worry, no heads are going to roll. Remember, this is Italy. Everyone will just shrug their shoulders, go out to a café and drink some wine."

"Maybe you should check into a psychiatric ward."

"I don't know how someone like you puts up with him, Father. He doubts everything, which isn't so bad. But his lack of imagination can be irritating. You'd think that after he was handed this assignment to write a new history about me and after he got my postcard from Moscow he'd be a true believer."

"Is that what this is all about? Writing a history of the Devil? Sometimes I wish I'd never been called to Rome."

"Forget the history. That was just my way of thanking you for helping me through my amnesia back in Virginia. I thought you'd look on Rome as your salvation. After they closed the monastery, you probably were going to be exiled to some third-rate parish church in the New Mexico desert for another twenty years before being pensioned off into poverty. I felt that would have been a waste of your talents. But, since you're still not convinced, try this on for size."

All at once, all the memories of what had happened at Blessed Skyline Abbey came back to Brother Gerald. They flooded his mind like water breaking free from a collapsed dam. The soup that boiled Brother Matthew alive from the inside. The way Brother Bruno's bones were crushed in a traffic accident. The snakes that bit Brother Anthony to death. The fire that consumed Brother Leo. The flowers that should not have been there. How every death could be linked to the feast day of a saintly namesake and to one of the Seven Deadly Sins. The suspicions, the conversations, the nightmare in which the man claiming to be the Devil apologized for the killings, but also justified them. The body of Nicholas that had been found in the Blue Ridge Mountains, minus the tattoo it once bore on his left arm. It was all happening again, this time in the form of the virtual reality promised by science.

"Enough," Gerald said sharply. He placed his hands over his ears and lowered his head.

"Didn't like your little trip down memory lane?" the cat lady asked. "Sorry to do that to you. You're not going to have a headache or any other uncomfortable after-effects. But it was necessary. I need you to believe."

"Why? Has your vanity been bruised by my doubts?"

"Still not convinced?"

"Yes, I am."

"And what about you, Father?"

"I don't know what it is you did to Brother Gerald, but from his reaction, I don't think I need it to be convinced."

"Good. Now that we're all on the same playing field, I can tell that something very big is close to happening. And your help, Brother Gerald, is needed. Of course, I supposed I'd be wasting my time trying to keep you out of it, Father. It's probably just as well, since the two of you seem to make such a good team."

"If whatever you're talking about is so big, why do you need my help? I'm only a priest, a monk at that, and not a very good one. Or is this some new sort of reward that you're going to punish me with?"

"You have a special attribute that could be very helpful."

"What? You need a wristwatch repaired? Or is it more research? What can I do that you can't?"

"Oh, I can't tell you. Not yet, anyway. That would be breaking the rules. In time, you'll probably figure it out yourself or with the help of someone else."

"Don't play games with me."

"Father, tell him this isn't a game."

Father William looked at Gerald and shook his head. Then, he turned to the woman and asked.

"Before I start wondering whether I should check into a psychiatric ward, too, I'd appreciate answers to a couple of things that have been bothering me."

"And they are?" the woman said.

*EARTHLY SPIRITS*

"There's an old man we call 'Il Professore'."

"You mean Mr. Renezzo. What a nice old gentleman. Never married. He died the way he lived. Alone in his small apartment."

"So, you're saying you took, or whatever it is you do, his body?"

"Oh, no. I wasn't in Rome. That was one of my aides. No sense telling him your name, you wouldn't be able to pronounce it. We're souls. I never did like the term 'fallen angels'. Just call him a devil. He was looking for Brother Gerald."

"Then why didn't he approach us in the restaurant?"

"I told him to contact Brother Gerald and set up this meeting. He took those orders literally. Because you were there, too, he wasn't sure what to do. It's not easy finding good help these days."

"And that man at the botanical gardens?"

"Very clever, Father. You only ask the smallest part of the question. A nice test. You mean the fellow who entered through the locked gate at the Gianicolense. You don't think locked gates or doors can keep us out. That was another one of my aides. Again, because you were there, too, he didn't want to risk interpreting my instructions to contact Brother Gerald."

"How many devils are there? Are you all in Rome?"

"Not enough to do the job we've been stuck with for these thousands of years. A couple of them have even died off. Souls live a very long time, but even they aren't immortal. No, we're not all in Rome, but it's our headquarters. You didn't think we'd be based in Pittsburgh?"

"All right," Brother Gerald said. "I don't want to hear any small talk. If this is so important, get to the point."

"See what I mean, Father," the woman said. "No imagination. And rude, besides. But, you have to admit that he's a practical man. A little creativity would help and I'm counting on you to provide that. You're going to need it and every other skill you were born with and have acquired."

She rose from the seat, turned to the two men, stretched her arms out from her body and said:

"Behold, I bring you what you believe are going to be tidings of great joy. The Second Coming. It's coming."

# CHAPTER 10

"Beer is a beverage for boys, my young friend," Father William said.

The old priest took a sip from his glass, paused as if to study what was left, then took another. He set the empty glass on the table and reached for the nearby bottle. He gripped the bottle firmly in his right hand as though greeting a friend, and held it halfway between his lips and the table for several seconds. An observer would have thought that he was about to raise it to his lips and drink straight out of it. Instead, he was studying the artist's rendition of a knight resplendent in an Italian Renaissance uniform of red and gold mounted on a colorfully caparisoned horse on the label. Finally, he poured a generous helping of the bottle's contents into his glass, sat back in his chair and took another sip.

"But wine is the beverage for men," he added.

"Young friends, too?" Brother Gerald asked.

"For all friends, even the young ones like you."

"Father, I'm pushing fifty. In a few years I'll be dragging it. And at the rate I've been going lately, it's likely to be heavy"

"That doesn't matter. You haven't reached sixty yet. Anyone under sixty is young to an old fart like me."

"You're drinking too much."

"Nonsense. This is only my second glass."

*EARTHLY SPIRITS*

"Sometimes one is enough."

"Two maybe, three probably. But never one. Besides, at my age, I've found it useful to stop counting."

"What's so useful about that?"

"If you don't count whatever it is you're expected to keep track of, then you can't forget what others expect you to remember. You'll find that out in about another dozen years or so. Sooner or later you start forgetting the small things, like where you left your wristwatch. For you that probably would trigger a panic attack. Just the other night I all but tore my bedroom apart looking for my reading glasses. Of course, I'd probably still be looking for them if I had as much space as you've got to misplace things in this apartment. You'll never guess where they were."

"You probably were just tired. Everybody forgets the obvious at one time or another."

"They were propped up on my forehead."

Brother Gerald interrupted his sip of wine with a laugh. It was the first time he had experienced humor in more than twenty-four hours. It felt good.

"Go ahead," William continued. "Have a good laugh on the poor old man who's taking his first steps into the world of Alzheimer's."

"I don't believe that for a moment," Gerald said. "Ever since you retired as abbot more than a year ago, you've been using your age as an excuse to get away with whatever you can. You eat and drink like a gourmet, walk for miles every day, visit historic old churches and Roman ruins, talk like an authority on everything to anyone who'll listen, watch too much TV and then complain about all of it. You love it when people think you're eccentric."

"At least you're right about the eccentricity. It's the best gift the Lord gives old people. It allows us to do and say whatever we want, and everyone else excuses it because old people are supposed to be eccentric. I'd refuse any offer to trade in aging for another shot at youth. Maybe Alzheimer's will even be a blessing; people doing all sorts of things for you that you once spent years having to do for yourself."

"What were you like when you were young?"

"Not at all like you. I was idealistic. That's one of the hazards that young people have to learn to surmount. But I also knew how to enjoy myself. I smoked, drank, played baseball. You know, everything you'd expect would interest a red-blooded American kid. I didn't think much about the priesthood until I was into my late teen years."

"Girls?"

"There were a couple of them in high school. But that's none of your business."

"Aha. I've finally found something that you don't want to talk about."

"The wine hasn't loosened my tongue enough to reveal all the secrets of my youth. And it won't, either. Which reminds me, you're in need of a refill."

Father William reached for the bottle as Brother Gerald sipped the last of the wine in his glass, then extended his hand. Father William's aim was less than perfect as he poured the monk another drink. Some of the red liquid missed its target and spilled onto the tabletop. Gerald grabbed a napkin and wiped it clean.

"Too bad we don't have a cat," William said.

"Why do we need a cat?" Gerald asked.

"So that none of the wine is wasted. When I was a boy, my family had a cat, a big, fat old tabby. That cat would lap up anything it could get its tongue on. Water, milk, beer, wine, even whiskey. It was a drinking machine. We should have asked Nicole to give us one."

"Who the devil is Nicole?"

"Now that's an excellent choice of words, Gerald. While we were walking in the Forum this afternoon, your friend Nicholas joked that he probably should take the name Nicole as long as he was going around posing as the cat lady. He has quite a sense of humor, you know. I could have sworn he also mentioned it to you, too."

"If he did, I probably blocked it out of my mind. Besides, Father, I've asked you not to refer to him as my 'friend'."

"Sorry, I forgot. See, that's proof that my brain has given birth to Alzheimer's. But, anyway, at least we've gotten back to what we're supposed to be discussing."

"The Second Coming? You don't really believe that, do you?"

"Let's just admit that I lean toward believing it and you lean in the

*EARTHLY SPIRITS*

other direction. Actually, you're leaning a lot more than I would've thought considering everything. If you think about that, it reflects our natures; my positive and your negative. But what either of us believes may be a lot less important than we think."

"Positive? You've all but accepted this person as Lucifer and his fantastic claim about the Second Coming and you call yourself positive?"

"Shhh. Don't shout. Who knows what kind of ears these walls have."

"Oh, right. Christ is supposed to be returning to Earth but only a few of us know about it and we're not supposed to tell anyone. That's a secret to beat all secrets. Just what I was looking forward to; more secrecy."

"We weren't ordered not to tell, just asked not to. He, or she, was much more polite than I expected."

"That's another thing. If this cat lady person really isn't just some third-rate trickster, why weren't we afraid?"

"According to the Bible, Jesus had at least two encounters with Lucifer. The first was when Christ went on that forty-day fast in the wilderness and was tempted by the Devil to seek power. The second was when Jesus was in the Garden of Gethsemane and was tempted again, this time to forsake what was supposed to be His destiny to die on the cross. Again, he refused. But, the Bible never mentions that Christ was frightened. The Bible tells us that Jesus was the prophesied Messiah, and the Church tells us that He was both God and Man. Yet, the Bible also clearly expresses His fear over being crucified. So, if Christ could fear crucifixion, why not also fear the Devil? I mean, according to our theology, there's nothing more frightening than Lucifer. He's supposed to be the embodiment of sinister evil."

"Father, you know that I can't debate the Bible with you. I've always had enough trouble explaining its meanings to anyone, yet alone understanding it."

"There's something else worth thinking about. If Lucifer was so evil, why didn't the Lord simply give him a dose of the same treatment He gave to the people of Sodom and Gomorrah? Maybe Heaven has rules like us. Humans kill the lower animals for food and even sport, but it's a crime to kill other people. Maybe Lucifer really was only more trouble to the Lord than he was worth having around. Maybe Heaven long ago abolished the death penalty for the angels and whoever else lives there. Then, consigning him to watch over things here on Earth might make sense. Sort of like life imprisonment. Can you think of anything else that would be more cruel or unusual punishment?"

"I'd love to watch you give that in the form a lecture to the College of Cardinals. Did you just make it up or have you been thinking about it for a long time as an alternative theology?"

"I've spent almost as much time pondering Church doctrine as I've spent praying over the years. And none of it ever gave me all the answers I wanted. That's one of the reasons I don't do it anymore. Now, for the first time, I feel like I might actually get those answers."

"From the Devil?"

"From whoever or whatever I can. Church doctrine has been more flexible than infallible. It's undergone a lot of changes in two-thousand years; sometimes to reflect Vatican policy, sometimes to pacify the cries of the faithful. That doesn't mean I'm questioning the teachings of the Church. After all, even the Vatican doesn't have all the evidence. Have you ever wondered what a priest really is? Or a rabbi, vicar or any other man or woman of the cloth?"

"Yes, but the definitions are always contradictory."

"The bottom line is that we're people who have only invisible means of support."

"Very droll, but can't we get back to why we're sitting here drinking."

"Hopefully, not to forget. And, I'm sure you haven't forgotten that you weren't afraid when he came to you in that dream you had back in Virginia. And don't say it was only a dream."

"No, because at the time it was only a dream."

"And since then?"

"We've been through all of this at least a dozen times. You know me better than anyone, maybe even better than I know myself. Now that I think of it, I'm not sure I really know much about myself anymore. Except that I feel like a rat swimming towards a sinking ship."

"I know you've got a doctrinal disbelief in superstition, which makes it difficult for you to accept the popular notion of what's superstitious. You might even want to believe, but aren't always able

*EARTHLY SPIRITS*

to. That's not unusual for someone who's served a long time in the priesthood."

"All my life I've been told that Lucifer is an evil liar. Now I'm supposed to believe that he's some sort of advance man for the Second Coming?"

"What do you expect him to do? Swear on the Bible?"

"I expect to be at least a little scared in his presence. I also expect him to tell us more than he did. All he gave us was some weak excuse that he didn't have time to explain anything because he was running late for another appointment. That seems like a convenient excuse to avoid answering questions."

"Maybe he was. As for being frightened, you've got a point. But, there are dozens of stories, even in the Scriptures, about people being unafraid and sometimes even comfortable in encounters with the Devil. Besides, we can't ignore the basic facts that we've learned between Virginia and here."

"Even if I accept everything you and he or she or whatever has said, including being given this assignment at the Vatican, there's one thing that doesn't make sense."

"And that is?"

"If the Second Coming really is going to happen, why should we be part of it?"

"Maybe he likes you and is giving you another favor."

"No, he said I had a special, what was it, 'attribute'."

"That did sound cryptic. But we'll know soon enough. He said he'd explain it all when we meet the night after tomorrow. You're not going to miss that, are you?"

"How could I? Even if I didn't go, you would. I couldn't let you do that alone. But it better be good. I'm tired of these intrigues. Did you see how everyone looked at us when we came back to the Vatican today?"

"I suspect that's mostly curiosity, with a touch of envy. We're a couple of simple priests and a lot of people who work have to wonder how we can have such a free run of the place."

Gerald nodded to the picture of the pope on the wall behind Father William.

"I wonder if he wonders," he said. "The Holy Father is supposed to be God's right-hand man on Earth. You'd think that the Almighty would have blessed him with some of His wisdom."

"I doubt that even the Lord works in that way. Wisdom isn't something that can be conferred on someone, not even on the pope. Besides, I don't think the Second Coming is something that would get a lot of advance publicity. I mean, the Angel Gabriel didn't announce the birth of Jesus to the world. He only told Mary. I'm inclined to believe the Holy Father doesn't know a thing about what we've been told. At least not yet. Why bother him with something he might refuse to believe. What cardinal or whatever Vatican insider is going to risk the clerical career he's worked so hard to nurture by passing on something so fantastic to the pope unless he can back it up with some sort of evidence? Besides, maybe we're the only two in the Vatican who know anything about it."

"You don't believe that."

"You're right. I don't."

"Finally, something that you don't believe."

"It's not the only thing I doubt."

"There's something else?"

"Yes. I doubt we're going to get another glass of wine out of this bottle. So, why don't you fetch another from that cabinet in your kitchen. We both can use a couple of boosters."

# CHAPTER 11

Ewan Sinclair wondered whether the science fiction writers and doomsday cultists had gotten it all wrong, then compounded their error by passing it on to the public. It was not the Martians who were going to invade and ravage the Earth. It was the morons. They already had invaded it and now they were running things.

That was bad enough. But now it was even worse than it had been two days ago. Sinclair felt that he had been drafted to serve in whatever cuckoo cause the morons had undertaken. So, that must make him one of them. Why else had he agreed to do what he was doing?

It all had come back so clearly. Not at first. Until he had boarded his connecting flight in New York, he had not done much more than obey his marching orders. Once the flight was airborne, his thoughts drifted all the way back to the beginning, encouraged by his unease about flying in a jumbo jet. He reluctantly had tolerated the flight from Halifax. The plane had been smaller and the flight took less than two hours to reach New York. But a jumbo jet? He would hurtle through the skies thirty-three thousand feet above the safety of the ground at more than five-hundred miles an hour in a metal tube that was packed with more than three-hundred people, some of them coughing bacteria into the stale air. Only one sort of lunatic could have devised such a hellish form of transportation. Obviously another moron.

He had been assigned a window seat. There, he could watch one of the massive wings to make sure it had not been jarred loose with each turbulent bounce in the sky. If the plane was so safe why were passengers given so many foreboding reminders? Like the location of the emergency exits. Or the glossy card with its printed layout of the aircraft and a list of emergency procedures. Why did they wait until after the flight was airborne to run the safety video? Why run it at all? Who would remember any of what they were supposed to do if the engines failed and the plane began plunging thousands of feet toward the ground? Worst of all was the sign above his seat. For nearly half of the long flight, its letters would light, sometimes accompanied by instructions from the pilot, that the passengers should fasten their seat belts. Every time the sign went on, it seemed like a warning that he was near his personal end of days.

There was none of that on a train.

So, for most of the flight Sinclair let his mind revisit his past. He was amazed how much detail was stored there and how easy it was to recall it.

How different might his life have been had his father not sprained his ankle that night twenty-seven years ago. Ewan was only fourteen years old then and, like some of his friends, seemed destined to be a fisherman. And why not? It was his father's trade and his grandfather's and great-grandfather's. He had heard all the sea stories and how the blood of fishermen had been running in the veins of the Sinclairs for centuries. Not only were they every bit as good as children's fairy tales, they had the added appeal of a role for him in them when he came of age.

The death of the other members of his fishing boat crew changed all that. Almost overnight, his father flipped the coin on the fairy tales and the only side Ewan ever saw again was stamped with hardship, danger and near poverty. No, his parents insisted, he would break the long family tradition. He would not follow in the shoes of the fisherman. There were plenty of others to do that. It might even benefit the community. One less fisherman sharing the catch might even put a few extra morsels of food on the table for some families.

By the time he was sixteen, Ewan was destined for a career in law. It had not been his choice. It had been chosen for him by the society, which was impressed with his grades; he was at the top of class all through high school. It was all the same to him. Like many boys of his age, he was not certain what to do with his life. He had mentally toyed with becoming a firefighter or police officer. The adventure of pursuing criminals appealed to him. As a lawyer maybe Ewan could prosecute them or even defend the innocent.

The society had other plans. Frank Conroy had the only law practice in the village and was closing in on his sixties. Though the practice was small, the society saw growth in its future. Conroy would lack the energy the society needed. His future was retirement. Besides, he was an outsider, who had come to the village years earlier to fill. In time, Conroy became a respected and appreciated member of the community, but he would never understand the heritage, traditions and goals of the society. That could be grasped only by someone whose family lineage made him part of it. Someone who would have a sense of duty when called. Ewan had become the ideal choice. He would be Conroy's associate and successor. He would do his duty all right. How could he refuse? Not only was he one of them by birth, he had willingly taken part in the secret ritual on his eighteenth birthday. Besides, he always would know that it was the society that paid the bill for his education.

Now the bill was due.

Why did it have to be Father John? Had anyone else in the society asked Ewan to make this trip, at least he would have been tempted to refuse. But Father John? No one ever refused him. The prizefighter looks chiseled into his face below eyebrows so thick that they cast shadows on his cheeks could demand obedience from anyone easily swayed. But his strength was in his voice. Loud and commanding, it was so hypnotic that even the most practiced doubter would hear truth in whatever the priest might say. Some who knew him wondered why he had chosen the priesthood over politics. Most of them were relieved about his choice.

Now that he was beyond the immediate reach of Father John, Ewan no longer knew what to believe. Father John had made his mission seem more important than the search for the legendary biblical Lost Ark of the Covenant. Now it felt more like a wild goose chase.

The priest had made him feel special by granting him admission to the secret room under Saint Andrew's Church. The legendary room where the select elders of what was left of the Knights of the Templar met. It was smaller and better kept than Ewan had thought. An old wood table and six straight-backed chairs were set in the center. A large display case lined most of one wall. Protected behind its glass shield were a handful of medieval weapons, a shield, coats of arms regalia and some old, leather-bound books. All looked their age. A small altar equipped with all the Church requirements for celebrating Mass and special services for the six faithful, who met there regularly, had been built on the opposite wall. A pair of medieval-style lamps hanging on each of the two otherwise bare walls provided enough light to make visitors forget that they were in an old basement designed in varying shades of decaying gray. The most interesting feature was a small, locked gold chest that sat conspicuously in the center of the altar. When he asked Father John what it contained, the priest became evasive, hinting only that it might be a sacred relic. At that moment, Ewan wanted to believe that it was the hiding place of the Holy Grail. If that claim were ever made public, the keepers of ancient Glastonbury Abbey in England were certain to issue a challenge.

Now that he was driving along the Pacific Coast Scenic Byway in Oregon, Ewan Sinclair neither believed nor cared that his village might be home to the Holy Grail or any other relic. For all he knew, the gold case back in Nova Scotia might contain nothing more than a piece of dried animal loin that the six old men of the society believed was the foreskin of Jesus.

He had an assignment to complete and the faster he completed it, the sooner he would return home and try to pick up what might be left of his law practice. Father John had made a convincing argument that his practice would not suffer. The society would see to that. It was the one thing about this trip that Ewan tended to believe. If nothing else, the society always could be depended upon to take care of its own. Fortunately, he did not leave behind any legal business that could not wait for a week or two. He was sure that he could do this job well within that range of time. And, even if he failed, who could dispute that his effort had been less than the best that anyone could have done?

Even though Ewan had not been given much notice, he had to hand it to the society. He had left Father John that night with a portfolio that

*EARTHLY SPIRITS*

included his airline tickets and a car rental voucher, background information on what was expected of him and a map of the northern Oregon coast. The only thing missing was the exact location that would mark the end of his search. That would be in one of the smaller towns, probably with fewer than five-thousand inhabitants. Still, unless Ewan got lucky, that could mean stopping at dozens of towns in the one-hundred-and-fifty mile stretch south of the Washington state border to Cape Fairweather.

He already had covered five small towns, two the afternoon of the day he had landed at Portland before finding a motel that had a rare available room for the night. It was the start of the tourism and festival season and most places were fully booked. After drawing blanks in three more towns on his second day, he took a lunch break at a small restaurant specializing in seafood. He lingered longer than he had intended, which meant he probably would be able to search only two more towns before calling it a day. The national and state registries would have made his task easier, but they were of no help. What he was looking for was too new to be listed in any of them. Local tourist offices were good sources of information, but not every town had one. All he could do was drive from one place to another, then when he got there, depend on legwork. If he should find what he was looking for, he still would have another problem. He was sent to get information but he could not reveal the reason for wanting it. Even if he could, who would believe him?

The afternoon drive was little different from what Ewan had experienced ever since he reached the coast the day before. Because he felt pressed for time, the legal speed limit of fifty-five miles an hour was frustrating. He could rarely reach that speed anyway because the road often was jammed with tourists gawking at the scenery or being careful because of road hazards they had not expected. The hazards of the highway dictated care. Sharp curves appeared out of nowhere, reminders that if he drove much faster he might not be able to slow down enough for his compact rental car to safely make the turns. Trucks hauling logs and other materials also occasionally burst from blind side roads onto the pavement not far in front of him. Deer, elk and other animals added to the hazards that materialized swiftly.

The coastal scenery was as picturesque as a series of postcards. The road wound along the top of rugged cliffs. The east side was mostly bordered by lush evergreen forests. To the west, Ewan often could see the Pacific Ocean, with occasional beaches below, some of them boasting sand dunes that could be mistaken for small pyramids at first glance from above. The unpredictable northwest weather was cooperative, laying out a canopy of light blue skies accompanied by mild temperatures, allowing him to drive with all the windows open. Except for the engines of vehicles driven by locals and tourists, the only other sounds he heard were the distinctive cries of seagulls cruising on the upper winds and of waves crashing on the shoreline below. Regardless of where his explorations took him, he promised that before returning home, he would indulge himself in a visual treat that he had never witnessed—the spectacle of the sun setting set beneath the distant horizon of the sea.

Ewan had driven for nearly half-an-hour when he saw the exit sign to Little Cove. It could not have been one of the larger towns because it was not even on his map. He did not hesitate deciding to leave the highway, partly because the mild effect of the two glasses of Oregon white wine that he had enjoyed with his lunch still had not worn off. He should have known better not to have the second glass. As a lawyer he was well aware of the consequences of being found with an illegal limit of alcohol in his blood had he been in an accident, even if it was the other driver's fault.

The narrow exit road ran off the highway and curved down toward the shoreline below. He was sure he was heading for another one of the down-home environments he had experienced. The sort of place whose hospitality and seasonal pleasantries rivaled those of Nova Scotia. What would it be this time? A lighthouse, marine museum or aquarium? Was he going to ride into a salmon festival parade clogging the main street? How many art galleries and gift shops awaited him?

Within minutes, he was on a two-lane road that was as straight as it was level. Just ahead he could see the first building, a gasoline station. A quarter-of-a-mile later, he passed a small elementary school and entered the center of what appeared to be barely a village. There were no lighthouses or marine museums or aquariums. No parades or festivals. The main street had an obligatory art gallery, two gift shops, a grocery

*EARTHLY SPIRITS*

store, general store, drug store, bookshop, antique shop, ice cream parlor, hairstyling salon, church and several houses that served as residences or businesses, some of them even both. A few tree-lined side streets that looked strictly residential intersected with the main street. Most of the buildings were whitewashed, all looked old, some looked recently painted. All were well kept.

He parked his car at a corner at the far end of the town in front of a yellow clapboard house that served as a municipal building and went inside. The only person he saw there was a gray-haired woman seated at a wood desk behind a counter, reading a newspaper. She wore a faded black dress with a floral pattern, the kind that looked fashionable only on elderly women. A light, white sweater was wrapped around her shoulders. Ewan guessed that she was in her sixties. She looked up at a clock on a nearby wall, then turned to Ewan as though she was surprised to see a visitor.

"I'm looking for somewhere to spend the night," Ewan said.

"Only one such place here," the woman replied.

She wore a slight scowl on her lips, which emitted a raspy voice that came from deep down a throat shrouded in a wrinkled neck. Every word sounded like it was spoken by someone who was easily irritated. He guessed that she was the town clerk, which meant that the mayor and council members did all the thinking, and she did all the work. But, almost as if she was physically disputing her natural crankiness, she carefully folded her newspaper, placed it on the desk, got up from her chair and motioned for Ewan to follow her to the door. They stood on the steps outside and she pointed down the street to her left.

"Is that your car?" she asked, pointing to his rental vehicle.

"Yes," he replied. "It's all right too park there, isn't it?"

"Park anywhere you want as long as you don't block anyone's driveway. Not enough cars come through here, so there's no need for parking rules. But you'll have to turn around."

"Did I pass it?"

"Yes, but you wouldn't have noticed it. It's not on the main street. It's one block back, on Cove Lane. Turn left there and look for the big white house on the right at the end of the first block. It's got blue shutters, blue

101

picket fence and a pretty flower garden. You can't miss it. They've got a couple of rooms for travelers, but I can't say whether they're filled up for the night. Just make sure you drive slowly. Cove Lane's only two short blocks long and runs straight into the beach. If you're not paying attention you could drive right onto the sand and get stuck. Then we'd have to call Elmer to haul you out. He has to do that two or three times every summer. Usually it's joy-riding kids who think they know how to drive."

"I'd like to leave my car parked outside here in front," Ewan said. "I'd prefer to walk there and take a look around your town. It seems very nice."

"Walk anywhere you want. There's no rules against that either."

The sedating effects of the wine had dissipated, leaving Ewan feeling mellow. He felt no need to rush. It was only twenty minutes past two o'clock. The sun would be king of the sky for at least another seven hours. That was enough time for two or three or more towns. So, he strolled, stopping to finger some of the postcards in a rack outside one of the gift shops. He moved along past two more doors and paused at the window of the antique shop. Its window was filled with old marine devices ranging from scientific instruments to ocean diving helmets, most of them restored to their original brass brilliance. He might buy something to add to his collection, maybe the brass sextant or the set of old irons from the brig of a ship.

Like the buildings on the main street, the houses on Cove Lane were old. But they were in such good condition that they gave him the impression of trying to look as though they had been recently built just for him to admire. This obviously was a village that had a sense of civic pride. He could see the beach and the sea ahead. His eye caught the house with blue shutters and blue picket fence in the middle of the block on the right. Then, he saw the sign. It was hanging from a white post next to the walkway in the center of the fence. He had to look twice before his brain processed the letters. They read:

"The Hitching Post."

He wanted to believe that he had gotten lucky. That was the name of the place that the proprietors had back in Virginia. Just in case, he put his hands behind his back and crossed his fingers as he stepped onto the walkway.

*EARTHLY SPIRITS*

A woman wearing jeans and a plain white blouse with a pair of garden shears in a gloved right hand was bent over a patch of red and white roses in full bloom. Chestnut hair tumbled gently down the back of a neck that nestled between softly molded round shoulders. When she heard his footsteps, she turned to him, smiling.

"Can I help you?" she asked.

"Yes, I'm looking for a room for the night."

"Well, you're in luck. Someone checked out this morning, so we've got one available. Is someone with you?"

"No, just me."

"Then, let's go inside and I'll show you around."

"I don't want to disturb your gardening."

"It's no bother. I'm, just pruning and clipping a few roses for the center of the dinner table. I can finish up later. By the way, what name can I add to our guest registry."

"Ewan Sinclair."

The woman switched the shears to her left hand, pulled the glove off her right, exposing a hand that looked too fragile for gardening. At the same time, it looked natural and, like her face, seemed to be a perfect fit on her.

"It's nice to meet you, Mr. Sinclair," she said.

As they shook hands, she added:

"I'm Teresa Lucci."

# CHAPTER 12

"Even with all these people walking by, this place always seems to lack the liveliness of other piazzas," Father William said. "With you sulking like a child who didn't get what he wanted for his birthday, you can make it feel downright depressing."

Brother Gerald's eyes swept the Piazza della Rotonda. He and Father William had a good view of it from where they were standing just outside the entrance to the Pantheon. People strolled in and out of the piazza through the maze of slender streets that fed into it from other sections of Rome's historic center. Except for one merchant selling souvenirs from what was little more than a narrow stall tucked in between old buildings, the piazza's shops were closed. It would be another half-hour before the piazza's restaurants opened for dinner.

"What do you expect?" Gerald replied. There was a hint of challenge in his voice. "The buildings are blocking the sunlight and we're standing outside a giant mausoleum waiting for someone who claims to be Lucifer. I wonder if it's going to be the cat lady again or is he going to have another sec change. Maybe instead of a he or she, this time we'll be meeting an it."

"Dressed for the occasion? Robed and hooded in black? Or is it red? Complete with horns, tail and cloven hooves? Now that would be a sight to behold. Something I'd like to see."

*EARTHLY SPIRITS*

"You take everything too lightly, Father."

"And you take everything with a good dose of despair, my friend. Neither of us has been threatened in any way. Even if he showed up in full satanic glory, neither would anyone else here. They'd probably think it was someone dressed for a costume party or some festival. Few people believe in the Devil anymore."

"Including me?"

"I can only go with what I've observed and what I've heard from you."

"Meaning?"

"You're sort of a reverse agnostic. On the one hand, you don't believe in the Devil, but you're hedging your bets just in case."

"And on the other?"

"You believe in the Devil, but don't want to."

"Well, if he's not here having fun at our expense by masquerading as someone we don't recognize, then he's two minutes late. It's six-thirty-two."

"It's good to see that you've regained some of your form. Such a stickler for time. I know just what you need to relieve your anxiety."

"Not another glass of wine."

"Still not recovered from last night?"

"That's just it. I am recovered and want to stay that way."

"No, not more wine. At least not for now. Something for your intellectual soul. Let's take a look inside the Pantheon."

"We're supposed to meet him outside."

"If he's really who or what he claims to be, I don't think he'd have any trouble finding us."

The two men took one last look around the Piazza della Rotunda, did not see a recognizable face, turned, walked between two of the eight monolithic granite columns that supported the massive front portico of the Pantheon and entered through the opening past the huge bronze main doors.

"I still don't get it," Father William said.

"Get what?" Brother Gerald asked.

"People are just coming and going as they please. No one's staffing the booth that sells admission tickets. I've seen it here, at the Coliseum and a few other places. What I mean is there doesn't seem to be any system or schedule for bilking tourists out of their money. One day they charge admission, another they don't. Sometimes you pay in the morning but not after lunch or vice-versa."

"There doesn't seem to be much security, either. Just the one carabinieri standing outside the door. He didn't seem to be paying much attention to anything. I didn't even see him bothering to check any handbags or shopping bags."

"Maybe that's because this building is blessed with divine security."

"It has its own guardian angel?"

"Oddly enough, it's the only ancient monument in Rome that was never sacked by the barbarians back in the days when the empire was collapsing. For some reason, it was left untouched."

"So, what you see now is what you saw, when, two-thousand years ago?"

"I'd like to believe that you knew that, but I'm guessing it was a guess."

"It was."

"The original Pantheon took two years to build and was opened in 25 B.C. Marcus Agrippa, who built it, wanted to dedicate it to Augustus, his father-in-law. When Augustus declined the honor, Agrippa dedicated instead to the major gods that were worshiped by the families of Claudius and Julius Caesar. They were Mars and Venus and, incidentally, the great Julius himself. The original building was a rectangle. The Emperor Hadrian added the great rotunda that we're standing in now somewhere around 120 A.D."

"He liked round buildings, didn't he?"

"You mean Castel Sant' Angelo near the Tiber River?"

"I mean Hadrian's Tomb."

"They're one and the same. For a moment I thought maybe you'd finally absorbed some of the culture of this city."

"I haven't had your freedom of movement," Gerald looked up from the rotunda floor to the great dome above them. "But I learn fast. This is an amazing achievement, even for engineers as skilled as the Romans were."

"What's even more amazing is that the cupola actually is supported by

*EARTHLY SPIRITS*

wooden frame. They applied a single coating of cement over it to give the impression that it's solid stone. Imagine, wood nearly two-thousand years old is the foundation for the dome. And these walls are about seventeen feet thick."

"Michelangelo is supposed to have used it as a model when he designed the dome for St. Peter's Basilica."

"He was so impressed with this dome that he's supposed to have deliberately designed the St. Peter's dome so that it would be a little smaller. I think the Pantheon dome is three or four feet wider in diameter. The Romans made their dome one-hundred and forty-two feet across, which is its same height at the center. It's the world's largest masonry vault."

"I wonder if the pope knew that."

"Probably not. At least not until it was too late. Otherwise, he would've made life miserable for Michelangelo, maybe even given him the boot and hired someone else to do the job."

"Isn't he supposed to be buried here."

"Wrong artist. It's Raphael."

Father William pointed to the left, where the great Renaissance painter's tomb was set between two of the niches that once had been reserved for statues of the ancient Roman gods. The two men walked to it.

"Cardinal Bembo composed the epitaph etched into the wall above Raphael's tomb," William said. "You can read Latin."

"Living great nature feared he might outvie her works; and dying, fears herself to die," Gerald read in whispering English.

"Raphael isn't the only notable buried here. Giovanni de Udine, Perino del Vaga, Annibale Carraci and a couple of others whose names I can't recall also have tombs. Oh, and so do two of Italy's kings—Vittorio Emmanuele II and Umberto I."

Brother Gerald's eyes swept the interior of the round vault.

"He's not here yet," William said. "Be patient. He's not going to stand us up."

Gerald then lifted his head again toward the great dome and stared at the oculus, the thirty-foot-wide circular opening in its center. For a few moments he forgot the reason why he and Father William were there. The fading sunlight that poured through the opening to the sky provided the Pantheon with its only illumination. He wondered what rites had been performed by the ancients inside this secret temple that had been conceived as a giant sundial. As the sun moved, its hours circled the center of the polished marble interior floor. It was now almost fifteen minutes to seven o'clock. Gerald checked the accuracy of the giant timepiece against the time on his wristwatch. It was an almost perfect match.

"How do they keep the rain from falling inside?" Gerald asked.

"They don't," a voice replied.

The two priests turned.

Facing them was a dark-haired man who looked like he was in his mid to late-twenties. He wore a dark blue business suit and an open collared white shirt. A mischievous twinkle hid behind the serious intensity of his light blue eyes that nestled in deep sockets on either side of the bridge of a sharply chiseled nose. He spoke again in an almost boyish voice that seemed to filter through thin smirking lips.

"Whatever is up sooner or later comes down, right onto the floor. They must spend a fortune in mops keeping it dry."

Brother Gerald and Father William remained mute.

"Forgotten me so soon?" the man asked.

"It's you," Father William said. "The man in the park."

"Well, yes and no."

"You opened the locked gate and walked past us. I remember you turned and nodded like you knew us. You were wearing blue jeans and a T-shirt then."

"Right body, wrong man."

"Is this another game?" Gerald asked.

"No, just another body that one of my devils was holding for me. I had to return the cat lady to the morgue. I couldn't continue cavorting around town like her. She was too well known in cat circles. Besides, her shoes hurt my feet. This fellow knew how to treat his feet. Expensive Italian leather."

"We're supposed to believe that you're…"

*EARTHLY SPIRITS*

"Will you ever be convinced? Here, take a look."

The man pulled back the left sleeve of his jacket. His forearm was tattooed with a red letter 'N' in a red circle."

"Do I have to give you another quick trip down memory lane?" he asked Gerald.

"No, that's all right," the monk replied.

"Who was it this time?" Father William asked.

"A small-time Russian hoodlum who'd stole some drug money from the Russian Mafia. He was hiding out in Rome. He got off lucky. Usually they make dying a long and very unpleasant experience. But the walls of his apartment were thin and some neighbors apparently heard enough noise to phone the police. So, he got lucky. He was dispatched with a single shot close to the heart. He died a few hours later waiting for treatment in a hospital emergency room. Must have been a busy day or they would have gotten to him sooner. We're always prowling the hospitals for likely candidate bodies, you know. Actually, we were more fortunate than usual with this one. Except for the bullet wound, he was in good shape. And that was easy to patch up. I can keep this body for as long as I need it. You should appreciate that."

"I hope you don't mean we're going to see a lot of each other," Gerald said.

"Brother, you cut me to the quick. But yes, we are."

"Why?"

"Questions, always questions." The man turned to Father William. "Is he always this way with you, too?"

"Yes, but I'd also like to know why," Father William said.

"I thought I'd explained that the other day."

"Of course," Gerald answered. His voice was splashed with sarcasm. "How could I forget the Second Coming?"

The man gave Gerald a stern look, followed with words that sounded almost admonishing.

"You'd best not forget it. This is no game. The Second Coming is coming all right. It's coming ahead of schedule. There's work to be done and, like it or not, your help is needed."

"If you're serious, I still don't understand why the two of us are so important," Father William said.

"You're about to find out. I'll explain it all at dinner."

"We're going to dinner together?" Gerald asked.

"Why not? You people have spent centuries dancing with the Devil. So what's the harm spending one evening dining with him?"

"Suppose I refuse?"

"Oh, you won't. If nothing else, you're curious to find out where this is all going. Besides, this is an invitation I know that Father William can't refuse."

"What happens, if after listening to you, I decide not to cooperate or do whatever it is you're going to ask?"

"You already know the answer to that. As with everything, you've got choice. But I'm betting that you'll get on board."

"Are we going to your apartment?" Father William asked.

"Oh, no, I can't go back there. Too risky. We're going to dine out."

"At a restaurant?"

"What's the matter? Are you ashamed to be seen in public with the Devil? God isn't going to strike you dead with a lightning bolt. He won't even consider it a sin. Only Bible thumpers and other religious fanatics believe that. He just hasn't wanted you putting me or anyone else on a pedestal higher than the one He occupies.

"I've reserved a quiet table in a rather unusual restaurant around the corner. The cuisine is superb and you won't find a better bottle of wine anywhere else in Rome. I'm picking up the tab, of course. This hoodlum had a lot of money hidden in his apartment. Credit cards, too. Not that I needed it. We do keep a reserve in a variety of currencies, you know, just in case."

"How are we going to talk about, you know..."

"The Second Coming? I'm surprised, Father William, that even you hesitate to speak the words."

"I thought we would meet somewhere privately, where no one could eavesdrop."

"That's exactly where we're going. You'll see. I know it goes against everything both of you have been taught, but... trust me."

"Okay, Nicholas, cat lady or whatever name you're using now, we'll go," Gerald said. "The sooner we get on with it, the sooner it'll be over."

*EARTHLY SPIRITS*

"You don't have to be so stiff collared, brother. The man was Russian. You can just call me Nikolai."

# CHAPTER 13

The old man tilted a weathered face toward the late morning sun, catching the rays from the sky. They added warming touches to the cool salt water spray that was sucked up from the clear turquoise waters of the Aegean Sea by the speeding hydrofoil, then dispersed in a non-stop shower onto its forward deck. His carefully brushed gray hair no longer was a neatly piled wave. The wind sliced into what had become a gray mass atop his head, tossing it upward like leaves on the end of a tree branch in a storm.

His eyes had been shut for several minutes, enhancing a rare feeling of freedom. It was a release from pressure felt for so long that it often blocked any memory of ever feeling free. Now the sensation seemed new, like a pleasurable emotion being experienced for the first time in a life that had known little enjoyment. His eyelids finally raised, revealing a pair of sad light brown eyes that struggled to regain a flicker of something more than mere existence.

Three weeks earlier, New York City was the starting point of what had become an long-desired odyssey. He had mused briefly about settling permanently in Greenwich Village. But that area of the American metropolis no longer had the Bohemian appeal of a half-century earlier. Besides, while it was easy to get lost among the city's millions, it also was

*EARTHLY SPIRITS*

easy to be visible there simply because it was New York. He had not gone there to stay, anyway, but to acquire an identity that would be difficult to trace. He knew that finding it would be easy, since people went there every day to escape or seek opportunity with new identities.

Stefano Petrandriou was the name on his passport. His face matched the photograph perfectly. A New York driver's license, Social Security card and birth certificate also bore the same name. So did the credit cards and bank account, with its substantial reserve of funds from the sale of the Petrandriou neighborhood restaurant. The documents all were genuine. He could pass through immigration and security checkpoints with little concern. He did not have to worry about family inquiries since the only relative was a distant cousin who lived in Athens. The old man had talked for years about going there to live with him. Anyone who ever listened to Petrandriou no reason to believe otherwise.

The weakening family ties and its strong heritage made going to Athens obligatory for someone trying to get lost. He wanted to visit it, anyway, but never intended it to be the end of the journey. He spent a few days there, admiring the Acropolis and other ancient Greek sites, then continued on, never looking up the cousin. Why bother? Their only contact in recent years had been the exchange of a few letters, none of which indicated when a reunion would take place. He had left no forwarding address with the Post Office, so any mail would be returned to sender. He would be presumed dead in time, then forgotten. By then it should be too late.

Nearly three-thousand islands in the Aegean Sea were potential havens. Fewer than one-hundred-and-eighty of them were inhabited. He first had thought of choosing one of the uninhabited on which to live out whatever years might be left. There was enough money to build a comfortable house. However, being the only resident sooner or later might attract more attention than being in a crowd. Besides, where one person built a house, developers were sure to follow. While no island guaranteed anonymity, one of the others probably would be a better choice. He could get a feeling for what could be the best refuge by spending a couple of days each on as many as possible.

Andros had been the first stop after leaving Pireaus, which for three-thousand years had been the port of Athens. Andros had the appeal of a place to get away from it all. But, even though it had no sandy beaches, it had become a popular destination. Athens was so close, that city dwellers packed the island on weekends. No, Andros would not do. It was too popular.

His next stop was nearby Tinos. Its picturesque mountain villages and charming harbor town were inviting. Not many tourists visited there. But, it was the most Roman Catholic of the Cyclades islands. Every year, thousands of pilgrims descended on it during Annunciation Day week in late March and Assumption Day week in mid-August. Many of them came seeking cures for ailments at Panagia Evangelista Church where the icon of the Virgin Mary had been reputed to work miracles on the lame and diseased ever since its discovery in the early Nineteenth Century. He left there after one day.

A place that beckons lovers of classical Greece, Mykonos sounded interesting. Its main town entwined its windmill-laced harbor with a picturesque labyrinth of narrow, cobbled winding lanes and alleys. Fishermen and tourists shared its port cafes that bustled beneath the balconies of whitewashed terraced houses. Beyond the main town, there were enough small villages, coves and beaches for anyone to enjoy for a lifetime. He was shocked, however, by the open hedonism of the place, especially its gay life. It could not be Mykonos. He could not be comfortable there and would go elsewhere. He also experienced the deep disturbing guilt of a long-dormant prejudice, but could not help it. He had forgotten much about human behavior. There was a lot to learn. He would have to adjust, adapt, accept. Otherwise, there would be little comfort in whatever years were left.

Naxos was not a planned stop. But, Stefano Petrandriou's ancestors had been born there. He wanted to visit the graves of the grandparents and great grandparents on the largest of the Cyclades. Life there in was blessed with an abundance of groves of orange, lemon, fig and pomegranate trees. It was reputed to produce the best wine in Greece. He had to agree. It also was a living museum for anyone addicted to history. Naxos had been the reigning power of the Aegean islands until 490 B.C. when the Persians all but destroyed it. He felt saddened by the loss of so

*EARTHLY SPIRITS*

much ancient marble architecture and monuments. But the Petrandriou family history made it impossible to stay there. He might be traced. Besides, the island attracted historians of all sorts. These included literary experts who wanted to visit the old school where Nikos Kazantzakis studied years before gaining fame as the author of "Zorba the Greek" and the Vatican's rebuke for his controversial novel, "The Last Temptation of Christ." He someday would have to read the latter.

Islands seemed to pass by as the hydrofoil sped across the Aegean. They were small and some could have been mistaken as uninhabited limestone rocks dotted with patches of green. Some were smothered in lush growth. However, unlike the other passengers enjoying the sea spray on the forward deck, the old man knew how to look. A small seaside settlement hugging a tiny cove hid just around the bend of one. A chapel dome glistened in the sunlight of another. Hillsides were tended with terraced vineyards and olive groves. All were washed gently by turquoise waters. The voyage almost was narcotic. He mused about it going on for an eternity, but the giant that loomed ahead ended the vision.

Santorini had come into sight. Stefano Petrandriou had been there as a child and the memory of it came back, blurred at first, then as clear as the waters of the sea. The immense rock hovered above two tiny black islands near the middle of its bay. They were built by the earthquakes and volcanic eruptions that had plagued Santorini for centuries. The nearly desolate port was not welcoming, but its meager facade was truly no more than a landing stage. High above its brown cliffsides, the capital town of Fira was strung out in an inviting chain of shiny pearl white buildings. Visitors could ride a donkey up the nearly six-hundred stone steps to the town. They also could take a cable car or an exhilarating taxi ride up the steep and winding mountain road in a vehicle recklessly driven by a young man with dreams of a future in the European racing circuit.

He would opt for the donkey, then rest here for several days, perhaps even a week, before deciding where to go next. His odyssey probably would not end on Santorini. More likely, the island would be only a temporary haven, a place to relax for a couple of weeks, giving time to decide on a more permanent refuge. He would go, go and go, then stop for a couple of weeks, and maybe go and go again before stopping for a shorter stay. That would break the rhythm of being constantly on the move, which could attract attention. He had the luxury of traveling light; just one medium-sized carryon bag. He wondered how travelers could haul two and three large pieces of unwieldy luggage everywhere they went.

He had begun to appreciate the irony of the journey. He was on the run. Yet, there was no anxiety, no fear. Physical fatigue was closer than any pursuers. He could outthink them. His aging body was in excellent health for its seventy-five years of wear. He had calculated that death could be at least ten years away. He would be left in peace before then. Sooner or later, they would give up their search, maybe in six months, certainly no more than a year. He would find the perfect hideaway soon. He had started the journey concerned about the potential consequences, but no more. He had done his best to leave everything behind in good order. He had done the best for far too long. He was tired of being tired.

The boat cruised into the harbor, docked and began unloading the passengers. He melted into the middle of the crowd, trying not to be conspicuous. He was ashore in less than a minute.

Looking up at the buildings of Fira clinging to the edge of the cliffs, the old man took a deep breath. He could not help but marvel at the resilience of Santorini's people. Earthquakes and volcanic eruptions may have shaken them, but only temporarily. One generation after another refused to surrender. He marveled at their resolve to live their lives the way they wanted. He would do no less.

He saw the men holding their donkeys by the reins. He went straight for the handler who looked like he had been around the most years. Not because the man might have been the most experienced, but because he was the oldest.

Stefan Petrandriou did not fear old age. He even had looked forward to it as it drew closer. He now expected to appreciate it more than anyone. Being born, getting old, dying. There was just one more of those experiences to go. The sequence was natural. Everything that had lived since the beginning of time had experienced it. What was wrong with that?

# CHAPTER 14

Three.

Brother Gerald felt it happening again, the way it had at Blessed Skyline Abbey. Everything once more was somehow coming up threes. There were three of them. Tonight was the third time they had met. They were on the third street they had turned into since leaving the Pantheon. The address on the door of the restaurant was the number three. He wondered whether the place had only three seats. He fully expected it to be named simply "Number Three" until he looked up and read the magenta letters on the sign over the large picture window.

"Maurice's."

Nikolai led the way to the door and stood there trying to look through the frosted glass framed by wood. When he did not reach for the handle to open it, Father William asked why he was waiting.

"The door's locked," Nikolai said.

"I thought locks were no problem for you," Gerald said.

"I catch a hint of doubt there, brother. Of course locks are no problem. But I don't want to disrupt protocol. The management would be very upset if I just opened the door and we walked in. I did tell you that this was an unusual restaurant."

After about a minute, a woman came to the door, unlocked it, opened it just enough so that they could see a slice of her face and asked what they wanted.

"Dinner for three," Nikolai said.

"You know this is not an Italian restaurant," she replied in an English that bore a heavy German accent.

"Yes, I know."

"And we don't accept credit cards. Cash only."

"No problem, madame."

She gave the two clerics harsh glances before opening the door all the way with just enough reluctance to make them feel unwelcome, and asked them to step inside. She then closed and locked the door behind them.

"Follow me," she said. It sounded like an order.

The woman marched the three between empty well-spaced tables about two-thirds of the distance between the door and a large, well-stocked bar that fronted the rear wall. When they reached a table against the gray stone wall on the right, she stopped, turned and said:

"Sit here."

They obeyed.

When she seemed satisfied that they were properly seated, she left without a word, leaving through a door just to the rear left of the bar.

Though the restaurant was larger than either Gerald of William expected, its décor gave it the warm, almost homey feeling that had been denied by the woman. The two side walls between the bar, and the huge front window and door were adorned with an eclectic mix of memorabilia, posters and souvenirs. One wall was finished in French, the other in German. They were seated on the German side, just below a large, hand-carved Bavarian cuckoo clock. Hung above the bar was a long row of German beer steins, most of them antiques. They were the only three people in the room.

"We're early," Father William said.

"So, can you get straight to the point before the crowd arrives?" Gerald asked, looking at Nikolai.

"No need to worry about that," Nikolai said. "First, a nice meal and some wine."

"You want us to have a feast like we're three friends out for the night?"

*EARTHLY SPIRITS*

"You're of the Benedictine Order, aren't you?"

"You know we both are. What's that got to do with it?"

"You've read more history than most people, brother. You should know the history of your order."

"Have I missed something?"

"Brother, I think he's referring to the Benedictine's medieval reputation as gourmets," Father William said.

"Close enough, Father," Nikolai replied. "Actually, they were more gluttons than gourmets. "In the Thirteenth Century, the daily ration of the Benedictines at Westminster Abbey in London included up to two pounds of meat, and equal amounts of fish and bread. Plus eggs and vegetables. And, each monk was allowed to top it all off with a gallon of wine or ale. It's astonishing that they had time or energy to do any soul-saving. Not that they did much."

"Sadly, brother, he's right."

"So, you brought us here to have some sort of Benedictine-style bacchanal orgy of wining and dining," Gerald said. He was trying not to be aggressive, but could not help it.

"Of course not," Nikolai said. "I've never been a Benedictine."

Before Brother Gerald could reply, a broad-shouldered man with a bulky midsection that looked as though it was struggling to burst the lower buttons of his light gray shirt, came through the door from behind the bar and began making his way toward their table. He seemed to totter unsteadily with each step on a pair of oversized feet clad in heavy black shoes. He wore a frown that looked like it had been permanently etched into a face that sagged from drooping eyelids down to his chin.

"Good evening," he mumbled in a French accent. "I'm Maurice. You already met my wife Gretchen. She will bring your menus shortly. Would you like a bottle of wine?"

"Brunello," Nikolai replied.

"An excellent choice," Maurice said. "Here comes Gretchen. I'll fetch the Brunello."

"I'm not familiar with Brunello," Father William said.

"It's the wine preferred by discerning people who produce and sell Chianti to the rest of the public," Nikolai replied.

The woman gave each of them a menu. Rather then leave to give them time to choose, she stood at the table, hovering over them. It did not bother Father William or Nikolai, but Gerald felt pressured.

"Is there anything particularly good tonight?" the monk asked.

"It is all good," she snapped. "But if you want a recommendation, I am sure my husband will be pleased to do so when he returns with your wine."

Gerald felt like covering his head with the menu. Instead, he opened it and pretended to read. To his relief, Maurice was on his way back to the table. Just as the man arrived, Gerald noticed for the first time that there were five chairs at their table, even though there were several tables with seating for three. Before he had time to wonder why, Maurice set the open bottle on the table and sat down on an empty chair. His wife took the other. One by one, he placed the five wine glasses he had been carrying in his other hand on the table, one for each of them.

The frown Maurice had worn when he first came to the table had been replaced by a genuine smile that seemed to lift the rest of his face except for his eyes. For the first time, Gretchen also smiled through thin lips in her thin face, though it looked forced. She kept the look through dinner and said little.

"Let's all enjoy some wine while you decide what you want for dinner," he said. He emptied the bottle into the five glasses, raised his in a toast and took a sip. "I'll bring another bottle later."

Father William and Brother Gerald took Maurice's recommendation, ordering a half-dozen escargots as appetizers and the Tuscan beef in Gorgonzola sauce as main courses. Nikolai ordered a small portion of steak tartare as an appetizer and finished with a full portion for his main course. At his request, Nikolai brought the raw beef, raw egg and condiments separately to the table, allowing Nikolai to mix his own. Brother Gerald tried not to look at the steak tartare, but fascination got the better of him and he glimpsed it a few times. Nikolai ignored the thin slices of bread that had been brought to hold spreads of the mixed raw beef. Instead, he ate it with a fork. He spoke only once during the meal. Maurice did most of the speaking as he and his wife sat at the table drinking from another of the non-stop bottles of Brunello that quickly

*EARTHLY SPIRITS*

replaced the empties until the three diners had finished with their dessert, a Black Forest torte from Germany.

The one time Gerald broke his silence was in the middle of the main course. Oddly, he was enjoying the food and wine along with Maurice's almost non-stop monologue, interrupted occasionally by questions from William and Nikolai. It occurred when four young people showed up at the front door, peering inside. Gerald had motioned for them to come in, then realizing that the door was locked, told Maurice that he had four more customers.

Maurice turned, looked at them, shook his head as though he was indicating that they should move on, then waved them away. His wife nodded in agreement.

At that moment, Gerald suddenly became aware that no one else had entered the restaurant since they arrived. A restaurant that served some of the best food and the best wine he had ever tasted? Had Nikolai somehow arranged that through some form of hypnosis or spiritual manipulation? Or was Maurice simply an eccentric? The French owner-chef answered the questions for him.

"I don't want those people in my restaurant," he said, turning back to his guests. "They probably want to use credit cards and I don't take them. Credit cards are a racket. They take a percentage and make you wait a day for your money."

"But, we're the only people here," Gerald said.

"Not to worry. The important ones come later. They always do."

"I don't understand."

"There's a lot you probably don't understand. Take the credit card racket. It's only one of many created to rob merchants and people like myself of the meager profit we need to stay in business. But it's not the biggest racket. Do you know what the biggest racket in the world is?"

"No."

"With all respect, my friends, it was started two-thousand years ago by thirteen Jews."

Father William tried to fight a laugh that was struggling to burst free. He lost the battle.

"It's funny, yes," Maurice said. "You see all that artwork, all that gold, all those gems and all those other precious objects at the Vatican. And all those churches around the world collecting all that money from the people. I'll tell you, the Church probably has more money than that place in America, what's it called? You know, the one run by the American Army with all the booty it's collected from all the wars."

"Fort Knox," William said.

"That's it. More money than Fort Knox."

Maurice may have been under some sort of hypnotic spell cast by Nikolai, but one thing was certain to Gerald. He was drunk. And it was not just from his generous share of the three bottles of Brunello. He obviously had started drinking before Gerald, William and Nikolai had arrived.

Nearly two hours after it had begun, the party at the table broke up, not because dinner had ended, but because Maurice finally decided to let more people inside. He went to the door himself to unlock it and personally welcome seven men. His wife explained that the newcomers were regulars. Five of them owned nearby restaurants and two were food critics for Rome newspapers.

"They come here twice a week," Gretchen said as she rose from the table. She was smiling warmly. "They know where to come for a good meal, good company and good conversation. We usually do not let anyone else inside on these nights. Not that we let just anyone in the rest of the time. But, how could we turn away priests even on this night? Just in case, you know. But, you do not have to leave. Take your time."

She went to the front of the restaurant to join her husband and the new arrivals at a table set for nine. Unless Gerald, William or Nikolai talked very loudly, they would not be overheard so far from the others. Maurice had turned on a compact disc playing French ballads sung by Yves Montand. Besides, the talk and laughter coming from the nine persons seated at the table was loud enough to shield anything else said in the room from the revelers.

"He's quite the character," Father William said.

"He's a lot more than that," Nikolai replied.

"Don't tell us that he's in on whatever game you're playing," Gerald said.

*EARTHLY SPIRITS*

"No, he's an eccentric, alcoholic restaurateur who happens to be married to a woman who, had she been around then, might have qualified as a guard at a Nazi concentration camp," Nikolai replied. "And, before I forget to mention it, Maurice is also a pervert."

"A pervert?"

"One of his talents that even I didn't realize until after we sat down."

"And how did you come to this realization?"

"He was stroking my thighs under the table. Not just once, but several times. He even grabbed my hand once and tried to pull it onto his thighs. Finally, just before dessert, I squeezed his hand so hard that he pulled it away from me and didn't bother me the rest of the evening. It's probably still stinging and won't feel right for a day or two."

"Maurice is a homosexual?"

"Not exactly. He's bisexual."

Brother Gerald looked at Father William, searching for support for something, though he did not know what.

"Why do you look so shocked, brother? You've had your share of homosexuals and bisexuals in the Church. Not to mention pedophiles and downright marriage-breaking adulterers."

"Why didn't you say anything?"

"With his wife sitting at the table? Not only would that have been bad form, it might have provoked a confrontation that would've ended our meeting. And we can't afford a postponement."

"So, are we finally going to know what this Second Coming business you've been hinting at is all about."

"Absolutely. But first both of you might want to have another sip of wine. Maybe I should even order another bottle. You're going to need it. You see, the Second Coming isn't supposed to happen for almost another thousand years. But, an unforeseen event has changed the schedule. Now, it could happen much sooner, perhaps in a few months. It's got to be stopped."

Father William and Brother Gerald looked at each other in disbelief. Finally, both turned to Nikolai, raised their voices and uttered the same word:

"Stopped?"

Nikolai took a quick glance at the other end of the room. There was so much chatter in the party of nine that none of them either heard the priests or bothered to pay attention.

"Calm yourself," he urged the two priests.

"This is nonsense," Gerald said.

"It's everything but nonsense. And you can't imagine how complicated."

"If what you're saying is true, it should be an occasion for joy. Its even at the core beliefs of most denominations. Why try to prevent what all of Christianity has waited centuries for?" Father William asked.

"Because if the Second Coming occurs now, billions of non-Christians aren't going to like it. And, neither will most Christians."

# CHAPTER 15

Cardinal Grosetti reached for the cigar box that sat atop the small cabinet next to his desk. He opened the lid and gently fingered three of the dozen Havanas before settling on one that met the moment's standards. He clipped off an end with the small cutting that he tool used only for such occasions, fitted the cigar firmly in the left corner of his lips and fired it up with the lighter that sat alongside the box. He took two long puffs, then took a few seconds to study the ash that was forming on the lit end of the tobacco stalk. When he was satisfied that it was burning evenly, he opened the cabinet door, retrieved a bottle of his favorite French cognac and poured a liberal amount into a brandy snifter.

The ritual was the closest that Grosetti could come to faithful prayer. While he never failed to pray when the occasion required it in the company of others, he had long ago concluded that it was a waste of time because it offered little hope of success. The cardinal still believed in a supreme being. But, he did not want to depend on a deity Who was tight-fisted with favors. No, the cigar and the brandy served him better. They cleared his thoughts. Since the cardinal lacked conviction, the tobacco and alcohol ritual enabled him to look at a problem the way he preferred—with an empty mind.

The problem was Brother Gerald. The monk was becoming a non-person. But Gerald was not yet aware of it.

Cardinal Grosetti was the first to pick up on the possibility and it had filled his mind with more information which, at times, seemed that even he could handle. Sifting through the evidence that he had collected, it was the only conclusion he could reach. And, his collection of what he considered facts was growing.

The first piece of the puzzle had been the assignment of Brother Gerald and Father William to the Vatican. It made no sense. One was a Benedictine monk whose long service in the Church could have been summed up in a single paragraph in which boredom was the most striking feature. The other also was a Benedictine who had been forced into retirement by poor health after leading his abbey down a path so economically ruinous that even an experienced administrative priest could not prevent its financial collapse.

The answer Grosetti was seeking had to be in the posting of the two monks to the Vatican. Researching and writing a new history of the Devil had taken the shape of an absurd cover story. That was no assignment for two immigrant monks from a defunct American abbey. The Vatican already had too many in-house experts on Satan. And, none of them had as free a rein to as much of the Vatican as did Gerald and William. The two even could disappear for days on end and no one would ask why.

The second piece of evidence seemed to be directly linked to the first. Even though the deaths of the four monks at Blessed Skyline Abbey in Virginia occurred after William's retirement, he had played a role in the investigation of them. So had Gerald. Since they had both served at the abbey for years, they must have worked closely together. Otherwise why would the two of them have been summoned to Rome? What could they know that the police and Father Shane did not? Grosetti wondered whether Shane was holding back a piece of vital information. He dismissed the notion. The young priest was too ambitious to be less than obedient. More likely, the two monks knew something that only one or two others in the Vatican knew. Cardinal Sforza most likely was one. The pope could be another, but that was less likely.

Cardinal Grosetti had been tempted more than once to confront

*EARTHLY SPIRITS*

Sforza directly on the matter. But the highest card he had been dealt in this game was a king. He was reluctant to play it for fear that Sforza held an ace.

If Grosetti had needed confirmation of his suspicions, which he did not, Father Monahan had given it to him with his telephone calls. No one Monahan had spoken with in America knew what had happened to Brother Gerald and Father William. Not any of the monks that Monahan had talked with, not even his sources at the archdiocese that once had technical jurisdiction over Blessed Skyline Abbey. The brothers may not have cared, but the archdiocese seemed interested. It all was hush-hush, according to Monahan, but someone high in the archdiocese seemed to be pulling out all stops to find the two Benedictines.

The cardinal had considered telling Monahan of the whereabouts of Gerald and William. That could be risky. Even though Father Monahan had proven his reliability over the years, Grosetti had reservations about the priest's loyalty. Monahan probably was telling him the truth about the blank he had drawn at the archdiocese, but if he told the priest that Gerald and William were at the Vatican, there was no guarantee that his spy would not sell that information to someone close to his archbishop. If the archdiocese did not know, someone in the Vatican must want to keep it a secret. Better that Grosetti keep the secret, too. It was the third clue to the puzzle that baffled him.

The more Grosetti had thought about it lately, the more he became suspicious of a conspiracy. Until recently, he had not paid much attention to the casual talk in the Vatican hallways. Lately, however, not only was there more than the usual amount of gossip common to bureaucracies, but it seemed more hushed. And, the chatter ended abruptly more often when he approached than it had in the past. He had wondered whether his natural curiosity was slowly sinking into paranoia. He suppressed the possibility each time that it awakened in his mind, but he could not banish it. The gossip that was running along the hallway grapevine had added to the evidence that something definitely was in the works.

Until a few hours ago, the links were clear, forming a trail that Cardinal Grosetti had found a frustrating enjoyment in following. Then, like a series of unexpected lightning bolts, three new pieces of information had landed on his desk shortly after lunch. Now the trail looked like it might branch off into three directions.

Grosetti glanced at his wristwatch. It was two-thirty in the afternoon. The time difference made it eight-thirty in the eastern United States and seven-thirty in Canada's Atlantic Maritimes. That probably was too late for any more telephone calls from that part of the world. Nothing of immediate importance was on the Vatican calendar, so he could count on solitude for the rest of the afternoon. His staff had been instructed not to disturb him unless it was urgent.

The cardinal tried to move. At first, his chair resisted the efforts of his substantial body, which at the same time, seemed to resist the order from his brain to shift. Finally, both brain and chair surrendered, enabling Grosetti to swivel around so that he faced the huge print of the Purgatory panel from Hieronymus Bosch's medieval rendering of The Last Judgment on the wall behind the desk. The cardinal enjoyed gazing at the work almost as much as he appreciated the hours sitting on his favorite bench in the Campo Teutonico of the Vatican Gardens. However, there he could be disturbed by visitors. Also, summer was about to set in with its usual severity and there was no air-conditioning outdoors. Besides, he found Bosch's concept of Purgatory more mentally stimulating.

He pondered the plight of the sinner being shod by one of Bosch's demons. He chuckled, imagining himself as the suffering soul being fitted with horseshoes for the trail he had taken in search of answers that were eluding him. His eyes shifted to the sinner escaping from Purgatory with the help of an angel. How convenient it would be if he had the same sort of guide. Bosch's demon preparing to fire a crossbow at the escapee gave birth to another chuckle. It reminded him of Cardinal Sforza.

After about fifteen minutes in Purgatory, where Grosetti managed to drink his cognac and smoke nearly half of his cigar, he decided to leave. He turned around again, this time with a body and chair that responded with remarkable obedience. He opened the thin drawer in the center of his desk and reached in for three sheets of paper. He closed the drawer and put the papers on the desk in a row next to each other. Then, he began pondering them, starting with the sheet on the left.

All three had been prepared by one of Grosetti's trusted clerks during

*EARTHLY SPIRITS*

the late morning. The cardinal read each of the messages before deciding that it would be better to have lunch before attempting to interpret their meaning. So, he went to his favorite restaurant, just two blocks from St. Peter's Square. It had been a typical Grosetti lunch, the sort his doctor often warned him against consuming. After an appetizer plate of fresh vegetables fried in olive oil, he moved to a generous helping of caprese salad, followed by a main course of Venetian-style liver and onions, then ended with a dessert of homemade tiramisu and a cup of cappuccino. All of it was washed down with a two-glass carafe of red house wine and a bottle of sparkling spring water. He knew he should have avoided the cheese in the caprese, the gravy in which the liver was soaked and the sugar in the tiramisu, but calculated that its effects would be neutralized by the quantity of olive oil, garlic and red wine that he had accompanied the meal. In fact, he even had briefly considered asking the waiter to do it all over again, only to surrender to nature, which had been creeping up on him through years of physical neglect.

After scanning the papers for a few seconds, Grosetti picked up the first and read it again, digesting each word as though it were a morsel of food. He loved papers. To him, all papers were documents. Like information, he hoarded them. Eventually, they all found their way into a bank of locked filing cabinets that had multiplied over his years as head of the Congregation for the Doctrine of the Faith. Only he and his most trusted aide had keys to the collection.

Like the other two, the first was handwritten. Not only was some information too sensitive to be typed by a clerk, it could end up etched permanently in a computer hard drive or be seen rolling out of a printer by a passerby. Any of the handful of sources who sent the information along Grosetti's grapevine could have made notes, but since only his administrative assistant knew the final destination of the information, no one was likely to give any of it special importance. Not even his administrative assistant knew why the cardinal wanted the information. Neither would the aide be likely to make notes or even a copy. He enjoyed the sense of power that came with his job being the cardinal's second set of eyes and ears.

There was no question that the piece of paper was an important piece of evidence. Father William and Brother Gerald had gone to Paris. It was all there; the airline, flight number, time of departure from Fiumicino Airport in Rome, scheduled time of arrival at Charles De Gaulle Airport in Paris. The information came straight from the Vatican travel office. What was so important that required going to Paris? It could not be a pleasure trip. The tickets were purchased only a few hours before the flight that morning, so the trip had to have been made on very short notice. Even more interesting, the ticket was open-ended, with no date for a return flight.

The evidence ended there. No lodging had been arranged in Paris for the two American priests. They would have landed in the French capital while Grosetti was at lunch and probably were met at the airport by someone who would provide them with a place to stay. But who? And why? And for how long?

Grosetti set the paper on the desk and picked up the next sheet. Its message was even more brief, but more tantalizing. It had been years since the cardinal had even had a passing thought about what was left of the ancient order of the Knights Templar. It had suddenly begun meeting several times a week. Normally, Grosetti would not have given the message more than a passing glance and dismissed it as the superstitious rituals of a cult that should have long passed into forgotten history. Knights Templars, indeed. What was it anymore but a small group of old men pretending to be hanging onto mystical beliefs stemming from a goblet presumed to have survived the Last Supper? Of course, the message still would have to find its way into the files with so many other insignificant papers awaiting the shredder that Grosetti expected would accompany his successor as head of the Office of the Congregation of the Faith.

But the last sentence in the message could give it a reprieve that would go well beyond Grosetti's tenure. It read:

"The Templars are rumored to be seeking the whereabouts of an unnamed American priest."

If the Templars and the archdiocese were looking for Brother Gerald or Father William or both, then there had to be a connection between the organization and the Church. If the link led all the way to the Vatican, that

*EARTHLY SPIRITS*

could surface in a day or two. Could Cardinal Sforza be the link? That was not likely, otherwise the curtain of invisibility would have been lifted from the two Americans. No, if there was a Templar in the Vatican, Sforza was being kept out of the loop. And if there was, how had it been kept a secret from Grosetti? Two secrets? No, that did not seem possible.

The third piece of paper was equally cryptic. A telephone call had been made to Brother Gerald after his departure for Paris. The caller had left only a name and telephone number in the United States.

Perhaps Father Shane knew the caller. If not, then Grosetti would ask Father Monahan. Certainly one of them could find out something about Teresa Lucci.

For the first time since he became aware of what he believed was a secret close to being a conspiracy, the cardinal felt he was about to pick up the scent. So what if the trail looked like it might be going in three directions. He was certain that if he explored them all, they would meet at the end. But he had to be careful. The trails might all meet at a pond of ice. And Cardinal Grosetti was well aware that some people at the Vatican would want to be there watching when the ice broke under his footsteps.

# CHAPTER 16

Brother Gerald had known better days.

Sure, he was in Paris, a city he long had wished to visit. Not only that, he was with an old friend who had been there before. The problem was the third party. After all, who could expect to be comfortable when the Devil was along for the ride?

Gerald, Father William and Nikolai had just climbed three flights of winding stairs to a small two-bedroom apartment in a building that had been converted into transient flats for visiting academics. It was on one of the few dreary streets on the Left Bank of the River Seine, where all the buildings looked like they had been designed by an incompetent Seventeenth Century architect, then left untended. Despite Nikolai's assurances of its integrity, the wood staircase looked like it needed repair. The hallway's rough stone walls certainly needed painting. To Gerald, the dimly lit hallway looked like the route to a medieval dungeon, only its stairs went in the opposite direction.

Nikolai took a key from a pants pocket, unlocked the door and ushered the two priests ahead of him into the apartment. He followed them in, closed the door and set his one piece of carry-on luggage on a coffee table in front of a sofa. He told the other two men to put their small carry-ons wherever they wanted. Then, he threw open the living room

*EARTHLY SPIRITS*

drapes with a casual flourish, revealing a small rear courtyard below. The incoming light revealed a bright sitting room that passersby could not have imagined was hidden behind the decaying walls of the old building. It was immaculate and cheerful. The luggage they had set down looked hopelessly out of place, like a homeless person who had been transplanted into luxury accommodations.

"This used to be a very nice apartment," Nikolai said. "But that was before they added all the modern conveniences."

He had started to talk again. Brother Gerald tried to block out the voice, which had droned on in a seemingly endless monologue through their flight from Rome and during the taxi ride from Charles De Gaulle Airport to central Paris. Even as they trudged up the long flights of stairs to the apartment, Nikolai would not shut up. What made it worse was that Gerald had heard much of it before, that final night at Blessed Skyline Abbey where Nicholas had lectured him in what the monk had wanted to be a dream. This time, Father William was Nikolai's target and the old priest obviously had listened with great interest. But nothing of what was said answered the questions that filled the monk's mind.

One thing had become clear, however. Nikolai, Nicholas, Nicole the Cat Lady or whoever or whatever he or she or it was, had at least one connection in the Vatican. Probably not a Devil worshiper, but a connection that must have served some practical purpose. Gerald and Father William had been told by Cardinal Verano shortly after waking that morning that they had only a few hours to prepare for travel. The befuddled Verano could not tell them where or why they were going other that that airline tickets would be delivered to them after breakfast.

When they boarded for their flight to Paris, Nikolai already was seated next to a window in a row of three. Brother Gerald took the aisle seat, letting an eager Father William sit next to the unwelcome traveling companion as a buffer. All Gerald could say was a laconic:

"Why am I not surprised?"

Other than to tell the monk that he would explain "as much as possible" when they arrived in Paris, Nikolai made Father William's ears his almost exclusive property for the rest of the trip.

*ED KONSTANT*

To Brother Gerald, who could not block out all of the conversation, the words sounded like those written for an unholy litany.

Nikolai had confirmed for Father William what the priest had heard from Gerald after his visit from Nicholas in the early dark hours of the last morning that the two had seen each other in Virginia more than seven months ago. Nicholas had come to him in what Gerald had believed was a dream to confess to killing the four monks at Blessed Skyline Abbey. Claiming to be Lucifer, he had blamed it on the aggressive side of his soul. He had told the monk that he had infiltrated the body of an alcoholic itinerant worker so that he could take a brief earthly vacation. When the worker was knocked unconscious by a mugger in a park it left him with amnesia; his soul split, leaving only its passive side conscious, while its aggressive side sought to bring the two together by planning and committing murders that puzzled everyone. It even had left clues, such as murdering only monks with serious moral and ethical flaws that matched a particular Seven Deadly Sin of which they had been deemed guilty, and only on days their names matched those of particular saints.

Nicholas had said that God had assigned him to Earth centuries ago to help guide the humans that were evolving after having been granted souls. The posting was supposed to be temporary, for a century or so, but because Lucifer and twenty of his followers had been troublemakers in Heaven, the tour of duty had become a condemnation stretching into an eternity.

He had denied blame for the despair of persecution, the horrors of war and other terrible acts that individuals and societies had perpetrated over the centuries. He blamed it on choice. It would have become even worse if, as Nicholas, he had died with a split soul that never could have been put back together. The soul would have been lost forever. Lucifer would have ceased to exist. Then, without guidance, humans would have been stricken with severe apathy, societies would have collapsed and the world would have come face-to-face with an Apocalypse that could have destroyed centuries of civilization building. At least, that is how Nikolai explained it.

On and on it went. Nikolai gave Father William a discourse on the necessity of intangibles to have opposites: light and dark, hot and cold, sound and silence, good and evil. He told him of his dabbling behind the scenes of centuries of world affairs and how his best of intentions often went astray because humans were not to have their choices overruled. Other than to mention that while souls lived a very long time and even they would die, Nikolai deftly avoided questions about the deity and any possibility of an afterlife. Father William was enrapt, feeling as though he was listening to the world's greatest authority giving him a personal intellectual lecture on the meaning of life. In a sense, priest was right. But he also recognized that it was more a matter of Lucifer having made acquiring whatever personality he needed for the moment into a fine art.

Brother Gerald was looking down from the apartment window when he realized that Nikolai had changed the subject.

"I don't know about the two of you, but I'm going to have a quick shower and a change of clothes," Nikolai said. "I still can't get used to all the dirt and perspiration that clings to these bodies even after such a simple activity as traveling. I don't know how you humans can take it."

"We can take a lot," Gerald replied. "We're here, aren't we?"

"Did I detect a bit of sarcasm in that?"

"We both did," Father William said.

"It's understandable," Nikolai said. "I'll be quick, then you can follow me, if you want. Then, we'll all sit down for a glass of wine before going out and I'll give you some of those answers that Brother Gerald has been so patiently waiting to hear. In the meantime, make yourself comfortable, watch TV and check out the closet in your bedroom. It has clothing in it. Civilian clothing. We can't have Brother Gerald wandering around in sandals and robe looking like a relic from a medieval monastery. That would attract too much attention. And, yes, brother, the shoes will fit comfortably. There are clothes for you, too, Father William, but you probably can get by with your usual priestly garb. Just shed the white collar for now."

Nikolai returned in about twenty minutes, garbed in a new set of clothes. He even had shaved, except for his chin. There, he had left a few hairs poking through the skin, trying to imitate the birth of a beard. William then took his turn showering and changing clothes, followed by Gerald.

Nikolai and Father William were seated on the sofa when Brother Gerald emerged newly clad from the bedroom. Both men looked at Gerald, then at each other and politely laughed at the same time.

"What's the joke?" Gerald asked.

"Just look in a mirror," William replied.

"Father William is being kind," Nikolai said. "You must have a vagrant's sense of fashion. If I didn't know better, I'd swear that someone tossed those clothes on you with a pitchfork."

"A pitchfork?" Gerald replied. "That's an apt pun coming from you."

"Very good, brother. I hadn't meant it as a pun."

"I'm not used to jackets and shirts with collars."

"Fashion is one of Gerald's shortcomings," William said. "Except for T-shirts and jeans when he delivered bread back at Blessed Skyline Abbey, I've never seen him in anything but robe and sandals. I'm sure we can fix him up easily enough."

"Forgive us for baptizing the bottle before you were done," Nikolai said. "Our father here looked like he wanted to get a head start. It's a Chinon vintage, made with grapes from a Loire Valley estate that produces only a few thousand bottles a year. It's an outstanding wine. Don't you agree, Father?"

"Actually, I think it's spectacular," William replied.

"Okay, I'll have some," Gerald said. "But will you finally get to the point of all this."

"Fair enough, brother," Nikolai said. "Or would you prefer I called you father?"

"I've been called brother for so long, why change it now?"

Nikolai poured some wine into a glass and handed it to Gerald, then motioned for him to sit in the easy chair across from the sofa. Nikolai leaned forward in a pose that made him look like a conspirator about to reveal a closely guarded secret. The two clerics followed his lead, like men about to hear something confidential.

"I've told you about the Second Coming, which Gerald here is reluctant to believe," Nikolai said. "But when you consider everything that has happened since that night in the Piazza Navona, I expect you're at least considering giving me the benefit of the doubt."

136

*EARTHLY SPIRITS*

"If the Second Coming really is going to happen, I don't see why we or Paris has anything to do with it," Gerald said.

"Everything in time. And time is critical now. Paris may be only the first stop."

"The first stop? You mean you're going to drag us somewhere else, too?"

"Wherever it takes."

"Why?"

"I've already told you that. To prevent the Second Coming."

"Yes, but I'm still waiting for you to explain why you need us."

"Well, I'm not sure you're ready to handle it, but what the Hell. This isn't going to be easy to accept, even for you, Father William. But, now is as good as any and time is becoming critical."

"Finally."

Nikolai took another sip of wine, let the liquid roll over his tongue and looked at the two priests. For the first time since they had met him in Rome, Nikolai was not smiling. He looked almost frightened.

# CHAPTER 17

It was the first of a series of mistakes. Stefan Petrandriou had made them before but none that ever threatened to have more personal consequences.

The old man never had acquired major vices, a remarkable accomplishment for someone seventy-five years of age. But minor vices were unavoidable. One was Petrandriou's occasional taste for an after-dinner cigar. He yielded to the temptation that beckoned from a window in a tobacco shop just off Fira's main street. He planned to dine in style to celebrate his newly discovered freedom. So, what was the harm in capping it off a good meal with a good cigar?

The second mistake was the choice of restaurants.

Most of the menus posted on the doors of the eateries in Santorini's town in the sky were similar. The specialties of the houses were lamb, chicken and seafood. The words that were written to describe each were phrased to tantalize the unwary:

"Lamb glazed with honey, sprinkled lightly with fresh capers and grilled to your taste;" "Chicken breasts stuffed with olives, raisins and almonds, slowly roasted to perfection;" "Fruits of the Aegean Sea, served on a bed of wild rice."

The prices matched the blown verbiage, especially for the seafood. He

*EARTHLY SPIRITS*

knew the Aegean no longer was a source of plenty. Nearly thirty centuries of fishing in its waters had stripped it of its once abundant stocks.

Most of the restaurants catered to the tourists who crowded into them, sitting almost elbow-to-elbow, congratulating each other with glasses of Greek wine on their discovery of the Aegean island way of life. In a sense they were correct since so many of the islands had become tourist traps.

He checked out nearly a dozen restaurants before settling on the Aegean Terrace at the end of an alley that ran parallel to and above the main street, and was accessible only by stone stairs at either end. His choice was more a matter of location than anything. True to its name, it had a small outdoor terrace and a few tables were empty, including one at the small barrier wall overlooking the Aegean. The sun would be setting soon, so why not dine with a view? It all seemed so idyllic that no one could have known that it was the only restaurant in Santorini that the old man should have avoided.

The menu that the muscular, dark-haired man in his late thirties brought to the old man's table was almost identical to the one posted on the bulletin board at the gate that led to the terraced dining area.

"Just one of you?" he asked. He was nervous, almost agitated, but was fighting it with a natural pleasantness. His liking for people was so obvious that it temporarily calmed what hid behind the discomforting dark eyes that were set restlessly deep in sockets under heavy eyebrows.

"Yes, just me," the old man replied.

"Would you like some wine?"

"What do you recommend?"

"We've got an excellent Macedonian white. It goes well with the fruits of the Aegean, which is particularly good today. Everything is freshly caught."

"I prefer red."

"Then I suggest you try the red from Crete."

"I'll have a half-bottle."

"Very good. I'll be back with it in a moment." He almost lurched as he left the table, then slowed after taking two long steps, looked back over his shoulder and said:

"By the way, my name is Triffon."

The old man saw the sales pitch for what it was. But, it had been delivered with such polite charm that it seemed genuine. Triffon was very likeable. The old man had recognized that Triffon was the restaurant manager, then quickly banished the thought. He had to be more careful under circumstances that were not familiar. It would take conditioning to avoid even thinking about the obvious. He could not afford the slightest slip. At least not until it would be too late.

He had to play the part of an aging man who never had left Greece. He had taken every precaution to insure that the role was perfect. He was dressed for it in a gray suit that had been carefully rumpled so not as to attract attention. He had toyed with the idea of wearing a Greek fisherman's cap, but dismissed it because it might catch the unwanted advances of a tourist with a camera. Photographs that could be passed around were definitely out. He could speak Greek fluently, with a touch of an Athens accent that would be discernible only to island locals. He had quickly adjusted to the European fashion of eating with a fork in the left hand and a knife poised for slicing in the right. Adjusting to whatever else any situation demanded should be no problem. However, one feature of everyday life was definitely going to take a lot of patience to accept: the never-ending tones of cell phones signaling incoming calls.

The old man placed the entire dinner order when the manager returned to the table with the bottle of red from Crete. He would start with a traditional tsaziki appetizer, then feast on the main course of the suspect fruits of the Aegean and finish with rice pudding for dessert. He dined and sipped wine with equal leisure, finding the seafood pleasantly tastier than expected.

He never felt alone even with the lack of a companion. He tried not to eavesdrop but could not totally ignore the conversation of the tourists who had begun filling the Aegean Terrace shortly after he was seated. Their words beamed across the tables like endless broadcasts of boring radio talk shows. He suspected that it would not have mattered whether two or twenty tables had been occupied. He wanted to avoid notice, but could not avoid Triffon. The manager returned to the table a half-dozen times, always lingering a few minutes to express views and ask questions that had nothing to do with dinner. The old man tried not to make eye

# EARTHLY SPIRITS

contact with him, but that did not matter. He was being paid attention that was not being given to anyone else. He knew that Triffon did not suspect anything about the odyssey, but the manager's persistence was slightly uncomfortable.

When the last spoon of rice pudding was consumed, it was time for the special after-dinner treat. He reached into the suit jacket breast pocket and pulled out the cigar. There was just enough wine left to sip while he puffed. He bit off one end of the cigar, neatly set it in the corner of the mouth, the realized that something was missing. He chuckled at the oversight. He had forgotten to buy matches.

He did not have to look up to know that Triffon was standing there. It was as though the manager had suddenly materialized at the table.

"Let me," Triffon said. He flicked the tab of the lighter in his hand, igniting a flame, then lit the old man's cigar.

"You shouldn't smoke," Triffon said. "It's bad for you."

"Do you know of a more enjoyable way to top off a good dinner than with a good cigar and a glass of superb wine?" the old man asked.

"No, but I know of a better way."

"And that is?"

"Don't smoke at all."

"I don't make a habit of it."

"Maybe not, but the habit has a way of winning."

"Like it has with you?"

"You noticed the cigarettes in my shirt pocket?"

"Yes."

"I never smoke when I'm working."

"But you try to discourage patrons?"

"Sometimes."

"If you feel that I shouldn't smoke, why did you come to my rescue with your lighter?"

"Courtesy and…"

"And what?"

"I couldn't help myself. It must have been the demon."

"The demon?"

Triffon suddenly became agitated, waving his arms and taking quick, short glances around the terrace. Then, just as suddenly, he became calm, bent toward the old man and lowered his voice.

"The demon inside me," he said. "I can almost hear and feel him urging me to light a cigarette. He's been at it for years and no matter how hard I try to fight him, I can't stop. So, he always wins."

"Do you really want to stop?"

"Of course. I've tried everything. Cutting back, patches, pills, even hypnosis. Nothing worked for more than a few days. Then it's back to the routine of two packs a day, sometimes more."

"Sooner or later that will kill you."

"I know. Sometimes I think it doesn't matter. We're all going to die. All we have to do is wait long enough and it will happen."

"There's a simple way to beat the demon."

"Advice from a fellow smoker?"

"No. I'm not a regular smoker. This is the first cigar I've had in a very long time. And I don't expect to have another unless it's a special dining occasion."

"Well, if you can tell me a secret I don't know and it works, then you can eat here free every night. I'll even provide the cigars."

"Thank you. That's a very generous offer. But I couldn't even consider imposing on your hospitality."

"So, there's no secret."

"No. Just a simple solution."

"I'm listening."

"Stop smoking."

"That's easy to say, but not very practical."

"Just try it tonight after you close."

His cigar still was burning when the old man finished the wine and paid the bill. He found a quiet lane along the edge of the town and enjoyed a walk along a personally detoured route back to the hotel. He marveled at how the stars tantalized anyone who bothered to inspect the sky.

He had made another mistake, but like the others, had not realized it. There was no reason to realize any of it. He was Stefan Petrandriou and expected that certainty alone to be comfort enough for the rest of whatever years were left.

142

# CHAPTER 18

It had been the sort of day that made Rick Erlandson wonder whether he ever could escape his recent past. Was it possible he never had left Washington? Maybe there really was a fourth dimension. Or even a fifth, sixth and seventh. Could he be trapped in one of them without knowing whether he was experiencing reality or being bluffed by illusion? Or was he traveling through each of them, one by one?

He had thought of little else during the last couple of hours. At least the weekly edition of the Cromer Chronicle had been put to bed before he had received the telephone call. Now as he pulled his dark blue two-door sports sedan into the driveway of his home, he was struck by a chilling realization. He could not recall a single thing along the ten-minute route he had just driven from town to the driveway of house on the cliff overlooking the Atlantic Ocean coast. Was that part of the illusion, too? Did he really have a wife named Robin and would she be there? Was she really expecting the birth of their first child? Would it be a son? If so, did they really intend to name him Gerald?

He exited the car and walked to the front door. Rick hesitated there for no more than a second, realized how ridiculous he had been thinking, reached for the doorknob, turned it and pushed the barrier open.

Everything inside looked the way it should. If Rick had any doubts as to where he was, they faded the moment. Dusty, their dark gray cat, slid from behind the short wall that separated the entrance hall from the living room. He reached down and gave Dusty a gentle pat on its head, reassuring himself as much as the cat that everything was all right.

He closed the door behind him and headed for the kitchen.

Without knowing it, Rick breathed a gentle sigh of relief when he saw his wife, Robin. She had just closed the refrigerator door, then turned toward him, brushed her auburn hair back from her forehead back onto the mass that tumbled to her shoulders and smiled. She threw her arms around his neck, hanging them there leisurely. She looked at him with inquisitive eyes waiting for him to speak. When he did not, she broke the silence with a soft question.

"Bad day?" she asked.

"What makes you think that?" he replied. She caught a tone of slight irritation in his voice.

"As bad as that?"

"Sorry. I didn't mean to take it out on you. Was I that obvious?"

"I'm surprised you have to ask. Have we ever been able to hide any of our feelings from each other?"

"You're right. Again."

"I also had help this time."

"Help?"

"The clock. You're about an hour-and-a-half later than usual on closing day." "Now there's a coincidence if I ever saw one."

Robin waited for him to explain the remark, but he just stared at her.

"If that's a riddle, I'm going to need a little more before I can even try to figure out the answer," she said.

"It's not a riddle," Rick said. "It's just that it involves someone who's got a reputation for being a stickler for time."

"Want to talk about it? Or would you rather have dinner first?"

"You didn't make dinner?"

"Of course not. Or have you forgotten that we dine out or get something delivered on Chronicle closing day?"

"Right. I never know when some last-minute problem with the week's edition is going to keep me later than usual."

*EARTHLY SPIRITS*

"Like today? Or should I say tonight?"

"There were no last-minute problems."

"Oh? Stopped off for a drink or two with Jeff?"

Rick let a heavy breath flow straight into Robin's face.

"I guess not," she said. "Then, are you going to tell me now or tell me later?"

"Let's order something to eat first," he replied. "We can talk about it while we're waiting for the delivery."

"Pizza, Chinese, sub sandwiches?"

"You're the one who had to wait, so you call it. Besides, you're the one who's pregnant. I can't keep up with the quirky appetite you've developed."

"It's been only three months. It doesn't show yet, does it?"

"If I didn't know, I wouldn't."

"That's sweet. While we're on the subject of sweet, I'd like a pizza with chocolate ice cream. But I guess I'll have to settle for one with pineapple?"

"Ugh. How can you eat something so inedible?"

"It's not for me. The baby wants it."

"I'd better order two small, one with pepperoni."

"Make mine a large."

"You're going to tell me you're eating for two?"

"No, but baby probably will want some for lunch tomorrow."

Their small talk had relaxed him for the first time since he had received the unexpected telephone call. Now he pulled her closer to him, holding her there as gently as he kissed her on the lips. He savored the moment, knowing that it would be swept away before their dinner arrived. Then, he gently removed her arms from around his neck, held her hands briefly, released them and went to the telephone to make the call for the pizza delivery.

They waited for dinner to be delivered in the living room. Robin had seated herself on the sofa, expecting Rick to sit alongside. When he took the easy chair across from her, she felt certain that something must be seriously wrong. She watched him stare at the window and wondered whether he was taking in the view it gave of the Atlantic Ocean as he did almost daily ever since they had moved back to Maine from Washington. After about a minute, he spoke.

"We closed an hour earlier than usual today."

Robin knew that was not what Rick wanted to say. It was just a preliminary opening, his way of trying to soften whatever blow was coming next.

"I got a phone call right after we closed," he continued. "It was someone I never expected to hear from again."

"You're going to tell me who," she said. "Or do I have to guess?"

"Teresa Lucci."

"That is a surprise. Is something wrong with her?"

"How would you like to spend a few days in Nova Scotia?"

The question caught her off-guard, like a prizefighter who had been on the receiving end of an unexpected counterpunch.

As if anticipating her response, he said:

"No, Teresa won't be there. She and her husband apparently are very content to stay three-thousand miles away in Oregon. Though, under the circumstances, it seems that three-thousand miles isn't far enough away."

"Rick, you never talk in riddles," she said. "You're scaring me."

"I'm sorry. It's just that I've been feeling disconnected from reality ever since I got that call."

"Well, then connect yourself and let me have it. I'm a big girl."

"It has to do with Brother Gerald."

"Oh, no."

"It's not what you're thinking. No one's been killed or died. He's very much alive and so is Father William and, I suppose, everyone else who lived through that bad time at Blessed Skyline Abbey."

His words should have been reassuring, but Robin felt as though her nerves had suddenly been stretched. She fought off the feeling before it had time to mature into a headache.

"Nobody from the old abbey is in Nova Scotia, either," he continued. "In fact, both Gerald and William are in Rome. At the Vatican, no less. I wasn't supposed to know that, but I pried it out of Teresa as a condition of what she asked me to do. So, if anyone asks, you don't know, either."

"Why should anyone ask?"

*EARTHLY SPIRITS*

"A man showed up at Teresa's front door looking for them."

"I don't understand. Why should anyone go to Oregon looking for Brother Gerald and Father William?"

"Because of the connection with Teresa and her husband, Chris. Remember, she once was a nun, and he was a monk at the abbey when Gerald and William were there. She thinks her visitor came from Nova Scotia to find them. Or, rather to find her and Chris, hoping that they could tell him where to look."

"All the way from Nova Scotia? That's ridiculous. I'd think it would be a lot easier to ask at the local diocese or whatever in Nova Scotia or even Virginia, which are a lot closer than Oregon."

"It's not quite that simple."

"Why is it I thought you were going to say something like that?"

"Apparently only four people in the United States know that Gerald and William are at the Vatican."

"Don't tell me. Teresa Lucci, Chris Lucci, you and I."

"Bingo."

"Why the big secret?"

"Teresa said the only thing she knows is that Gerald told her that he and Father William had been assigned to the Vatican just before the Virginia abbey closed and he couldn't tell her why."

"So, we're going to Nova Scotia to…."

"Are you ready for this?"

"I have a feeling that I'd better be."

"She asked me to try and confirm that the Knights Templar are looking for Gerald and find out why."

"The Knights Templar? I don't like the sound of that at all. It sounds very medieval."

"In a way, it is."

"In what way?"

"Teresa tried giving me a five-minute crash course in the Knights Templar. It seems they were created during the Crusades, then fell into disrepute when they returned to Europe, were persecuted and what was left of them fled to Nova Scotia. They're supposed to have landed in the New World before Columbus."

"Like the Vikings?"

"Not exactly. According to the story, the Templars stayed and over the centuries established themselves first as a religious organization, then began dabbling in economics and politics. It's supposed to be very ritualistic and so secret that the only people who know who is and who isn't a Templar is another Templar."

"Teresa and Chris Lucci?"

"No. Teresa told me she was making an educated guess. The third day he was there, he made what she called a 'clumsy' effort to steer a conversation they were having about travel in the direction of Virginia. He was going on about how much he liked the Shenandoah Valley, especially this monastery he supposedly stayed at. He even mentioned the names of one of the monks who impressed him, a Brother Walter. When she asked Chris about Walter, he told her that no brother had that name while he was there and neither did any after he left. If there ever had been a Brother Walter, he would've had to have been there when her guest was a very young boy, probably no more than six or seven years old.

"It was then that she put everything together. Him showing up alone, unexpectedly. His name, Ewan Sinclair, which could be a modern version of Saint Clair, an old Templar family. His Nova Scotia accent. Then there was the ring. He was wearing a ring the day he arrived, but he'd removed it since. She didn't get a good look at it, but it was one of those society-style rings, like the Masons wear. Swinging to conversation to Blessed Skyline Abbey was the clincher. Like a good news reporter, and she was pretty good, she didn't like what seemed too many coincidences."

"Didn't he ask her about Brother Gerald."

"No. But he hasn't checked out yet."

"You're sure about going to Nova Scotia?"

"Yes. You're not worried, are you?"

"I'm not sure. But don't be surprised if I start."

"I could always go alone."

"Don't even think about that."

"Then be ready to leave tomorrow morning. For four, maybe five days. It's the slow news season and Jeff can handle things without me. Besides, the boss should be able to take a few days off now and then."

*EARTHLY SPIRITS*

The front door bell rang. The pizza had arrived.
Rick rose from the chair and went to get their dinner.
Robin did not move. She had lost her appetite.

# CHAPTER 19

Penko Lazar signed the guest registry card and handed it back to the clerk behind the desk in the simple lobby of the small hotel.

The clerk squinted as he read the personal information that Lazar had penned onto the card. Most people would have been confused enough to ask the writer to decipher the words. But, Alberto had clerked for so many years at so many hotels in the city that his eyes had become experts in translating the letters of any alphabet into sound with the exception of Oriental, Arabic and Hebrew characters.

"Thank you, Mr. Roussel," Alberto said. "Will you be taking dinner with us tonight?"

"Not tonight," Lazar replied. "Perhaps tomorrow."

The clerk handed him the keys to his room. "It's number twenty-two, one floor up. The lift is down the hall to the right. Have a pleasant stay, Mr. Roussel."

Thank you," Lazar said, with a smile that was as pleasant as it was genuine.

He lifted his carry-on luggage off the counter and headed down the hall. He smiled all the way to his room. After all these years of doing the same work, he had found nothing to compare. Not travel, not eating, not music, not literature, not sex. Not the career success or even the money,

*EARTHLY SPIRITS*

which now that he was in business for himself, had become plentiful. No, nothing matched the enjoyment of the deception of being someone else. He sometimes wondered whether he would find another pleasure as rewarding when he retired and would have to be the same person for the rest of his life.

His hotel room was not the sort of place that attracted millionaires. It was small with walls that recently had been painted coral. Besides the single bed, the only other furniture was a nightstand with a drawer for personal items, and a wardrobe for storing clothes. A telephone and an old clock radio sat on the nightstand. The ceiling light was supplemented by a wall lamp above the bed. Hung next to the lamp was a small framed print with an Italian countryside scene, all but mirroring in detail a similar print on the opposite wall, except that the latter was hanging at a slight angle. A window with shutters had been left open. It looked out onto a small courtyard with a bench surrounded by potted plants, most of them with a wealth of large leaves and poverty of small flowers. Exposed pipes ran along two walls near the floor in the bathroom to a simple sink, toilet and shower. All the fixtures looked tired. It was one of those places that brochures described as comfortable, which meant adequate for tourists on a budget. But, it was clean, quiet and well located for why he had come to where he was. Penko Lazar could not have wished for a better place to stay.

After setting his luggage on the floor, and tossing his jacket onto the bed, he straightened the picture on the wall and went to the bathroom to freshen up after his flight from Paris. He splashed several handfuls of cold water on his face, ran his fingers through his thick dark brown hair and looked in the mirror. For the first time in the twenty-seven years he had practiced his profession, he was less than certain that he was doing the right thing this time.

He never had experienced doubt in the past. Not from the beginning, when he was pulled out of the ranks of the Bulgarian army as a twenty-two-year-old corporal by a senior officer who had detected the young man's special potential and was willing to gamble both their futures on it. Technically, Lazar remained in the army for years afterward, though never again in uniform.

The first year of his new job as a specialist was boring. He had grown up speaking his native Bulgarian. In school he had learned obligatory Russian and a smattering of English. But most of that first year was spent perfecting his English and learning to converse in French. He was a fast learner.

His first field assignment quickly followed. He was ordered to join a small but vocal political movement that was going nowhere but still made the Communist Bulgarian government nervous. He quickly ingratiated himself with the movement's leadership. Shortly later, he received another order that was unexpected. He never questioned it. Instead, one week later, he slipped a knife through the ribs of the organization's leader as they walked through a cheering crowd of a few hundred followers in a town near Sofia. Before anyone had realized what had happened, Penko Lazar had planted the weapon in the coat pocket of a young farmer he had befriended and brought with him to the rally.

The farmer took the fall for the crime without ever knowing why he had suddenly been elevated to the leadership of rival opposition movement. His confession no doubt had been encouraged with the help of Bulgarian secret police interrogation. Still, a show trial had to be held. Witnesses swore that they had seen the man do the deed. Bulgaria's Communist government-controlled media dutifully reported the proceedings to a disinterested public. Of course, the rival opposition movement was a work of fiction for the masses. The day of the farmer's execution, the rival party vanished as easily as it had been created by the government. The enemies of the state had been defeated. The people's republic had been preserved.

A few months later, Penko Lazar was posted to the Bulgarian Embassy in Paris. Officially, he was listed as a consular attaché and he sometimes actually performed some of the duties of his official position. At first he thought it was a good cover, but quickly learned that the French believed that most Eastern European Communist embassies were little more than nesting places for spies. It was not long after that he realized they were right. To keep his cover, he was ordered to spend as much time in consular work, whether those duties were real or simple paper shuffling. Most of all, he was to avoid the Paris café circuit where agents of the

*EARTHLY SPIRITS*

Russian KGB, American CIA, British Secret Service and other countries met to exchange meaningless trade secrets that made them look good to their superiors.

Penko Lazar was not destined to be a spy, but he did not realize it yet. He was a foreign diplomatic bureaucrat who processed papers for a suspicious consular chief. Four months after he had been at his embassy desk, the first of the special telephone calls came through. Like the one or two others that would follow each year for more than a decade, it was from a general in Sofia whose authority no one dared challenge.

Lazar then learned that he would be something far more important than a spy. He had to attend secret meetings, of course. Usually they were in the early hours of the dark morning. The city where he was working at the time did not matter. The locations always were the same—under a bridge, in an alley, on a park bench. Places where few people ever met before daybreak. No one ever was there to meet him, but arrived minutes later, always standing behind him. He never saw their faces, but sometimes recognized a familiar voice.

During the early years of his career, Penko Lazar sometimes wondered if his secret contacts knew his identity. He eventually came to realize that they did not. Every time he was assigned to a new embassy, he had been given a new name and new background, including all the necessary official documents. And, just before every special job, three or four other persons would be posted to the embassy where he worked, then be recalled within a week or two of the completion of his assignment. That would insure that one of them would be blamed, perhaps even eliminated by an agent of the host government eager to make it known that it could be counted on to retaliate.

One more precaution all but guaranteed that Lazar would remain anonymous. His special talents sometimes would be contracted out to Third World clients, so that there would be little reason even to try tracing anything back to any of the Bulgarian embassies where he worked under so many different identities. His services had become in great demand not only in the power circles of the Eastern European Communist bloc, but in selected capitals of Asia, Africa and Latin America. Penko Lazar had graduated from the ranks of a Bulgarian assassin for the KGB. He had

*ED KONSTANT*

become a hit man for hire, a valuable commodity, a Communist experiment in capitalism. Of course, he never knew that large amounts of money had been paid for many of his assignments. Those funds went into a secret bank account in Switzerland, where a Bulgarian general was amassing them for his own retirement.

What political ideals guided Lazar through the early years of his profession had stopped haunting him long before the Iron Curtain collapsed into the scrap heap of European history in 1989. But if the end of European communism no longer meant much to him, something else did. He was about to become unemployed.

Hanging onto his sham job at the Bulgarian Embassy in London, where he was at the time of the communist collapse was not much of an option. He could continue to process papers in the consular section for expatriate Bulgarians and starry-eyed Britishers eager to explore the brave new world of Sofia. At best, that was a temporary way to earn a living. He could be replaced at any time by the new Bulgarian political structure. Even if he was not, he would tire of being a bureaucrat. And, sooner or later, his true identity risked being discovered. Penko Lazar had long drifted into obscurity and he was content to leave that identity there. He did not relish the thought of standing in the dock before an international criminal tribunal at The Hague.

At first, Lazar tried contacting the Bulgarian general who had guided him into and along his career. When his telephone calls remained unanswered, he knew that he was on his own, perhaps even hung out to dry in the winds of political upheaval. Then, an embassy acquaintance, who had been known to be a spy in the guise of a press attaché and also was concerned about his own future, suggested that they look into a new opportunity that had arisen out of the ashes of the Communist collapse.

"You're kidding," Lazar had said.

"Not at all," his fellow ex-Communist replied.

"Bodyguards? For British businessmen?"

"Property investors. They're heading east, from Britain, France, West Germany, Italy. Even America, I'm told."

"Why do they need bodyguards?"

"To make sure that their money is secure."

*EARTHLY SPIRITS*

"I don't understand."

"They need people who know the territory and can speak the language or find other reliable people who can. And, they travel with cash. You know, British pounds, German marks, American dollars. Hundreds of thousands, maybe even millions of them."

"Why not bank drafts? They would be safer. What are they going to do, carry all that money in their luggage? That could create problems at the borders. It all sounds fishy to me."

"You know our people. Do you think they would accept bank drafts or checks?"

"You're right. They won't."

"That's why it's got to be cash. Besides, you show a Bulgarian or a Czech or a Hungarian a briefcase filled with western currency, and it's more money than he's ever imagined seeing in his lifetime. It's an instant sale. And there's no problem at the borders. Slip a customs agent a few hundred pounds or dollars and you're in with no questions asked."

"So much property is still owned by the government."

"That's going fast. Anyone who can convince the bureaucrats in the east that their family once owned a place, it gets cleared and fast. The new governments are eager to prove to the west that they're ready to join the capitalist democracy club."

It was the start of a new gold rush and most of the entrants were from the industrial west. Not the big corporations, who already had staked marketing claims of their own. This race was for property that could be purchased at bargain prices, converted into commercial, residential and industrial space and sold at huge profits.

So, for the next year, Lazar and his new partner went from Sofia to Prague to Budapest and other Eastern European capitals. They stood outside locked doors while their British entrepreneurs were inside closing a bargain basement-priced property deal. The pay was good, better than Lazar ever had earned. Then, one day when he returned to his London apartment, he found the message on his telephone answering machine.

"Would you be interested in resuming your old career? The pay is very good."

The voice was unmistakable. The general was calling from

155

Switzerland. He left a telephone number where he could be reached only at a certain time on specific days.

Now, nearly fourteen years later, Lazar stood in front of the mirror of the bathroom of the small hotel. He was pushing fifty years of age. This might not be his last job, but he was getting close to it. The money he was being paid for this assignment would push his Swiss bank account to nearly five million dollars. Six million would be a nice round figure. He could reach that in another year.

It had been a good fourteen years, better than those he had during his days as a government assassin. He was no longer under orders. He had been able to choose only those assignments he wanted. He could slip into whatever identity fit his whims or needs. The general no longer was his boss. Instead, he had become his agent, who took a cut. Lazar never knew how much and did not care. He was paid far more than he ever had dreamed before going into business for himself.

With that money, he could retire in luxury. Not in Paris, though he had loved the city since the day of his first embassy posting there many years ago. He expected that the Mediterranean coast would become more appealing the further behind he left his middle years. He would be ready for the milder weather, the easier lifestyle. Would it be the Portuguese Algarve, the Spanish Costa del Sol or the Italian Riviera?

Italy was the leading contender. Far more Russian and other Eastern European political and government leaders who had taken their money and left after communism's collapse had settled in Spain and Portugal. In Italy there was less chance he ever would be recognized. The Italians also were less likely to be interested in outsiders who obeyed the law and Penko Lazar was going to be very law-abiding. Once the necessary papers had been prepared they probably would be filed away and forgotten. The Italian government might not even bother to demand that he pay taxes.

All he needed was to get through this assignment and maybe two more. Then, he no longer would need the dozens of sets of passports and other identity papers. One would do. No more contracts, no more plastic explosives, no more high-powered rifles, no more knives. Still, he would keep one gun, just in case.

He wished he could use a handgun for this assignment. It would be

*EARTHLY SPIRITS*

quick and cleaner. But he was told that it would not do. This time it had to look like an accident or death by natural cause. An accident would be difficult because everyone and everything would have to be in the right place at the right time with zero margin for failure and no second chance. So, he had decided on poison, something that would look like a fatal heart attack or stroke.

It was not going to be easy. But if anyone could pull it off, he could. He was the best. He never asked questions, never left a trail. He never cared who the prey was or why he had been targeted. Bulgarian political troublemakers, South American generals, African warlords, European diplomats. They all were the same to him. In the early years of his profession, he had been told that each assassination was a public service. In time he came to believe that assassination was the highest form of public service.

But this assignment was different. Penko Lazar could not understand why he had been sent to Rome to kill an American priest.

# CHAPTER 20

Brother Gerald flipped through the pages of the old book as though he was disinterested, then carefully replaced it where he had found it in the middle of the row of other volumes packed tightly into the shelf of the bookstall.

"You haven't read that one, too?" Father William asked.

"Of course not," Gerald replied.

"I thought you'd read every book there was to read about Napoleon."

"Only about a hundred."

"Only? How many others are there."

"About fifty-thousand. And I could never handle the one I just put back."

"Why not?"

"My French is limited to about a hundred words, most of them learned in the three days we've been here. That old tale about how studying Latin can help you learn English certainly doesn't apply when it comes to French."

"Actually, it's a fable. Latin doesn't help you learn English, either. It can be useful if you want to understand the origins of English or French or Italian or whatever. Latin was one of those languages that the English stole words from in the late Middle Ages and incorporated into the

*EARTHLY SPIRITS*

language they were building. They would have been better off stealing a good cuisine. Studying Latin only helps you learn Latin and even though priests still learn it, not many of them use it anymore."

The two men turned and resumed their stroll along the River Seine. As they approached where the Pont de la Tournelle crossed the river, the vast curve of the apse of Notre Dame came into full view, its unmistakable buttresses extending out from between high vertical stained glass windows like the legs of an enormous spider. William pointed to the cathedral.

"He was crowned there," the old priest said. "But I suppose you knew that."

"To be precise, he crowned himself," Gerald replied. "Shocked everyone and embarrassed the pope. But the occasion wasn't quite the spectacle that a lot of history books and all the Hollywood movies have made it out to be. The place was pretty run down back then and Napoleon was too busy fighting wars and building monuments to give it any attention. About forty years later, the government finally got around to restoring it and that's only because Victor Hugo's novel, 'Notre Dame' was such a big hit that the public put pressure on the authorities to save the place."

Father William could not suppress the smile that ignited his face.

"What's so funny?" Gerald asked.

"I didn't know you had it in you," William replied.

"Whatever it is, I'm sure you're going to tell me what."

"In all the years I've known you, I've never heard you speak enthusiastically about anything until now. And it's also the first time you've given me a history lesson instead of the other way around."

Father William pointed across the river again just before they reached the next bridge. "It's a good thing we got there early in the day," he said.

Long lines of tourists waited outside Notre Dame, some patiently and others not, in a sun that was rapidly heating up the early afternoon. It would be another half-hour before those at the ends of the lines would pass through the Gothic portals leading to the interior of the Twelfth Century cathedral. And then, the lines still would be as long because others would have replaced those whose patience finally had gained them entry.

"I wonder how many of them are there for religious purposes," William added.

"Not many, I'd guess," Gerald said. "Most of them probably are gawking tourists. Even those who might look pious probably aren't. It's easy to look religious when the sun is shining."

He stopped at another of the bookstalls. It was not much different than the two dozen or so that he had browsed over the past hour. Permanently mounted atop the wall along the River Seine, hinges at its base allowed the front door to be closed when the owner was elsewhere. When shuttered, it looked like an oversized gray box. When the owner opened it for business, the door was unlocked and pulled down into a position similar to a large desk leaf that held a variety of old magazines and prints. Two shelves built into the stall were filled with books, mostly hardbound, mostly old and all in French. The rarest of the rare were carefully encased in large, clear plastic envelopes that hung on hooks at the top and down the sides of the bookstall. Brother Gerald gently removed one hanging at the upper left corner of the stall and briefly studied the cover of the rare old edition of the Paris Match magazine inside before replacing it.

"I'm not knocking Notre Dame," he said. "It's certainly worth a visit. But I prefer being outside in this city, especially on such a nice day."

"In my wildest dreams I could never have imagined you of even thinking such a thing," Father William said. "Coming from such a recluse who's spent years burrowing under books in dark corners, it's almost like listening to blasphemy. It's the lure of the bookstalls, isn't it?"

"They do have a magnetic charm. Each one is like an old corner of a giant outdoor bookshop. How many are there?"

"I don't know, but I'd guess a couple of hundred."

"All of them along the river?"

"On both sides, with an occasional break here and there."

"Are they all like those we've seen today?"

"As I recall from my first trip here twenty years ago, this end of the river has the best. The closer you get to the center of the city, the more commercial they become, especially on the right bank past the Paris City

*EARTHLY SPIRITS*

Hall. But you still can find something you like even there. You just have to look harder."

"I haven't seen anything I don't like. The old books, the magazines, even the old prints are all wonderful. Where do they find all of it?"

"Probably the same place people who run junk shops and even legitimate antique emporiums find what they sell. Yard sales, garage sales, estate sales, classified advertising announcements, word-of-mouth. You name it."

"Sounds like a fulltime job."

"For some people it is. But a lot of these vendors have other jobs, usually at odd hours so that they can run these bookstalls during the day when they're not at work."

"That doesn't sound as romantic as it looks."

"It probably isn't."

They resumed their stroll, Gerald stopping to mentally soak in the printed wares at four more bookstalls. He was about to check out a fifth when Father William tugged at his left arm and said:

"There's a break in the traffic. Let's cross here."

Gerald started to resist, then gave in and followed the old priest out into the street. He saved his protest until they reached the sidewalk in front of a small, fenced park. He waved an arm toward the river across the street they had just crossed.

"There must be dozens of bookstalls that were still ahead of us," he said. "Why are we going this way?"

"You can't do all of them in one afternoon, William said. "We can pick up on them later."

"We're not going to another church?"

"Well, sort of. At least for me."

"And me?"

"There's something else to amuse you while I visit a couple of neighborhood churches. You're going to like it."

"I like the bookstalls."

"Stop fretting like a spoiled child. The something I'm talking about is very special for you and it's just around the corner. You're going to like it every bit as much as your precious bookstalls. Probably even more.

Besides, I need you to stay in one place while I'm making my rounds. If I leave you to the bookstalls, you'd probably be somewhere past the Louvre by the time I'm finished and I don't want to have to go hunting for you."

"How long will you be gone?"

"About an hour, maybe an hour-and-a-half at the most."

"I might get bored."

"You won't."

"Is that a guarantee?"

Father William pointed a finger.

"No. That is."

About fifty feet ahead on the left, Brother Gerald saw a half-dozen people standing in front of a shop with green-framed windows. They looked like refugees from the nineteen-sixties. Three were listening to a bearded man wearing black slacks and a black sweater. Two were browsing through a small selection of books resting on a makeshift table that looked older than Father William. Brother Gerald looked at the sign above the shop windows. It read "Shakespeare and Company."

"It's a bookstore," Gerald said.

"This isn't just a bookstore," William replied.

"Don't tell me it's also another souvenir shop."

"For someone so well read you are a literary illiterate."

"I feel another lecture coming on."

"Shakespeare and Company is the bookstore to end all bookstores. It's a literary institution."

The two clerics paused outside the first of the shop's two doors. Beyond it, shelves filled with what obviously were rare old volumes lined the walls of a small room. Brother Gerald tried the door. It was locked.

"You can't get in there without an invitation or asking someone at the desk in the main shop," Father William said. "Besides, I doubt that you'll have enough time to browse on this side."

"Why not?"

"Wait until you get a look at the rest of the place."

"It can't be better than this room."

*EARTHLY SPIRITS*

"It is. After all it was started in the early nineteen-fifties by George Whitman."

"Who's he?"

"The grandson of Walt Whitman."

"You mean…"

"None other."

"This place was almost a second home to some of the great writers of the Twentieth Century. Ernest Hemingway, Virginia Woolf, Henry Miller and a lot of others sometimes held court here. You can almost sense their ghosts hanging around inside. They still get a lot of visiting writers here. And some tumbleweeds."

"Tumbleweeds?"

"Yes. Tumbleweeds are what we used to call the motley crew of mostly transient aspiring writers from all over the world. Usually they have little money to afford a place to stay in Paris. So they stay here."

"They live in a bookstore?"

"For a few days, sometimes even a few weeks, in exchange for a few hours of work. Upstairs there are dusty old sofas, studio couches and whatever tucked behind bookshelves. It's everything but luxury. Sort of like your old monastic cell back in Virginia, but surrounded by all the books you'd ever want."

"This place doesn't look that big."

"It isn't. Whitman obviously is creative at interior design. Downstairs it's a tightly packed labyrinth with old creaking shelves from floor to ceiling filled with books old and new. Probably ninety percent or more of them are in English, which is what you'd expect in a place named after Shakespeare. But look for a familiar title and you just might see a half-dozen or more of the same book side-by-side, each in a different language. In the back you'll find a narrow staircase that looks like it's ready to collapse going upstairs to where the owner sometimes lives, the tumbleweeds stay and where visiting writers, usually of little repute, are hosted."

"You've been here before?"

"I was a tumbleweed."

"You?"

163

"Don't look so surprised. I may have been your father abbot for a long time, but I've got a personal history that predates that."

"You were a hippie?"

"More like a beatnik. I was in Paris for a week in the late nineteen-fifties on a summer break from the seminary. I heard about this place like most of the other tumbleweeds, word-of-mouth. It sounded like it might be more enjoyable than spending my entire time in a church dormitory."

"Was it?"

"Definitely. I felt like I was a character in a book. Not one of those slick-jacketed popular hardbacks. More like a book filled with mystical poetry, the kind that university students carry in their backpacks and recommend to their friends, but rarely read."

"I never would have known."

"There's a lot you don't, but I have a feeling we're both soon going to know more than we want. I'll be back long before you've had your fill of the place."     Father William wanted to add "before we meet up later with Nikolai." But why ruin the simple earthly delight that Brother Gerald was experiencing for the first time since Nikolai had created their trinity?

At the same time, William wondered what Nikolai was dabbling in all day. That morning, he had been insistent that the two priests spend the day without him doing whatever they wanted. William only hoped that whatever Nikolai was up to, it would not take a tragic turn like those he had blamed for so many past earthly ills.

Still, William reluctantly admitted to himself that he missed having Nikolai around. That made the priest feel guilty of having committed the most mortal of sins.

# CHAPTER 21

The boat glided smoothly from the concrete bank from which it had been launched and headed across the smooth surface of the water straight toward two others that were on a collision course. It slid deftly between the other boats just before the bow of one broadsided the other.

"You're cheating," the voice said.

"And you enjoy sneaking up on one," Nikolai replied. "By the way, I'm not cheating. Just entertaining the youngsters with a little magic act. Watch this."

The miniature boat that he had launched turned around, circled the two that had their disaster in the pond at the Tuileries Gardens, then sailed straight back to Nikolai. He lifted it out of the water and handed it to an eight-year-old boy who looked at him with eyes that were as wide as he ever would open them. The youngster placed it back into the water and gave it a push.

Nikolai raised himself from the edge of the concrete ring that encircled the pond and turned to face his visitor.

"That boy's going to be disappointed when that boat won't do for him what I could do for it."

"Well, you could give it a little push," the other man said. "I'm sure it would make the boy smile."

165

"That would be breaking the rules. I'm not supposed to interfere. Besides, he might as well start learning to deal with disappointment while he's young. He's going to have his share of it over the years."

"How have you been?"

"What a question. But, then again, you've always been the eternal optimist."

"I like the name you're using. Did it come with the body or is it simply that you can't resist using some version of Old Nick?"

"He was a Russian hoodlum. What do I call you?"

"Raphael, of course."

"It's refreshing to know that you haven't been afflicted with originality."

Raphael extended his right hand, but Nikolai ignored it. Instead, he grasped Raphael lightly by the shoulders and gently brushed him check-to-cheek on both sides in an imitation of kissing before Raphael could pull away.

"Don't be embarrassed," Nikolai said. "It's not the kiss of Judas. When in France, do like the French do. Or at least like some of them still do when they meet old friends. We once were friends."

"That was a long time ago," Raphael replied. "A very long time ago."

"Too long."

"I hope this isn't going to take too long. I can't spare too much time."

"Then let's take a stroll. There's something I'd like to show you. We can talk while we're walking and even more when we get there."

They turned away from the children's toy boat pond and walked along a wide path toward an arch.

"That's the Arc de Triomphe du Carrousel," Nikolai said. It's a smaller version of the Arc de Triomphe that you probably saw in the distance beyond the pond. The two are lined up almost perfectly. This smaller one ahead was modeled on the Arch of Severus in Rome. Napoleon built it about two-hundred years ago to commemorate his victories over Austria. The bigger one behind us also is dedicated to the military. It's inscribed with the names of thousands of French officers who died in the Napoleonic wars. It's also the largest arch on Earth and under it there's France's Tomb of the Unknown Soldier. They only had room for one,

*EARTHLY SPIRITS*

from the First World War. Plenty of other unknown French soldiers died in the two big wars of the Twentieth Century. But I suppose you know all about those."

"You could have prevented them."

"You know that's not in my job description."

"Free will?"

"That's what He told me when He stuck me in this God-forsaken world. Pun intended."

"Did you ever think that you may have interpreted it too literally?"

"You know there's no other way I could have interpreted it. If He didn't like the way I was doing my job, He could have fired me."

"I'm not here to debate you. Anyway, I'm not sure anyone else could have done any better. Interfering might have prevented some of the disasters I've heard about, but who knows what others it might have created?"

"You have no idea."

They passed under the Arc de Triomphe du Carrousel into an enormous courtyard flanked by Sixteenth Century buildings that stretched along both sides and a massive building of similar age at the far end.

"This used to be a royal palace complex and Napoleon lived here for a while after the French Revolution," Nikolai said. "He sometimes reviewed his Imperial Guard on parade here. Now, it's the Ministry of Finance and the Louvre."

"The art museum?" Raphael asked.

"The finest. I'm surprised you know it."

"I don't. A tourist told me to take the Metro to the Louvre station when I was trying to find out how to get to where you suggested that we meet."

"I'm surprised you were only a few minutes late."

"The public transportation system here is very good."

"See that giant glass pyramid. That's the entrance. We're going inside."

"There must be two-hundred people standing in that line in front of it. If we have to stand there, we'll be wasting a lot of valuable time. We won't be able to discuss what I came here for. Besides, why go to an art museum?"

"I'd think you'd have enough faith in me to believe I know what I'm doing."

"Faith in you?" Raphael let a wisp of a smile emerge from his lips. "Now there's heresy, if I've ever heard it."

"That's more like it. I haven't seen you smile in a long time."

"We haven't seen each other in a long time. And, it's not my smile. It belongs to someone else."

"The body you took. It's not too bad. About forty-five, maybe fifty years old. A little paunchy around the middle. Let me guess. Liver failure."

"You noticed the slight touch of yellow in the skin."

"Where did you get it?"

"One of the hospitals. I'm not used to this sort of thing. I can't control every minor physical function as easily as you. But I'm sure that's only because you've had more practice."

"More than you realize."

Nikolai motioned for Raphael to follow him. The two men took a diagonal route to the left and crossed the cobblestoned courtyard to a passage. They emerged from the other side onto the busy Rue de Rivoli, turned right and came to a stairway that led to an underground shopping area.

"This is the express lane to the Louvre," Nikolai said.

They passed a couple of brightly lit shops and went straight ahead to one of the museum ticket booths with the shortest line. Nikolai bought the two tickets needed for admission from a bored clerk.

"Follow me," he said.

"I still don't understand why we're going into an art museum," Raphael protested.

"Because there's something I want to show you."

"Does it have anything to do with why I'm here?"

"In a way. Humor me. I've got an ego I'd like to have massaged."

"This had better be important. We don't have much time."

"How much time do we have?"

"Two months, maybe three."

"That's cutting it a lot closer than I expected. And a lot closer than I'd like to think about."

*EARTHLY SPIRITS*

"I would've thought that you'd be worried the most since all Hell is going to break loose in your territory. But you don't seem very concerned."

"Shit happens. It's something people say."

"Is that what they call linguistic evolution here?"

"No. That's what they call reality."

Nikolai led the way, up a flight of stairs to the main level.

"It's a shame we can't stop here," he said. "This floor has a wealth of ancient Greek antiquities. Even you might even recognize a few. The Greeks loved to sculpt statues of beings they believed were gods. But, since you're in a hurry, we've got to go up another flight of stairs."

The stairs opened at the next level into corridor hung with paintings. They followed it through a series of rooms, passing by hundreds of the more than five-thousand paintings of old masters that rivaled even the collection of the Vatican. They bypassed the works of Dutch and French painters that dominated the Salle des Sept Metres, a room named for its width. From there, the lofty Grande Galerie, where huge paintings of French artists dominated the walls along both sides of its nearly four-hundred-foot length.

"We're almost there," Nikolai said. He paused and extended his hand toward an entrance at the right of the Grand Gallerie. "Be my guest. After you."

They entered another large room. Masterpieces of Italian painting assaulted the eye, especially Paolo Veronese's "Marriage in Cana," a giant work measuring twenty-one feet high by thirty feet long.

"Forget that one," Nikolai said. "It takes too long to study. And, by the way, since you're in such a hurry, we probably shouldn't bother to look at the Raphaels, either. Two of his best are here. We want the painting at the far end of the room, where all those people are gathered."

Nikolai gently nudged his way through the middle of the small group of Japanese tourists, at the same time opening a space for Raphael. They gazed at the portrait of the woman that had been hung alone on the wall as though it were an object of sacred religious importance. Disappointed that none of them could take photographs of the painting, the Japanese tourists soon had their fill and went on their way. When they were out of earshot, Nikolai broke the silence.

"She's supposed to beautiful, but I've seen thousands of better looking women her age."

"Isn't that the famous Da Vinci painting?" Raphael asked. "The…"

"The Mona Lisa."

"Right. I've heard of it."

"I thought whatever interests you may have developed in art would be limited strictly to religious works. You're even painted in one of them somewhere in this room, though it's not a good likeness. The artist was a romanticist."

"I still don't understand why we're here."

"Take a good look at the Mona Lisa. Especially the face. What do you see?"

"That smile. It's supposed to be famous."

"It is. What else?"

"And those eyes. They go with the smile. The artist has painted a secret into her face. There's something familiar about all of it."

"Correct again. And?"

"You're not going to tell me…"

"Who else?"

"You painted it?"

"You are a clod. Of course not."

"You gave Da Vinci the idea. You interfered."

"Not exactly. The inspiration, maybe."

"Take a good look at the painting, then look at me."

"Oh, no. It can't be. Is it you?"

"Very good. You see, Da Vinci's model died shortly after he started work on the painting. I just happened to be around and needed a body. She was available. Da Vinci was such an artistic genius, among other things, that I couldn't very well let him down. Besides, it was a chance to have myself painted in a good light for a change. You should see how a lot of other artists think I should look."

"It is you. I can see it now."

"How else do you think this painting could've become so famous. But let's go. Here comes another group of gawkers."

"Okay, so you've let me in on your little secret. But I'm not here to

*EARTHLY SPIRITS*

attend art appreciation school. I'm trying to stop a war. Maybe the most catastrophic war ever fought."

"Could it really come to that?"

"Not only do you know very well that it could, you're well aware of the consequences."

Instead of replying, Nikolai raised his eyelids just enough to accent the smile on his face. Raphael recognized the Mona Lisa in his lips.

"You have something," he said. "You've got a secret, haven't you? An answer to our prayers?"

"If you want to call it that, just maybe. I'd have thought by now that you still wouldn't have been hung up on prayer. I prefer to call it an ace in the hole. That's something else that people say."

"You're going to tell me, aren't you?"

"I'm going to do more than that. I'm going to show it to you."

# CHAPTER 22

Cardinal Sforza and Cardinal Grosetti were living intangibles. Both lived in the shadows, otherwise they were nearly complete opposites.

Sforza was mostly straightforward, Grosetti almost always manipulative. Sforza was often dour, Grosettti usually jovial. Sforza was a believer, Grosetti generally doubted.

Their differences also extended to the physical. Sforza was short and wiry, with a face that sometimes seemed like it should have been worn by a ferret. His movements matched his furtive demeanor, like those of an animal stalking its prey, not for the food, but for the kill. No one could miss Grosetti coming. He lumbered painfully on a body that he had subjected to years of abuse at the dining table. His lumpy face looked like a caricature out of a medieval painting.

So, when Cardinal Sforza invited his scarlet-robed colleague to a late lunch, Cardinal Grosetti was certain that his suspicions about a big secret circulating through the Vatican had to be true. Sforza rarely invited anyone to lunch and never to a restaurant outside the Vatican.

Because he knew that Sforza frowned on all excesses, Grosetti arrived at the restaurant on the Via di Concilizacione forty-five minutes ahead of their scheduled meeting. That would give him enough time to savor a bountiful appetizer plate of sliced meats and vegetables fried in olive oil.

*EARTHLY SPIRITS*

And, a small bottle of Brunello, the best of the red wines in the house. He knew that Sforza would know that he had begun his afternoon feast early. But he also knew that Sforza could at least tolerate Grosetti's gluttony as long as he did not practice it in his presence.

Sforza arrived ten minutes late. While that was out of character for the cardinal, it pleased Grosetti, giving him time to think, something he almost never let interfere with dining. Grosetti had to be prepared for whatever Sforza might ask or reveal to him. He saw the meeting as a bout between clerical heavyweights. He would need all his skills to go the distance. Because Sforza had allowed Grosetti to choose the site of their meeting, the latter felt that the familiar territory of his favorite restaurant added to whatever edge he might have. Besides, what did the no-nonsense Sforza know about dining?

Cardinal Grosetti had spent so many years accumulating Vatican experience that he had all but evolved into a new life form. Nearly half of him had become a politician who knew how to deftly maneuver in the Vatican's convoluted corridors. Nearly half of him had become a bureaucrat, almost subservient to his desk. Little room was left for the priest. He felt that this gave him a slight advantage over Sforza, who still had as much priest in him as politician. If it were not for Sforza's position as head of the Vatican Secretariat of State and was someone who had the ear of the pope, Grosetti believed he would win with a knockout.

After pausing to have a word with the restaurant's owner, Sforza made his way to the small alcove that was set aside for Vatican clientele. In a breach of protocol, Sforza motioned for Grosetti to stay seated. The two men shook hands, exchanged the usual pleasantries and Sforza sat in a chair across from Grosetti. Only their close associates would have recognized them. They had exchanged their scarlet robes for black suits whose white clerical collars were the only clues to their vocations.

"I apologize for being late," Sforza said.

"No need to apologize," Grosetti replied. "I've set aside the rest of the afternoon. I'll work into the evening to catch up."

"I appreciate that. There's a lot to talk about."

Cardinal Grosetti would have known that even if he did not believe some sort of important secret was circulating among a handful of Vatican insiders. Sforza never met with anyone socially. And even Sforza knew that arranging the meeting during the late afternoon hours would be convenient because restaurants in the Vatican City closed after lunch and would not reopen until dinnertime. Like so many others, he also knew the restaurant owner had a long-standing policy of keeping the doors open for cardinals and other high-ranking Vatican personnel. To insure the privacy of those who wanted it, he had installed a heavy curtains that could shield his Vatican clientele from the ears of anyone who might be at another table. Grosetti had used the alcove several times and sometimes wondered whether it was bugged. He even had thought of bugging it himself.

"I've only been here a few times and not since last year," Sforza said. "I'll leave the ordering up to you. Besides, you're the gourmet."

Grosetti did not know whether to feel flattered or insulted. He decided to go for the compliment.

"The Venetian-style liver and onions," Grosetti suggested. "The sauce is outstanding. It's a house specialty. I doubt they make it as good in Venice. For a starter, you might consider…"

"No, no. The main course will be enough. That way I might have some room left for dessert, if I choose to have anything else. And, please, you select the wine."

Grosetti signaled the owner, ordered for himself a repeat of the appetizer plate he had sampled earlier, two portions of liver and a full bottle of Brunello. He asked that the wine be brought quickly, suggesting that there was no rush for the food. The owner gave him an understanding nod.

Cardinal Sforza flicked the switch on the lamp on the wall to his left, turned in his seat, reached for the curtain and pulled it to the right until it reached the edge of the alcove. He had shut in the two of them. While it made Grosetti slightly uncomfortable, he knew that the privacy meant that he was going to learn something important. At last.

"Now we can talk without concern over prying eyes and finely tuned ears," Sforza said.

"Then it must be something very important," Grosetti replied. The remark was strictly conversational. Except for ceremonial affairs that his office required him to attend, Sforza never met anyone privately unless it was important.

"What we talk about here must remain here, at least for the time being," Sforza said, lowering his voice.

"No one in the Vatican is more discreet than the two of us," Grosetti replied.

"So, let me get straight to the issues at hand."

Grosetti wanted to ask whether there was more than one issue, but thought better of it. There must be. Cardinal Sforza never was known to have made a slip of the tongue. He always was so careful with his choice of words that they could be taken as gospel. Grosetti's only disappointment was that Sforza was going to be who he was. There would be no meaningless conversation to open their meeting, no preliminaries. Grosetti enjoyed feeling out his opponent. He was a master at parrying while looking for a weak spot. It was a psychological game. He wondered how someone so dull could rise so high in the Vatican. He let his colleague continue.

"The Holy Father is going to summon you tomorrow to a private audience. Just the two of you."

Grosetti wanted to interrupt. A private meeting meant something big was up or about to occur. But if Sforza knew about it, he must already have had a private session of his own with the pope. Envy crept up Grosetti's spine. But he remained quiet, curious as to why Sforza would tell him about it in advance. His anxiety was stretched a little tighter when they were interrupted by the owner, who had returned with the Brunello, pouring a glass for each before leaving them alone again. Even wine could wait.

"The Holy Father wanted to meet with us separately this morning," Sforza continued. "But his schedule wouldn't allow it. So, it will be the first thing two mornings from today, right after Mass. After that, he plans to have a brief audience with all the heads of the other Vatican offices under the Secretariat. Then, later in the day, we'll both be summoned to another audience, just the pope and the two of us."

So that's it, Grosetti thought. Sforza wants to avoid a battle in front of the pope. He wants Grosetti's support for whatever Sforza has on his agenda.

"As you probably gather, something very important has arisen," Sforza said. "And meeting like this seems rather irregular, but you may know something that you're likely to be asked tomorrow."

"By the Holy Father?" Grosetti asked.

"Yes."

Sforza sensed Grosetti's concern. Briefly, he wondered what new web had Grosetti woven that he feared might snare him. Under different circumstances Sforza would have been unable to resist the temptation to play some of the game that he knew Grosetti loved so well. But, letting the thought slide, he said:

"Oh, it's nothing to worry about. It's that American priest, the monk, Brother Gerald."

"Brother Gerald?"

"Yes. The Holy Father wants to talk with him, probably sometime early next week. He stressed the importance of seeing him."

"Importance? He's a simple monk, a priest who doesn't seem to have ever had any ambition. I don't even know what he's doing in the Vatican. I mean, I know what he's doing, I just don't know why he was chosen to do it."

"Neither do I," Sforza said. "Yet, I'm the one who is supposed to have signed the letter offering him the position in Rome. And I don't even remember signing it. I only saw a copy of the letter for the first time an hour ago when I asked Cardinal Verano if he knew anything about it. He had the copy in his files."

"Someone forged your signature?"

"No. It's mine all right. But then, I sign so many pieces of paper that are put in front of me without reading them. But, considering the nature of this monk's work here, one would think that I would remember it."

"Why ask me about him?"

"His research on the devil does have a connection with the Congregation for the Doctrine of the Faith. So, you must have talked to him."

"Well, yes, but only once. We met at my office to discuss the progress of his work."

"Then you have one up on me."

*EARTHLY SPIRITS*

"You haven't met Brother Gerald?"

"Until the Holy Father asked about him today, I'd never even heard of the man. In fact, he seems quite elusive."

"More like a hermit. From what I gather, the only people in the Vatican that he's associated with are the old abbot who came with him, Father William, and the young American priest, Father Shane. And, of course, Cardinal Verano."

"No, I meant elusive. We have to find him. It seems our Brother Gerald is missing."

"Missing?"

"Yes. He and Father William have flown off to Paris."

"Paris? Why would they go to Paris?"

"I thought you might know."

"I don't. Maybe Father Shane or Cardinal Verano know."

"Shane doesn't. Cardinal Verano knows only that he gave them the airline tickets, with an open date for a return. They were issued by the Vatican travel office."

"An open return? Well, Verano should know where they're staying. He can contact them and tell them to fly back to Rome."

"That's not as easy as it sounds. Verano gave them only airline tickets. There were no hotel reservations."

"Who authorized their travel?"

"It came from the Congregation for the Doctrine of the Faith. The paper had your signature."

Cardinal Sforza reached into his inside jacket pocket, pulled out a folded sheet of paper, opened it and passed it across the table to Cardinal Grosetti.

"This is your signature, isn't it?" Sforza asked.

To Grosetti, the words sounded like those of an inquisitor. He took a long, close look at the paper, focusing on the signature.

"It can't be," he said, nervously. Just as quickly, he regained his composure. "It looks like mine, but it must be a forgery. I signed no such document. The date on it is only four days ago. I couldn't forget something that happened so recently. Besides..."

"Yes, I know," Sforza said. "You never sign anything without reading it first and thinking about at least twice. It looks like we're both victims of an intriguer."

"But, who? I can vouch for everyone in my office."

"So can I in mine."

"Which means…"

"Someone outside our domains. Someone who has access."

"Access to who? Not the…"

"I doubt the Holy Father would be involved in something like this. He's not the conspiratorial type."

"It could be someone close to him."

"I've considered that. It makes sense that it must be someone who has influence. Someone who can come and go as he pleases without attracting attention."

"I should be able to find out easily enough."

"And how do you plan to do that?

"I'll ask my chief of staff, Umberto, to inquire around the office."

"My chief of staff says he knows nothing about the letter I supposedly signed. Of course, he's conducting his own investigation in my office, but I don't expect results."

For the first time that he could recall, Cardinal Grosetti felt that he was being outplayed. A nondescript monk from the United States and his sidekick priest were doing whatever they pleased. And a mysterious third party was pulling the strings. If it was not Cardinal Sforza, who could it be? Would the pope give him the answers to the puzzle that had frustrated him? He took a generous sip of wine witthout bothering to savor the taste just as his appetizer had arrived.

"What can you tell me about this Brother Gerald?" Sforza asked.

"Probably not much more than you already know," Grosetti replied. He related what he knew about Gerald's background, Father Shane's investigation of the deaths at Blessed Skyline Abbey in Virginia and the meeting with the monk in his office. Sforza already knew most of what Grosetti told him. However, Grosetti was careful to omit any mention of Father Monahan or the telephone call from Teresa Lucci.

"What about this Father Shane?" Sforza asked.

"You don't think he's our mystery man?" Grosetti replied nervously.

*EARTHLY SPIRITS*

Shane was his creation and it was unthinkable that he could have had a clerical mole in his service.

"I don't know what to think," Sforza said. "But it seems like this priest worth looking into."

"You can be sure I'll do that," Grosetti promised.

"I thought you would," Sforza said. "I'll also have a discreet investigation under way in my office and in the other offices of the Curia. But let's put Brother Gerald and our forger aside for the moment. There's something else far more important that you should know. Something that can't possibly involve our American monk and his unknown benefactor."

"More important?" Grosetti asked. The words came out with a slight touch of resignation. Was it going to be more bad news? He raised his eyebrows.

"The pope is going to call a council," Sforza said.

Grosetti wanted to reply, but a torrent of thoughts cascaded through his mind, flooding any attempt by words to escape. There's going to be another ecumenical council. The Holy Father had one only a few years ago. Once should be enough for one papacy. What is it going to be this time? An end to the priestly vows of celibacy? The welcome mat for homosexuals? A relaxation of the rules prohibiting abortion? The priesthood for women? Millions of Catholics, especially in the United States, already weren't paying much attention to these strictures. He might as well just strike a dozen or so names from the Church's approved list of saints. At least that would not be controversial.

"You're thinking an ecumenical council," Sforza said.

"What other kind is there?" Grosetti replied.

"The Holy Father wants to sit down at the table with the heads of all the major Christian denominations."

Grosetti suspended the fork with the roasted peppers midway between the table and his mouth. He did not speak, but looked straight into Sforza's eyes with eyes that were lit with disbelief.

"Yes, you heard me correctly. Oh, the Jews will be invited, too. You know, the old Judeo-Christian ties. And the Holy Father is even also seriously considering asking the Muslims."

"The Jews? The Muslims?"

"And the Anglicans, Baptists, Lutherans, Methodists, Mormons and all the others that have substantial numbers of followers."

"Why?"

Cardinal Sforza refilled Grosetti's glass with more Brunello.

"You'd better have another sip," Sforza said. "You might even want to empty the glass."

"He's going to propose reunification? That's it. But, then why invite the Jews and Muslims?"

"Not exactly reunification. But he's going to ask them to be as united as possible. To prepare."

"For what?"

Sforza hesitated. Once he had formed his lips into what he felt was an undecipherable smile, he said:

"The Second Coming."

# CHAPTER 23

Loyalty. That was the virtue Ewan Sinclair had been taught to hold dear above everything else from as far back as he could remember. His father was the first to teach it to him. As he grew older, others repeated it to him as though it were a sacred vow. Younger listeners were expected to at least nod their heads in assent. In recent years, only Father John and a handful of other secretive old men preached loyalty anymore.

Since returning from Oregon, the doubts that always had been fettered in the corner of Ewan's mind had broken free and escaped their shadowy existence. Loyalty was one thing. But blind loyalty was another. The first recognition that he may have been brainwashed to be obedient rather than loyal was coming to life in his mind.

Now, as he sat across the table from the journalist from Maine, Ewan Sinclair felt like he was sinking into a mental quicksand of uncertainty.

"Your wife is very attractive," he said. It was small talk and before he was tempted to say anything else, he took a sip from the pint of ale that the waitress had brought to their corner table at the Knights Inn

"I think so, too," Rick Erlandson said.

"She's also intelligent."

"That she is. Does she wear that on her face, too?"

"I think so. But she did give us some lame excuse about going shopping. She obviously felt I'd be more comfortable talking to you, one-on-one. She's going to be disappointed."

"How so."

"Most of the shops are going to close in fifteen minutes and I suppose you'd planned on just the two of us talking for more time than that."

Rick let his smile give way to a mild laugh. He raised his glass as if toasting Ewan.

"I wouldn't worry about that," Rick said. "She's also creative and adventurous. She'll find something to do. A little sightseeing. Probably take the car for a drive up to that church on the cliff. I understand it's quite interesting. A lot of history."

"I suppose so." Ewan suddenly became defensive. "That's why you've come here, isn't it?"

"Partly," Rick replied. "Look, don't worry. I'm not here to do a story about this village, your church or the Knights Templar. Or any kind of a story. Your friend at the Halifax newspaper said you were the person to talk to. I'm sure he must have mentioned when he telephoned you that whatever we discussed would be off the record."

"Yes. Roland said you wouldn't write anything. That all you were looking for was information about the Templars. We were both students at the same university. Fraternity brothers, too. I believe him. He believed you. How do I know I can?"

"No honor among thieves? Do they teach you how to talk that way in law school?"

"Yes. It's in that book that we all get when were accepted. It's our version of the book that all females get just before they get married. You know, the one that tells them to tell their husbands to think about the money they saved when they've bought something they didn't need because it was discounted. Or, how they can win arguments by using their emotions to run roughshod over logic. Don't journalists have a book of their own that no one else ever sees?"

"I'd hate to have you going up against me in court. But, for now, will you at least hear my case? Otherwise, why did you agree to meet me?"

"Curiosity, self-interest, timing. Your point is well taken."

*EARTHLY SPIRITS*

Ewan scanned the dimly lit pub, his eyes searching the crowd for faces he knew. The few he recognized had little or nothing to do with the Templars. The rest all were tourists. He let out a short sigh, turned to Rick and told him he would answer whatever he could. They ordered two more pints of ale and Ewan gave Rick a brief discourse on the history of the Knights Templar.

"That's quite a tale," Rick said when Ewan was finished. "It's more than I ever would have learned in my lifetime. Except..."

"Now we're finally going to get to the heart of the matter," Ewan said. "I didn't think you'd come this far just for a history lesson."

"You left something out."

"What's that?"

"Your last name."

"Not that thing again."

"I'd think you'd be proud of it. Sort of like the descendants of the people who came to Massachusetts on The Mayflower."

"All right, so I'm a descendant of the Saint Clair family that fled continental Europe to Scotland during the persecution of the Knights Templar and eventually settled here. But since you brought up the subject, you obviously knew that already. That was so long ago, it might as well have been something that happened on another planet. You know, in a galaxy far, far away."

"Why is a descendant of the Saint Clair family trying to find Brother Gerald and Father William?"

The question was as unexpected as it seemed impudent. Ewan was briefly lost for an answer, so he let Rick continue.

"I hope you're not going to try to deny it. It's all over your face."

"How did you know?"

"I got a telephone call."

"From who?

"You're clever enough to figure that out."

"Teresa Lucci?"

"Since I hope you'll be open with me, yes. We worked on the same newspaper when we were in Washington. She's also a friend."

"I didn't think I was that obvious."

183

"You weren't. But you made a couple of mistakes. And she's very smart."

"Mistakes?"

"She got a glimpse of your Knights Templar ring. Is that it? The one on your right hand?"

"I should've taken it off before meeting her. And tonight, too."

"Also, there was no Brother Walter at Skyline Abbey in Virginia."

"She knew that?"

"Her husband used to be a monk there."

"A nun who gave up her vows married to a defrocked monk?"

"You knew she'd been a nun?"

"Oops. Another slip of the tongue."

"But not that she was married to an ex-monk?"

"Obviously I didn't have all the information."

"I don't get it. Why would the Templars be interested in Gerald and William."

"I don't know."

"Next you're going to tell me you were only following orders."

"Look, the Knights Templar is nothing more than a group of old men hanging onto a tradition that's been dying for centuries. Give it another generation or two and it's going to be nothing more than a social club. But for now, I owe it a lot. Without it, I might be on a fishing boat right now, competing like the few fishermen still here for what the big corporate trawlers haven't pulled out of the Atlantic."

"You really don't know."

"Nothing I can back up with facts."

"Well, someone must. I doubt you went off to Oregon on a whim. I don't suppose you'll tell me who does."

"You suppose correctly."

"If I've reached a dead end with you, I suppose I'll have to start digging elsewhere. Or would you rather tell me as much as you feel comfortable with."

"If I knew anything that I felt was important…"

Rick took another sip of ale, slid his chair back quietly along the floor and started to rise.

*EARTHLY SPIRITS*

"It's been nice meeting you," he said. "But it looks like I've got a lot more ground to cover, so I'd better be on my way."

Sinclair took a quick look around the room and tapped the table with his right hand.

"Don't go," he said. "Please sit down."

Rick sat back into the chair he had just vacated and slid it back into position close to the table.

"If this is going to be a confession, I'm in the wrong business," Rick said.

"Call it legal curiosity, which probably isn't much different than journalistic inquiry," Ewan replied. "But I'm also having some lingering doubts about what I've done. So, I'm going to trust you."

"We're still off the record."

"First of all, I'd like to know what makes these two priests so special?"

"I don't know. Except that they were involved last year in the investigation of a series of deaths at their monastery in Virginia."

"I've been told something about that. But before I say anything more, I'd like to hear your version."

Rick had no trouble recalling the details. He told Ewan about the deaths of the four monks, how they had occurred, their relationship to the Seven Deadly Sins and the name days of the saints, Father Shane being sent by the Vatican to investigate and the death of the prime suspect, a drifter named Nicholas."

"That's one Hell of a tale," Ewan said after Rick had finished.

"It was one Hell of a mystery," Rick said.

"I somehow get the feeling that you don't believe that this Nicholas person was the murderer."

"Let's say that I'm not entirely convinced."

"Don't you think it's odd that after the monastery was closed, that the Church sent this Brother Gerald and Father William to some place where they can't be found. I mean, no one seems to know where they are. What's the big secret?"

"Nice try, counselor. But there really is nothing I can add. If there's a big secret, I'm not in on it."

"But, you know where they are."

"I only found out a few days ago."

"So did I."

"For a landlubber, you're making a good attempt at fishing."

"They're in Rome."

Rick went silent. How did Ewan know?

"Teresa Lucci."

"I don't believe you. She wouldn't have told you."

"Not directly."

"Then how?"

"I'm a lawyer. I know how to get information even when the client isn't being candid. I called her telephone company the day I checked out and pretended I was her husband, Christopher. I wanted to know what long distance calls had been made from 'my' telephone in the past forty-eight hours. They were reluctant to give it out, but I bluffed my way through. I called the number they gave me. It was the Vatican."

"Well, I'll be…"

"That makes two of us. It seems to me that Brother Gerald and Father William are very important. Otherwise, why would they be assigned to the Vatican and then have that kept a secret? Could there be a link between their being posted to Rome and what you told me happened in Virginia?"

"I don't know. I wasn't really that much of an insider then and I'm still not. But that still begs the question."

"Of why the Templars want to know where they are?"

"Yes."

"I don't have an answer for that."

"Then it looks like I've reached the end of this trail."

Rick took a small sip out of his still half-filled glass of ale, gently slid his chair back away from the table again and started to rise."

"I guess I'm going to have to look somewhere else, maybe even dig a little deeper," he added.

Ewan's reaction was swift and unexpected. He reached out and grasped Rick's right hand.

"Please don't go," Ewan said.

Rick paused for a moment, pretending to be unsure. Than he sat down

## EARTHLY SPIRITS

in the chair he had just abandoned and slid it back into position at the table.

"Something you forgot?" Rick asked.

Ewan leaned forward, lowered his voice to a whisper and said:

"There's something I can't get out of my mind. Something so fantastic that I wouldn't blame you for thinking you came all this way just to hear a lunatic tell you a fairy tale."

""I hear fairy tales all the time in my business," Rick replied, also in a whisper. "Some of my readers even accuse me of writing them."

"You've got to swear that you'll never reveal my name as the source of what I'm about to tell you. Or reveal where you heard it and promise not to pay any visits to the local church or the pastor, Father John."

"Those are stiffer than usual conditions."

"It's that or nothing. And, if as you've said, you're not here searching for a story, but to help your friends, then why not? You're not likely to learn anything more from anyone else."

"If I'm not, then why bother to tell me what you're holding back?"

"If you start digging, some people here might start looking in my direction."

"Good thinking, counselor. All right, I solemnly swear."

"It all goes way back to the Crusades. The Knights Templar believe that something they've been waiting for ever since then is about to happen."

"You're not going to tell me that they think they're going to be powerful again. Like maybe getting one of their own elected as pope? So what? Do you remember what Stalin said during World War II when he was asked not to offend the Vatican?"

"No."

"He said 'how many divisions does the pope have'?"

"I'm sure the papacy is involved somehow, otherwise why would those two priests be at the Vatican undercover? I doubt either of them are Templars, otherwise the society wouldn't sent me across the continent to try to find them. They already would've known that they were in Rome."

"Well, then what do the Templars think is going to happen that they've waited for so long?"

"Jesus."

"Jesus Christ? I don't get it."

"They believe the Second Coming is going to occur by the end of this year, maybe earlier."

"You're right. It's a fairy tale."

"I'm not saying I believe it. But the elders of the Templars do."

"So what?"

"They also believe they're going to have an important role in it."

"What's that supposed to mean?"

"The only other thing I know is that the Templars will do whatever they feel is necessary to protect and promote their goals. And, they've got the resources to do it."

# CHAPTER 24

Brother Gerald was studying a striped gray tabby cat in the courtyard below the Paris apartment where he and Father William had been brought by Nikolai. Face up, the feline was stretched to its full length on a small red bench, soaking in the thin shaft of sunlight that managed to knife its way into the small space surrounded by old buildings with faded and streaked walls.

It was Gerald's way of pretending to ignore the conversation that was flooding the rest of the room. If Nikolai was not talking, Raphael was. Father William encouraged it with what seemed like an endless supply of questions. Gerald had heard much of it before, years earlier at the seminary. Some of it he had believed, some not. Now, he was not sure whether he had gotten his beliefs and disbeliefs right.

At least Raphael was being modest, leaving Nikolai to recite his biography to the two clerics.

"He's the angel of prayer, you know," Nikolai said. "If you want light, love, health and joy, you pray to him. Those are his specialties."

"You're also supposed to help travelers," Father William said. "Is that why you're here? To help us?"

"No," Raphael replied. "I came here to get a briefing from Nikolai. I've got to get back tonight. Too much is happening for me to stay away too long. I'll be back again, but for now, you're in Nikolai's hands. Besides, he's been here so long, no one knows the territory better."

"But so many religious scholars have said you have great ability to intervene in mankind's affairs."

"A myth."

"The Old Testament says you assumed human form before, accompanying Tobias in his travels, protecting, saving and healing him. Is that a myth, too?"

Raphael looked at Nikolai.

"He knows the Bible from A to Z," Nikolai said. "He knows that you, me and the others once lived in bodies similar to theirs. I've had to tell them a few things, otherwise they'd never have agreed to get involved."

"Let's just say it's a story," Raphael said, turning back to the old priest.

"What about the others? The archangels. The Bible mentions only three."

"Four," Raphael replied. "Nikolai here once was one."

"Technically, I still am," Nikolai said.

"I'm sure he's given you his version of what happened."

"I told them the truth."

"That you were a pain in the ass?"

"Yes. And that I was posted here with my contingent of devils for arguing against giving souls to monkeys. We've been stuck here ever since."

"Why do you insist on calling yourselves devils?"

"We didn't choose the name. The Church did. So it stuck. Besides, I think the word has a nice ring to it."

On and on they went, the discussion turning next to Michael, the fearless warrior of Heaven and for thousands of years, the most prominent and venerated of the archangels.

"And how is Michael these days?": Nikolai asked.

"Steadfast," Raphael said. "You're still not holding a grudge, are you?"

"I admire his loyalty."

"I mean over that incident with Moses."

"Had Moses listened to me instead of Michael, his people would have found the Promised Land a lot sooner. But that's ancient history. Besides,

*EARTHLY SPIRITS*

Michael was only following orders. He's always been a stickler for that. Considering current events, he must be in a wilderness of his own confusion now. Or, as Milton wrote in 'Paradise Lost,' is he getting ready to sound the trumpet for the Last Judgment?"

"You know he isn't."

"The Second Coming without a Last Judgment?" Father William asked.

"Not exactly," Raphael replied. "Someone else is ready to do it."

"Who?"

"Gabriel."

"The angel of the Incarnation?"

"The very same. The one who gets to make the announcements that are supposed to be joyful."

"I should have known that. Gabriel is mentioned four times in Holy Scripture and each had something to do with the coming of Christ."

"Oh, I don't doubt that he's eager to break the news," Nikolai said. "After all, he is the patron saint of communications workers."

The best Brother Gerald could do was fifteen minutes. When irritation finally gained control of his feelings, he turned from the window and snapped at the others, who were seated in the room.

"Listen to yourselves. It was bad enough listening to Heckle and Jeckle for the past three days. Now, I've got to put up with the Three Stooges."

"You'll have to forgive Brother Gerald," Nikolai said to Raphael. "He's a born doubter and he's had a difficult time trying to cope with everything. First it was me, then the big event, the search and now you. He's just blowing off steam. He'll come around."

"Blowing off steam? Is that what you call it? Maybe you're right, but what else do you expect? Now I'm supposed to believe that the angels have landed?"

"Well, his name is Raphael, after all. And I don't mean the Renaissance painter. Or would you have preferred Ralph?"

"Maybe I shouldn't have come," Raphael said.

"Your curiosity wouldn't have let you stay away."

"Why is he here?" Gerald demanded.

"To observe."

"Observe what? Father William and me? To see if we're up to the job of following you to the ends of the Earth or wherever it is you're taking us?"

"Aha! Then you believe my friend is none other than the Raphael."

"I didn't say that."

"Brother Gerald would like some proof."

"Like what?" Raphael asked.

"I think he'd like to see your wings."

Father William laughed. Raphael smiled.

"Just like I think he's secretly wished that he could see me sprout horns, cloven hooves and a pointed tail."

"That wouldn't hurt," Gerald said. His voice was calmer.

"Raphael could give you a small demonstration like the one I gave you in Rome at the Forum ruins," Nikolai said.

"No thanks."

"Then how about this?" Raphael asked.

Suddenly a ring of light appeared hovering over Raphael's head.

"Just like in all the Church paintings," Nikolai proclaimed.

The ring vanished almost as quickly as it appeared.

"I saw it, too," said an astonished Father William.

William looked at Gerald, who approached Raphael and passed his hand over the visitor's head.

"You're not going to find anything," Nikolai said. "It was just an short energy burst from the brain. Something we all did a long time ago to amuse your ancestors. You know, the savages that evolved from monkeys after God granted them souls. Actually, it scared the Hell out of them."

"It also made them true believers," Raphael said. "What about you, Brother Gerald?"

"Do I really have much choice?" Gerald replied. "It could be a magician's trick, but what's the difference? I've been dragged nearly halfway around the world in the past six months, asked to believe in things that challenge logic and told to be patient without knowing why Father William and I are here."

"You won't have to wait much longer," Nikolai said.

A look of surprise flashed across Raphael's face. "You know something?"

192

*EARTHLY SPIRITS*

"Let's say I have what you might call a good lead."

"How good?"

"The best I've had so far. But even if it's a false alarm, it's essential that we leave Paris early tomorrow morning."

"What's the rush?" Father William asked.

"We've only been in Paris for three days," Brother Gerald said. "I'd like to spend a few more here."

"Has the well run dry in Paris?" Raphael asked. "Or is your lead so good that unless you go tomorrow morning, the trail will get cold?"

"Both," Nikolai replied. But there's been a new development that has nothing to do where we're going next."

"There you go again," Gerald said. "Can't you ever say anything that doesn't have a riddle attached to it?"

"It may not be safe to stay here much longer."

"Not safe," Gerald said. "For who? You? Father William? Me? Who's going to risk tangling with Lucifer?"

"No one. But even I have my limitations."

"I want a better answer than that."

"So do I," said Father William.

Nikolai looked at Raphael and raised his bushy eyebrows. "Our two friends obviously have forgotten what I've told them. Maybe they'll listen to you."

"I think what Nikolai is trying to say in his inimitably convoluted fashion is that he's bound to the doctrine of non-interference," Raphael said. "He can guide, but not directly act on something or prevent events from occurring."

"Exactly. That's one of the constraints that I've had to operate under. If I'd been given more flexibility, this world would be a lot different."

"However, I'd also like to know what he's talking about."

"Like I said, it's got nothing to do with where we're going. But, it has everything to do where we came from."

"The Vatican?"

"Oh, things are happening there. But what's happened outside the Vatican walls is more of an immediate problem."

"What have you been holding out on me?"

"Nothing. I should have told you earlier, but there was so much else to talk about that I was going to tell you later. Apparently, we've left a trail of our own behind us."

"Someone's following you?"

"Someone's following Brother Gerald. And if whoever was clever enough to send this person to Rome had to have known he was there. Now it's only a matter of time, maybe as little as a day or two, before they figure out that we came to Paris."

"You're not making sense again," Gerald said. "Who's following us?"

"A Bulgarian assassin."

"You can't be serious. You're just trying to frighten us into following you to who knows where."

"I'm dead serious and dead is what one of us could be if he gets close enough."

"One of us?" Father William asked. "Which one?"

Nikolai hesitated. He turned to Raphael with a face that seemed to be asking for guidance.

"Speechless for once?" Raphael said. "It's who I think, isn't it?"

"Yes," Nikolai answered.

"Well, this is your show, not mine. Tell them."

Nikolai tried not to make eye contact as he shifted his face to Brother Gerald. His movement was so obvious that he did not have to speak.

"I don't believe you," Gerald said. "Why would a Bulgarian assassin be interested in me?"

"He wouldn't," Nikolai replied. "He's only a contractor."

"A contractor? You make it sound like he's going to remodel my living quarters."

"That's the terminology used in the trade. He's been hired by someone else."

"Now it's 'the trade'. You think that maybe your friend's magic halo didn't impress me, so you've decided to play the assassination card. And if he's only a 'contractor,' who hired him and why?"

"Some fanatical members of the Knights Templars."

"This is really good. Now the Knights Templar are after me. I suppose the Knights of Columbus or Opus Dei are right behind them."

*EARTHLY SPIRITS*

"Of course not. And it's not the Knights Templar organization that everyone and most of its members know about, with lodges or chapters or whatever they call them that meet for business lunches and do charity work. It's a very secret group of about a dozen zealots inside the Knights Templar who've been waiting for the Second Coming."

"And because the Second Coming is supposedly going to happen, the Knights Templar want me out of the way? Am I to be shot with an arrow, decapitated with a sword or will it be something more contemporary, like being gunned down in the street?"

"Nothing that obvious. Any publicity could cause repercussions later. It's almost certainly going to look like an accident or natural causes. You could be nudged onto the tracks of a train or into the street in front of a truck or bus. Or, you could be walking in a crowd or alone in a park and be pricked by a needle laced with a poison that simulates a fatal stroke or heart attack."

"You think you always have all the answers, but you always dance around the one question without an explanation."

"You must mean why you're the center of attention."

"Yes. Why?"

"Maybe you should tell him," Raphael said.

"Go ahead," Gerald said. "Give it your best shot."

"I can't," Nikolai said. "You'll find it out for yourself soon enough. Maybe even tomorrow."

"Now you won't even tell me why you won't tell me."

# CHAPTER 25

Cardinal Grosetti forced a smile that had just the right blend of benevolence and malevolence in it to make a saint think twice about the joys of martyrdom. He smiled without moving for a calculated number of seconds before opening the drawer in front of him. Then, he reached inside, withdrew a folded sheet of paper and nudged it across the top of the desk until it reached its intended destination under the nose of Father Shane.

"Open it," Grosetti said.

While Shane unfolded the paper and studied it, the cardinal tilted his chair back and rested his head against the wall just under the Purgatory panel of Hieronymus Bosch's medieval depiction of the Last Judgment. Grosetti folded his hands as in prayer. He was trying to strike the pose of an inquisitor awaiting a recantment.

"Do you know what that is?" the cardinal asked.

"It looks like a copy of a purchase order for airline tickets from Rome to Paris for Father William and Brother Gerald," the priest replied.

"Do you recognize the signature?"

"It looks like yours."

"It does indeed. But there's only one problem."

"What's that, your eminence?"

*EARTHLY SPIRITS*

"I didn't sign it."

Shane looked at the signature again, then at the cardinal.

"I don't understand," Shane said. "Is it a forgery?"

"If I didn't sign it, then it must be. A very good forgery. I didn't realize we had anyone so talented at the Vatican."

"Why would anyone want to do that?"

"I was hoping you might be able to tell me."

"Me? Your eminence, I swear I had nothing to do with this. I've never seen this paper before."

"I never thought you did."

It was almost a lie. Father Shane suspected that it was and he thought quickly in an effort to change the course of their conversation. He replied with words designed to open the door to other possibilities, and spoke them in a voice intended to reassure the cardinal of his innocence and loyalty.

"There are four possible explanations."

"That many?" The cardinal tilted his head in feigned surprise. I can't wait to hear you tell me about them. So, please go on and be candid."

"First, your eminence, and I don't mean any disrespect or to imply anything, one possibility is that you signed it."

Even before he was finished saying the unforgivable, Shane braced himself for a reaction from the cardinal. But there was no outburst, no remonstration, no surprise, no denial. Grosetti did not budge. Even his smile remained intact through a moment of silence between the two.

"I did ask you to be candid," the cardinal said. The words came out of his mouth almost in the form of a hiss. "Don't stop now."

"I only mention that as the remotest of possibilities," Shane said. He knew that he should have phrased his response differently. But, he was tired of being the pawn in the games that Grosetti had been playing with him since the cardinal assigned him to investigate the Virginia abbey deaths eight months ago. Yet, his self-preservation instincts took charge of the priest, forcing him to automatically add that he wanted to get all the explanations out on the table so that they could begin eliminating the weakest. Shane knew that it was not much of a recovery, but he did not feel like searching for anything that sounded more

197

convincing. When he realized that the cardinal was not going to speak, he continued.

"Another possibility is that someone on the staff of the Congregation for the Doctrine of the Faith is the culprit. Someone who either was able to forge your signature or used the misdirection practiced by magicians to get you to sign your name."

"I never sign anything without carefully reading it," Grosetti replied. "But that's an interesting theory."

"Then someone in your office must have forged it."

"You're looking at a copy. The original document is in the hands of an expert. If it's a forgery, I should know soon enough. As for those who work for me, I've already launched an investigation; But I don't expect it to be successful. I have confidence in the loyalty of everyone on the Congregation staff."

"Of course, your eminence."

It was the safe reply. Shane could have pressed the issue, but he suspected that Grosetti was acknowledging that everyone under the cardinal had been subjected to a background check not only before they joined the staff, but regularly since then. He wondered how many people Grosetti employed to do the dirty work of spying.

"If no one on your staff is responsible, then it must be someone else inside the Vatican," Shane said

"That's exactly my suspicion," Grosetti replied. "Do you have any of your own that you'd like to share?"

"Naturally, I'd have to give it some thought. The most logical possibility is the Vatican travel office. After all, it issues all travel tickets."

"I've considered that, but it's doubtful. Only three people work there and since they'd be the first to be suspected, I doubt any would be so brazen to take such a risk. Besides, all three have been there for a long time. There's nothing in their backgrounds to suggest that they're involved."

"If it didn't originate there, it had to have been someone clever enough to forge your signature on a purchase order and submit it to the travel office."

"I've covered that, too. The tickets were issued by the travel office.

*EARTHLY SPIRITS*

There was a record of them in that computer they use and office receipts for the tickets, but no one there recalls issuing them or anyone handing them the purchase order with my signature."

"If it's no one who works in the travel office, then it must be someone with access to it. Someone who forged your signature, gained entrance to the office after closing and printed the tickets."

"Then why leave the incriminating evidence behind?"

"Someone who wants you to know what they did."

"You mean someone is taunting us?"

"Yes."

"That would have to be someone very bold."

"Who do you know who might have private access to the travel office."

Grosetti lifted his folded arms above his head and thought for a moment.

"I can't imagine who," he said. "Do you have someone in mind?"

"Cardinal Verano?"

Grosetti wanted to reply that Verano lacked the skill for such an enterprise. He was dull, even servile. He never read anything but religious material. He never watched movies or listened to music. He did not understand art. He had no sense of humor. He did not appreciate cuisine. He did not drink anything other than sacramental wine during Mass. He did not smoke. He never questioned anything. He had so little to say that he had no close friends. He was the bureaucrat's bureaucrat. In anyone else, his social and cultural shortcomings would have been the perfect cover for a Vatican mole. But not Cardinal Verano. He enjoyed the drudgery of daily existence too much to be imaginative.

"No, it couldn't be Verano," Grosetti said. "He wouldn't even be the last person on my list."

"I agree, your eminence."

"Then, we're back to where we started."

"There is another possibility."

"I thought you might have something else. Does it have anything to do with our two missing priests other than the fact they're missing?"

"I always felt there might be something more to what happened at

Blessed Skyline Abbey in Virginia. But I only got there before the death of the last brother."

"Something you left out of your report."

"It was nothing that I could include in it, your eminence. It was only a feeling."

"You're not going to tell me we're dealing with the supernatural."

"If none of the other explanations fit, then perhaps we should consider what's unexplainable."

"What's this feeling you're talking about?"

"Well, I never was fully satisfied with the police report that blamed the abbey handyman, Nicholas. I know the killings stopped after he'd left the abbey and that they later found his body along some mountain trail. I know everything pointed to him but no one ever explained how he was able to kill the four monks."

"You mean the methods he used, like the punishments that were supposed to have been meted out for the commissions of four of the Seven Deadly Sins."

"Exactly. Not just the way they were murdered, but the timing of the deaths on the name days of the saints."

"All of those could be explained."

"But then all of a sudden Brother Gerald and Father William show up at the Vatican. And, now they're missing."

"From what I understand, neither of them had the opportunity to commit the murders."

"That's right."

"So, you're telling me that all of this still may be connected to them but you don't know what it is."

"As I said, it's only a feeling."

"In light of that, my son, I'm going to give you another special assignment. You're probably the best qualified person in the Vatican to handle it. It's not going to be easy and you'll be on a very short leash timewise. But I'm going to give you a lot of extra rope to work with."

Father Shane wondered about the rope. Was the cardinal hinting that he'd give him enough to hang his stalled career if he failed at whatever was in store for him? Unlike in the past, Shane did not respond

*EARTHLY SPIRITS*

with enthusiasm. All his face showed was that he was waiting to hear more.

Grosetti leaned forward and opened his desk drawer again. This time, his pudgy fingers came out of the drawer with an envelope. He shoved it across the desktop to the American priest and told him to open it.

"Those are airline tickets," the cardinal said. "You're going to Paris. I want you to find Father William and Brother Gerald and bring them back here."

"Me?" Shane asked. "How can I do that?"

"You're probably the only one who can. No one else in the Vatican seems to know them as well. You spent time with them in Virginia. You know what they do when they go out into the streets of Rome. We can only assume that whatever is they did there, they're doing the same thing in Paris."

"They mostly visit churches. At least Father William has. I think maybe Brother Gerald has been doing some of that lately, too."

"Yes, I know about Father William's wanderings. He talks to priests, nuns, laymen, asking questions about possible supernatural occurrences. They're supposedly doing some sort of research for a new history of the Devil."

"That's what they told me, your eminence."

"Do you believe it?"

"I've no reason not to. Is there something I should know?"

"Nothing that we both already know."

Father Shane knew that could not be true. What he did not understand was why Grosetti was lying if sending him to Paris to find Brother Gerald was so important.

"How much time do I have."

"Today and two, maybe three more."

"That's all?"

"It should be enough, if they're continuing along the same path in Paris as they were here."

"But, there are dozens of churches in Paris. Maybe hundreds."

"I've already arranged considerable support. My staff has been making telephone calls, sending telegrams and even that thing called e-mail to every priest on the books in Paris. They've been notified to expect you, and if Father William or Brother Gerald turn up, then they should try to detain them or find out where they might be headed next. You'll have a private car with a driver to meet you at the airport and take you wherever you go. You'll get a cell phone and a list of churches with addresses and telephone numbers so you can be in touch with anyone who's been in contact with them. Also, I'll want to hear from you regularly, at least every three hours. If you find out anything useful or need anything, then call me at any time, even if it's three o'clock in the morning."

"This sounds urgent."

"It is."

"What if they don't want to return immediately?"

"Then tell them that the Holy Father wants to meet them. I think that should override any resistance they might have."

Shane had not expected to hear that. The look that almost instantly splashed across his face betrayed the doubt in his mind.

"I'm serious," Grosetti continued. "And I'm trusting you not to tell that to anyone except Father William and Brother Gerald, and then only if it's necessary to convince them to cut whatever they're doing short and get back here immediately."

"But why should the pope want to meet them?" the young priest asked.

"Your guess is as good as mine. Perhaps it has something to do with their work here."

"Maybe." Shane could not hide the lack of conviction in his response. Why should the pope want two nondescript American priests to brief him about their research into the Devil? That was more along the cardinal's line. Grosetti had to be holding back something. Ever since his first contact with the cardinal eight months earlier, he had suspected that Grosetti never told anyone everything. That was one of the secrets of the cardinal's power. Yet, this time he sensed that Grosetti was genuinely up against the wall for whatever reason. So, Shane played his last card.

"What if I can't find them?" he asked.

Grosetti rubbed his hands together like a baker kneading a small ball of dough. He looked straight into Father Shane's eyes and said:

*EARTHLY SPIRITS*

"I've considered that possibility. But only as a possibility. I know you'll find them. How does that phrase go, the one about failure that your American politicians are so fond of using?"

"Failure is not an option."

"That's it. Now go. Your flight leaves in two hours. A car is waiting near the bus stop in St. Peter's Square."

"That doesn't leave me much time to pack."

"That's already been taken care of. You'll find your clothing and all the necessities in a carry-on bag on the back seat of the car."

As he left, Shane wondered how thorough his quarters had been searched by whoever Grosetti had sent to pack his travel needs. The thought of his privacy being invaded bothered Shane, but it was soothed by his knowledge that there was nothing incriminating to be found. Even more soothing, that was certain to perplex the cardinal. And probably irritate him, too.

# CHAPTER 26

Neither of them knew it, but Cardinal Grosetti and Brother Gerald were sharing common concerns. Both were losing a night's sleep. Both were looking at the same unfinished picture. Both had doubts about what they were seeing. Because they were viewing it from different vantage points, neither could see it all.

Grosetti was having the worst of it. Wracked with pain and pounds from years of physical abuse, his rotund body resisted the involuntary efforts of the sleepless to shift from one position to another in the vain search for the one comfortable spot on the bed. For the most part, he was restricted to lying on his back in the sagging center of a soft mattress. It was not the recommended position for someone whose search for sleep was tormented by relentless worries.

After about an hour, the cardinal finally surrendered. He rolled to the side of the bed like a wounded walrus trying to escape to land from the pursuit of a predator, sat up and, using a nightstand for balance, rose. His body stood for a few seconds on his heavy, shaking legs. When he was sure of his footing, he took slow lumbering steps to an easy chair in a far corner of the room and carefully lowered himself into it. He allowed a few more seconds to go by, then opened the door of a small cabinet alongside the chair, reached inside and retrieved a glass and a bottle of French

*EARTHLY SPIRITS*

cognac. He uncorked the bottle and poured himself a generous portion. He set the bottle on top of the cabinet within comfortable reach for refills, wriggled in the chair until he found a bearable position and took a sip of the cognac. He rolled the liquid around his mouth to get the maximum taste before letting it slide down his throat, then sat there studying the darkness. Now he could think logically.

He thought it best to set everything that he knew in sequence, so he let his mind drift slowly back to where it all had begun. He was now in his mental element.

It had started with Cardinal Sforza. Grosetti drove his suspicions the cardinal out of his mind. He did not want them clouding his thoughts. There would be time enough for that later, when the pieces he would arrange in their proper order would cast revealing shadows of their own.

It was Sforza who had first alerted him to what was happening at Blessed Skyline Abbey in Virginia after the death of the second monk, Brother Bruno. That was October sixth of the previous year, just a little more than two weeks after the death of the first monk, Brother Matthew. Cardinal Grosetti chuckled at a self-satisfied thought. Sforza may have known of both deaths earlier, but Grosetti had been the first to realize that they had occurred on the feast days of Saint Matthew and Saint Bruno. Even before the third death, of Brother Anthony, also on the feast day of his saintly namesake, Grosetti had set in motion the wheels for an Vatican investigation, just in case. He had ordered a probe of his own, a quiet look into the background of likely candidates to send to Virginia should the Vatican Secretariat order an investigation. Father Shane's credentials as an expert in demonic possession made him the ideal choice. Shane also was an American and young enough to be expendable should the Blessed Skyline affair become a public relations disaster for the Church.

Grosetti also congratulated himself on being ahead of Sforza on recognizing the possible link of the deaths to Seven Deadly Sins. When the fourth monk, Brother Leo, died during a fire, Grosetti was convinced that each of the brothers had been killed by methods similar to those that were supposed to have been the punishments proscribed for commission of specific sins. When the police reported the death of a prime suspect, a

205

drifter named Nicholas, that settled the matter. Father Shane's conclusions reflected those of the police. Grosetti had wished for a conclusion that pointed to the supernatural. It was not that he believed in demonic possession or anything supernatural. But that would have made another investigation mandatory. Only the Congregation for the Doctrine of the Faith had the ability to conduct such an investigation. That would have added to Grosetti's influence. It could be like the old days of the Inquisition. While his office probed, he would be second only to the pope.

Instead, two of the players in the drama had turned up at the Vatican, ostensibly to research and produce a new history of the Devil. Was Brother Gerald really doing that in the labyrinthian halls of the Vatican Secret Archives? Was Father William really searching for tales of the supernatural at all the churches that he had been visiting in Rome? If so, why them? There was nothing in their backgrounds to suggest they had special qualifications for their work. Was the signature on Sforza's letter summoning Brother Gerald to Rome really forged, as Grosetti's had been on the travel order for Paris? Or was Sforza playing some sort of game of his own, setting Grosetti up for a fall? But why? To eliminate him as a contender to succeed the aged pope, who was in poor health? No, that could not be it. Everyone at the Vatican knew that Sforza was the strong favorite to be the next pope. Besides, they also knew that Grosetti had no papal ambitions. Being pope was like being kept in the dark. Grosetti preferred living in the shadows on the edge of the world of light where information was a dream that no inside trader would want interrupted.

The cardinal took another sip of cognac to help him clear his mind of the doubts that had returned to plague his sleep. He poured himself a refill.

The key to what was happening had to be with Brother Gerald and Father William. They had gone off to Paris, apparently without a word to anyone. And the pope wanted to see them. What made that especially significant is that the Holy Father wanted to talk to the two Americans before issuing his ludicrous call to the religious leaders of the world to a council in Rome. Was he planning to tell them in advance why he wanted to meet? If he announced plans for a council, he risked international

*EARTHLY SPIRITS*

ridicule. Who would bother to come except maybe a television evangelist? The Second Coming. Really. If the pope went through with this plan, it could lead to a crisis that would make the Church the laughing stock of the world and could severely damage its stature and authority. Grosetti had no doubt—senility had set in on the Holy Father.

Rumors of the rebirth of the Knights Templar, plans to announce the Second Coming, signatures forged on documents, a couple of has-been American priests doing whatever they pleased at the Vatican, diocesan interviews of those monks who had been dispersed after Blessed Skyline Abbey had been closed. Somehow, they all had to be linked. And what about the deaths of the four monks? Could it all go back to them? That seemed so unlikely. Yet, that is exactly where it all started.

Yes, Brother Gerald and Father William were the keys. Why else would they be at the Vatican? And why was that woman, Teresa Lucci, trying to reach Brother Gerald by telephone? Father Shane had said that she once had been a nun and was married to a former monk. Only in America. Perhaps Gerald had uncovered something in the Secret Archives that he, and whoever his patron was, believed had great religious significance. If it had been passed on to the pope, it would explain why he had become a champion of the Second Coming. Otherwise, why bother to want to speak with them at a time when he was getting ready to announce the Second Coming to the world? That had to be connected. Who were these priests claiming to be? Advance men for Jesus?

An hour later, Grosetti fell asleep in the chair. When he awoke to the sound of his alarm clock just before dawn, he still was clutching the empty glass in his right hand. He shook the cobwebs out of his head, struggled to his feet and pulled aside the drapes. The sun was beginning to cast its light on the dome of Saint Peter's Basilica.

He wondered what surprises the new day had in store. As ordered, Father Shane had telephoned twice from Paris the day before, each time to report that he had not been able to pick up the trail of the two priests. Perhaps today, Grosetti would find a message or two waiting for him at his office from some French parish priest who might have seen Brother Gerald or Father William. For now, the only thing that Cardinal Grosetti feared was a certainty was that when he called,

Father Shane would not have found any of the pieces still missing from the puzzle.

If not today, then tomorrow the pope was going to ask about Gerald and William. Grosetti wondered if he could count on Cardinal Sforza to be discreet.

# CHAPTER 27

While Father Shane was taking a needed rest at a small hotel from his day on the streets of Paris and Cardinal Grosetti was wrestling with sleeplessness, Brother Gerald was standing on a balcony outside of the room he was sharing with Father William.

It was nearly midnight and the moon was in full bloom. Its light reached all the way down to the Aegean Sea, as though blessing its waters. Even the black sand of the beaches below glistened. In the distance, the sparkling lights of a town still very much awake competed with the moonlight for attention.

"It's a spectacular view," William said, stepping onto the balcony behind Gerald.

"For one of the few times in recent days, I've got to agree with you," Gerald replied. "Do all the islands have views like this?"

"I wouldn't know. When I was a young priest and visited Ephesus in Turkey, where Mary spent her last years, the tour included stops here and another place whose name escapes me. But if I had to take a guess, I'd say this view is unique."

"Why was this stop on the pilgrimage?"

"The priest who organized it was hooked on religious icons and the prophet Elijah. There's a Fifteenth Century icon of Elijah in the monastery church on the Profitis of Elijah, that mountain over on the left. The one with the ugly communications tower. If we get the chance, we should go there."

"I'm not particularly fascinated by icons."

"Not for the icons. The monastery has a unique collection of the bones of the brothers who died there. Wouldn't you like to take a peek at what we're going to look like a couple of hundred years from now?"

"I'm more concerned with what I'm going to look like when all of this is finally over. I feel like I've aged twenty years in the past week."

"Are you nervous about tomorrow?"

"Of course. But it would help a lot if I could figure out what this is all about."

"You still don't believe Nikolai."

"It's hard not to. Let's just say I don't trust him."

"Whatever, there's no doubt he's been holding back on something. Even he admits to that."

"That's exactly what I mean. Assuming everything he's said is true, and I'm not acknowledging that, the question he won't answer is why I have to be involved. He could have picked someone else with prestige, like a bishop or cardinal."

"The office doesn't always make the man. Sometimes the man makes the office."

"Oh, really. Then maybe you can tell me what special qualifications I have that makes me so important."

"I can't think of a single one. Except honesty."

"So I'm the last honest man? You're becoming even more cynical than what you accuse me of being."

"You're not going to sleep, are you?"

"I'm hoping that the view from this balcony will clear my mind enough to help me put things in some sort of perspective."

"It may be relaxing, but it might be even better if we tried to work this out together. Over a glass of wine."

"It's always over a glass of wine. You're becoming an alcoholic. If you keep it up, you're going to shave a few years off your life."

"At my age that really doesn't matter that much. The years I might lose

*EARTHLY SPIRITS*

would be the crappy ones, anyway. Besides, a glass or two might help you to sleep."

Father William left Brother Gerald to resume enjoying his view alone, then returned with two glasses and the bottle of Cretan wine that Nikolai had purchased for them earlier in the evening. He poured some of the red liquid into each, gave Gerald a glass, set the bottle on top of the waist-high balcony wall and settled into one of the two chairs that were in each corner.

"So, Father, where do we begin?" Gerald said.

"We begin by dropping the formality of 'father'," the old priest replied. "It's about time you started calling me Will. That's what friends and family called me most of my life, even after I became a priest. We've been friends for a long time and I'm not your superior anymore. You're my boss now."

"I'll drink to that, Will."

"This has to have some connection to what happened back in Virginia."

"Not that again."

"If you want to make some sense out of this, we've got to look at who started painting the picture where. It obviously began with Nicholas, Nikolai or whatever name he's going under. And, you."

William raised a hand, signaling for Gerald to hold onto the protest he was about to make. Then, the old priest continued.

"Hear me out. Like it or not, the two of you are connected. As Nicholas, he came to you in your monk's cell and essentially confessed to killing the four brothers. Whether he intended to kill them or not is immaterial. Forget about the police report. The law's arm isn't long enough to reach into the supernatural, so the police really couldn't do anything but close the books on the case with the death of Nicholas.

"Next you get an invitation to take a plush job at the Vatican. Face the fact that Nicholas, Nikolai, Lucifer, Satan or whatever he's calling himself at the time, had something to do with it. Then, he shows up in Rome specifically to get you to join some sort of crusade to stop what he says is the Second Coming. And here we are flying from one place to another in Europe as though we had free passes to go anywhere we want."

211

"You mean anywhere Nikolai tells us to go," Gerald said.

Father William ignored the interruption and said:

"Now he tells us you've been targeted by an assassin who's been hired by some cabal in the Knights Templar. And tomorrow we could be at the end of this odyssey."

"Oh, that was really something I wanted to hear. Not that I believe it. He could have made it up just to get us to leave Paris. Or to keep us from going back to Rome. And what about the pope?"

"You mean what Nikolai told us about the pope wanting to see us before he announces the Second Coming of Jesus?"

"Yes. If the Holy Father really wants to see us, and I don't know why he would, shouldn't we be on our way back to the Vatican."

"Under any other circumstances, yes. But if he's right about tomorrow, then even the pope will have to wait."

"Tomorrow. Oh, yes, what should we expect then? Another Raphael with a halo over his head? More stories about a war between the angels in Heaven, wherever that's supposed to be? I wonder how the nightly news is going to cover it?"

"It all does sound fantastic. But I believe it."

"Then why are we so important?"

"You actually. I'm just along for the ride."

"Then why me?"

"That's precisely why I believe it. Everything that's happened to you since the last months in Virginia have happened for a reason."

"You're not going to tell me it's God's plan, one of those mysteries the Church has preached for so long that we'll learn only after death."

"Definitely not God's plan. And from all that you've experienced, it's certainly no mystery, either."

"Then what?"

"Simple logic."

Gerald could not hide the cynicism in his laugh.

"Go ahead, laugh all you want," Father William said. "But consider this. You can't really believe that Nikolai is just an ordinary person or some sort of trickster. That he and Raphael are a couple of guys who are staging all of this as an elaborate hoax. What makes you think you're so

*EARTHLY SPIRITS*

important that so much time, energy and money—not to mention murder—has been concocted just to make you the fall guy of a practical joke?"

"They could be lunatics," Gerald replied. "On the run from men in white coats."

"You know that isn't true."

"I know. But, then we're back to where we started. If I'm not that important to be the victim of a lavish practical joke, then I shouldn't be so important to be needed tomorrow. And if I was so important, why did he go alone today?"

"He said he had to be sure we'd come to the right place and, if so, that we couldn't just walk in unexpected."

"How could we not be expected?"

"We'll find that out tomorrow, won't we?"

"If I make it to tomorrow."

"Why, are you nervous?"

"Who wouldn't be. But that's not what I meant."

"Are you expecting to die before then?"

The monk swallowed the wine that was left in his glass and held it out toward Father William for a refill.

"No," Brother Gerald said. "I'm expecting to get drunk."

# CHAPTER 28

"This must be some kind of a gag," Brother Gerald said.

"I don't think so," Father William replied.

"It's not," Nikolai added.

Four place settings

Sets of cups, saucers, plates, juice glasses, knives, forks, spoons and napkins had been carefully arranged in front of four seats at a table in a corner of the café, near a large picture window that looked out onto the Aegean Sea with a sailboat in the distance. A large pot of coffee sat in the middle. Next to it was a platter of freshly baked bread, croissants and pastries, accompanied by a tray of butter, cheese, preserves, jam and a small pitcher of milk. An old man in a gray suit sat nearest to the window. It was a few minutes before nine o'clock in the morning, time when most people in Santorini were having breakfast. But the only people in the café were Gerald, William, Nikolai and an old man in a gray suit, who had the table seat closest to the window.

As soon as he saw the three enter the room, Stefan Petrandriou rose from His seat. The old man pretended not to have heard what they had said. He extended his right hand toward Brother Gerald. The monk hesitated for a few seconds, looked at William and Nikolai, and said:

"Oh, what the Hell."

*EARTHLY SPIRITS*

Then, he shook Stefan Petrandriou's hand. It felt remarkably normal. Next in line, Father William also accepted a handshake. Nikolai simply sat down in a chair opposite of the old man. Petrandriou motioned for the two priests to sit at the chairs on either side of them and sat down again.

"Well, how did that feel?" Nikolai asked the two priests. Before either of them could respond, he added:

"It's not every day that you can reach out and actually touch the hand of God."

"Nikolai has always been like that," Petrandriou said. "I suppose he's subjected you to what seemed like endless daily doses of puns and bad jokes during all the time that he's told me you've spent together."

Father William nodded in assent. Brother Gerald just sat there. Neither spoke. After all, they were meeting God face-to-face for the first time. What could they say? Actually, Gerald had a lot that he wanted to say to the old man, but an overwhelming sense of better judgment suggested caution. Instead, he turned to Nikolai.

"There should be more people here," he said. "Why are we the only ones? Is this another one of those places like that restaurant in Rome, the one owned by the pervert? Or is another one of your tricks to make me believe?"

"Oh, it's my doing, all right," Nikolai said. "I arranged it so we could talk in private. And it's not a trick."

"Then, how?"

"Simple. I booked the entire place."

"You paid off the owner?"

"Of course. How else could I guarantee privacy?"

Stefan Petrandriou smiled. "Nikolai has always been an idea man," he said. "Very resourceful."

Father William laughed. Even Brother Gerald could not repress a smile.

"You're a doubter, my son," Petrandriou said. "That's a good quality. Otherwise you'd end up being opinionated. On the other hand, Father William here is more of a believer. Oh, he doesn't just take leaps of faith without at least some facts. And he's not as opinionated as he likes to pretend. Anyway, I'm not here to try to convince you that I'm the Almighty."

"Then why are you here?" Gerald replied. He was careful to phrase the question as simply as possible, with no hint of the challenge that had been gnawing at him ever since he had awakened.

"Curiosity. This meeting wasn't my idea. It was Nikolai's."

"Pardon me…" Father William said, interrupting the budding conversation between the two.

"Just call me Stefan," the old man replied. "Not Lord, not God, not Allah, not Jehovah, not any of the other, mostly unpronounceable, names I've been given by your different cultures over the centuries. The one I liked best was what the ancient Greeks called me—Zeus. I'd tell you my real name, but I'm pretty sure you'd have trouble saying it. For now just call me Stefan. That's who I intended to be for the rest of whatever life is left in this body."

"The rest of your life?"

"Obviously Nikolai didn't tell you everything. He only learned the truth last night. He thought that maybe I'd had an accident or been attacked like he was last year and had lost my memory or taken an extended vacation. It's not that at all. I came here to stay. To enjoy my newly found declining years as a human before dying a natural death. Before the end of this year, my soul will have been permanently fused into this body. Once it is, it won't be possible to go back."

"But, if you're God, how can you die?"

"Nothing lasts forever. I could have stayed around for about another thousand years, but I've been around for so many millions already, another ten centuries or so really shouldn't seem like much. Besides, I've always wondered what it was like to be human. It's not bad at all, especially when you don't have to experience all the problems of youth."

"But, why?"

"I would've thought someone your age would've figured that out. But, then, even Nikolai didn't at first and all you had to go on was what he told you. I was tired of being God, so I decided to retire. To put it in earthly terms, I was burned out."

"Burned out," Gerald said. A trace of sarcasm had escaped into his voice. "Now that's a good one."

"You can believe it or not," Petrandriou replied. "If I hadn't made

*EARTHLY SPIRITS*

those stupid mistakes, we wouldn't be here and in a couple of months it would all be over."

"Mistakes? I thought God made miracles."

"I don't do miracles. Any miracles you may have seen or heard about where either coincidence, natural occurrence or interference by some angel who should've known better. You have no idea how many of them I've had to discipline."

"Then you don't listen to prayer?"

"Sorry to disappoint you, my son. Prayer is a part of theology, which has nothing to do with Heaven. Besides, I've never had the time, not with millions of prayers directed at me every day, just from your world alone."

"You're telling me there are people on other worlds?"

"Do the mathematics. In your galaxy alone, there are eight-billion stars. If only one in one-hundred of those had planets that would leave eighty-million solar systems with planets. Then, if only one in one-hundred of those systems had planets that could support life, that would give you eight-hundred-thousand planets. Next, if only one in one-hundred of those had planets with conditions that could support intelligent life, you could have such beings on eight-thousand worlds. And, that's just in this galaxy alone. There are millions of other galaxies."

"There are people living on eight-thousand planets?"

"I didn't say that. Just mix a little imagination with a little logic. I hope you're not so arrogant to believe that you're the only intelligent beings in the universe. And, I didn't say they were people as you know them. Some of them might be offended by the word. But I'm getting off the track. As for my mistakes, all you have to do is take a look at your Earth to see them."

"Souls for Adam and Eve were His first," Nikolai said.

"It was the temptation of that cigar that started it," Petrandriou said, ignoring the interruption. "Then going to that restaurant where the owner was a chain smoker. I told him he should stop smoking, without thinking that my suggestion was enough to actually make him quit. Naturally, within two days, he was telling everyone in Santorini about it. I didn't realize it until after one of Nikolai's men, a devil, learned about it and passed the word on to him. His spies are all over the place. I was planning to leave here today, but he got to me last night and convinced me to stay because of you."

"So, again it's all about me," Gerald said. He folded his arms across his chest in a posture of defiance. "Well, I'm not moving, saying another word or listening until You or Nikolai tell me why I'm supposed to be so important that I've been dragged halfway around Europe to meet someone whose supposed to be the Lord Almighty and help stop the Second Coming. How I can't imagine. And it better be good because I haven't been convinced about anything, but no one is leaving here until either I make up my mind one way or the other."

"I think our Brother Gerald expected You to be something more," Nikolai said, looking at Petrandriou.

"Something more?" the old man replied.

"Maybe a long white robe, white beard and stern eyes."

"I certainly didn't expect God to be so matter-of-fact," Gerald said.

"You mean like me when you found out who I was back in Virginia?" Nikolai asked.

"No one is like you. At least this man, or whoever or whatever He may be, is polite."

"Of course he's polite. How else do you think He became God?

"That's enough, both of you," Petrandriou said. "Either we're all going to learn the truth now or we're all wasting our time. My time, especially. If I stay here too much longer, Raphael, Michael and all of their followers will find me and start twisting my arm to go back. Then, I just might do that to get some peace. Nikolai knows there's only one thing that can change my mind."

"I've already explained that all to You."

"Yes, but you've become such an expert in making mistakes, that the only way I can be certain is to find out for myself."

Stefan Petrandriou turned to Brother Gerald and looked at the monk with eyes that were filled with kindness and trust.

Gerald glanced at his wristwatch and reached for the coffee pot. "It's fourteen minutes after nine," he said. "It's about time you got to the point."

"This won't hurt a bit," Petrandriou said. "And it won't leave you with

*EARTHLY SPIRITS*

any unpleasant after-effects like that business in the ruins of the Rome Forum with Nikolai when he was the Cat Lady."

Before Gerald could protest, he no longer was sitting at the table. He found himself in Paris, then in Rome, then in Virginia during the last months of Blessed Skyline Abbey. He was not there as an onlooker, but as a participant. The sights and the sounds and the smells. The joys and the disappointments and the monotony. Especially the monotony. Though he had a strong feeling of deja vous, he was unaware that he was living life again in what seemed like real time. Curiously, it did not even feel unnatural to him that he was living it in reverse.

The years passed by, eventually reaching back into his twenties when he was a seminary student. At first he did not know why he was at a seminary, though he knew he had to be there, otherwise he could not have become a priest. He did not yet know that in the life he had lived before this one, he had been able to block the memory from his mind. Then, one day, he remembered. It was his father. The father into whom the child Gerald had poured so much faith. Again, he experienced the youthful pangs of the days ahead when the man would betray and abandon his mother. The act would steal his faith from him one more time and send him seeking a new faith in a seminary. Oddly, now the event had lost its importance. He still was experiencing every detail of everything he had lived before, but now he was going back even further, to a happier childhood. All of a sudden he became afraid and tried to slow the process as an aging person might try to hold off the approach of death. He knew that this life had no death for him to fear. Its only fear had become birth.

At birth, he drifted back to an even earlier time. Decades passed, followed by generations, then centuries. He was not moving fast, but as though he was living and reliving different identities at the speed of normal everyday life. It allowed him to absorb details. Some were familiarly pleasant. Some others that he recognized were unnerving. Finally, after what had seemed an eternity, the trip braked to a sudden stop and paused for a moment as though to allow him to ponder the end that also was the beginning. There, in a small village whose stone houses and narrow alleys were surrounded mostly by sand, he found a truth that he could not deny. But his talent for doubt had survived the backward voyage of life and now it poked tauntingly at him, tearing him between the fear of destiny and the comfort of denial. Before he could surrender to it, he no longer was where he had gone, but back at the breakfast table with the three others.

# CHAPTER 29

Father William's voice was the first that Brother Gerald heard.

"Well, are you going to just sit there holding that pot and staring into space?" the priest asked. "Pour yourself some coffee and pass the pot around."

Brother Gerald looked at Father William, blinked his eyes and took a quick look at where he was. The cups, saucers, plates, juice glasses, knives, forks, spoons and napkins had not been disturbed. Neither had the platter of freshly baked bread, croissants, and pastries. The butter, cheese, preserves, jams and pitcher of milk still sat neatly arranged on the tray. The panorama of the Aegean Sea looked the same—the sailboat had barely moved. Stefan Petrandriou sat near the window where he had been before. Nikolai, wearing his annoying smile looked as though he had not budged. Gerald looked to his left and right. There was no one else in the café.

"I trust you found your experience informative," Petrandriou said.

Gerald's hands were shaking as he filled his cup with coffee and passed the pot to Father William.

"It was an incredible dream," Gerald said. "The most realistic I could imagine having. I must have been out for hours."

"Out for hours?" Father William said, raising his eyebrows. "What are you talking about? You weren't even out for minutes. All you did was reach for the coffee pot and sort of froze there like a Greek stone sculpture for two or three seconds."

Gerald looked at his wristwatch. It read a few seconds before a quarter past nine. He then glanced at the clock on the wall to his right. The time it displayed seemed almost mocking to him: a quarter past nine.

"It isn't possible," Gerald said. His voice trembled slightly and he looked as bewildered as someone who had just landed in a foreign country and could not understand the language.

"Oh, yes it is," Nikolai replied.

"Another dream, just like in Virginia. Except this time it seemed even more real."

"That was no dream and you know it."

"Neither was this one a dream, my son," Petrandriou said. "I was there with you the whole time."

"I don't remember you being there," Gerald replied. His remark seemed more like a question asked by someone who had lost his confidence.

"I was. No matter what theology teaches, I can't know everything and be everywhere all at the same time. But I had to be with you to be sure."

"Don't say I didn't tell you so," Nikolai said. His face betrayed self-satisfaction.

Stefan Petrandriou turned to Nikolai, gave him a weary look and said:

"You have always been a pain in the holy buttocks. So, for just this once, will you shut up?"

Until now, none of the four had sampled any of the breakfast that had been laid out, not even the coffee. Father William broke the fast by taking a sip from the cup he had filled, set it back on the table and said:

"Pardoning your Lord..."

"It's Stefan," Petrandriou said.

"All right, Stefan. I'm as much as a simpleton as Brother Gerald seems to be, so could you please tell us what's happening?"

"You weren't supposed to be here, Father. But Nikolai made it quite clear to me that Brother Gerald would not come without you. That whatever he learned would have to be shared with you. That's

*EARTHLY SPIRITS*

remarkable loyalty. If only the people of Sodom and Gomorrah had been like that. It's not that I've demanded worship. I only wanted a few simple laws obeyed so that people could create a civilization where they at least would learn to someday respect each other. I didn't expect it to be perfect, just workable. Even Heaven has its shares of problems. Like it's having now."

"You mean that what Nikolai has been telling us about the Second Coming and a war between the angels is true?"

"Sadly, yes. Let me see if I can explain it in terms you'll understand. As the Almighty, I could live for another thousand years or so. Then, when I pass on, my son would succeed me."

"Jesus?"

"Yes. And please don't ask any more questions until I'm finished. After all, I'd think that God should deserve a little courtesy, especially from a priest."

Stefan smiled. So did Father William. Stefan continued:

"If you recall, one of the things the Bible got right is that when my son ascended into Heaven, he would sit at the right hand of God. Actually, it was his soul that ascended. Your ancient and medieval kings understood the meaning of the right hand seat well enough to reserve it for the children who would succeed them. Well, souls are tricky things. They're every bit as alive as you feel you are. Once a soul experiences corporeal life, it never completely loses the desire to try it again. It's sort of like a person who quits smoking after years of doing it. He may have hung his tobacco out to try, but the desire to light up is still inside him. For the most part, it remains, but every so often demands attention. Let me tell you, I've had quite a few urges for a real body over the last few millions of years. Unlike our friend Nikolai, I've been able to resist the temptation. Well, in fairness to him, finding an occasional body to fill has been an occupational necessity. As I told you earlier, I'm worn out. Being God isn't as simple as the words 'Thy will be done' from that prayer of yours. I can't just will things and consider them done. Heaven is the biggest bureaucracy in the universe and it makes as many demands on me as those of mine that it ignores."

"I can vouch for that," Nikolai said, turning to Gerald and William.

"The paperwork alone that I have to submit would sink any of your governments."

Stefan gave Nikolai a disapproving look, which he and the two priests understood to mean the old man wanted no more interruptions or flippant remarks. The Almighty then continued.

"Two months ago, I decided to make a run for it by telling my confidants that I was taking a vacation. I know, it was a lie, but not a malicious falsehood designed to harm anyone. Because I'd never been gone for more than a couple of weeks, I knew that any absence longer than that would raise suspicions. So, I had to act fast. I was lucky to find the perfect body in New York City, a Greek American widower with only one living relative, who was about to die alone in a hospital bed.

"Once I assumed his identity, he experienced a remarkable recovery. I sold his restaurant and closed out his affairs. Had I stayed put in New York, Nikolai might not have found me. But, the city didn't appeal to me. Neither did the suburbs. I wanted to retire where the pace was more relaxed but not boring. I thought being Stefan Petrandriou would allow me to keep a low profile. Eventually, my son would have taken my place and I could have lived out the rest of my new life in blissful peace. Essentially, that's how it was supposed to work out. Then I made that mistake with the cigar. Once more, it proved that battles aren't necessarily won by who has the most brilliant plan, but by who makes fewer mistakes. And so, here we are."

"Speaking of battles, aren't you ignoring something?" Nikolai asked.

"Heaven has had its share of battles and survived them all. I even survived the revolt you led against me."

"It never came to that."

"That's because I sent you here before you could act. It would have failed, you know. You didn't have the support you needed. You never could have beaten Michael, Gabriel and Raphael. I know you thought Gabriel was straddling the fence, but in the end he was loyal."

"Not anymore."

Stefan Petrandriou pretended to ignore Nikolai's last remark. Instead, he looked at both priests and spoke directly to them.

"It seems that Gabriel is urging Michael and Raphael to declare my

*EARTHLY SPIRITS*

throne vacant and form a triumvirate that would rule until the six-month abdication law is declared to be activated."

"What does that mean?" Father William asked.

"Simply put, if whenever a ruler of Heaven is absent for six months, abdication is declared and the next in line automatically assumes the throne."

"Jesus?"

"Yes. He's my only son."

"Then he would return to Earth?"

"What you call the Second Coming probably would follow two or three months after he ascended the throne. That doesn't sound like it's enough time to prepare, but they've been working on the plan for a few hundred years. Still, in order for it to work without upsetting the power structure in Heaven, Michael, Gabriel and Raphael would have to be on the same team."

"Don't forget me," Nikolai said.

"Nikolai, too. But he tells me the others are divided. Gabriel, who can be a hothead at times, wants it to happen now. Michael wants to wait until it's supposed to happen. If it comes to a test of force, even though Michael is the best commander, Gabriel probably could balance that with numbers. He'd have more followers. Raphael is the key. He could side with either or stay neutral."

"A war in Heaven?" William said.

"The worst kind you could imagine. And even if it somehow could be avoided, and the Second Coming occurs centuries before its time, the repercussions of its arrival on Earth could stretch all the way to Heaven. What religion would accept it? Not Judaism, not Islam, not Hinduism. Not even Catholicism. Oh, some branches of Christianity would, at first. Especially the evangelicals. But they'd quickly be very disenchanted once they learned that the Second Coming wasn't going to be a Christian event. My son wasn't a Christian and like me, doesn't subscribe to any religion organized by man. But the Second Coming would bring a new brand of organized religion to the world. It would be very organized, complete with justice. Only, for most people, it would seem like the injustice of an invasion and occupation. Millions of them would oppose and try to fight it. And they could never win a war against Heaven. Jesus wouldn't want that but even he would have trouble controlling the forces of Gabriel and also maybe those of the other two once they were unleashed. Angels fighting people, angels fighting each other, even people fighting people. It would be the Armageddon."

"If that's the case, then the Second Coming is doomed no matter when it happens."

"No. Humanity just isn't ready for it. Just look at your United Nations. How often does it agree to do the right thing? Given another thousand years, people should develop more tolerant religious views. Not to accept any one religion, but to treat each other the way they wished to be treated. At least, that's how it's expected to work. When that day arrives, the Second Coming will be the main event of a new era, which humans already will have created for themselves. Of course, love always could be imposed on everyone as a last resort, but then it probably would develop into an incurable disease."

"Then, you've got to go back."

"I know. That's what I'm going to do."

"Just like that? Why? What's this been all about?"

"Our young friend here knows. Don't you, Gerald?"

"No, I won't accept it," he said, breaking his silence. He no longer seemed to be struggling with the metaphorical demons inside him. He had become agitated.

"It can't be true," he continued. "It's not fair. Why can't it be someone else?"

Stefan Petrandriou placed his right hand gently on Gerald's arm. Immediately, the monk was calm. He looked questioningly at the old man.

"It's not like I'm asking you to be crucified," Stefan said. "And, just to set the record straight, I never asked that of Jesus. I begged him not to go through with it. But I couldn't break my own law of non-interference. Besides, he was always impulsive, so he sought martyrdom on his own far before completing his work here. He believed his death would change the world. He was right about that, but it didn't turn out exactly the way he wanted. While he's a little impatient, he's a good son and loyal. He will

*EARTHLY SPIRITS*

gracefully accept that his time hasn't come. As for you, all I'm asking is that you return to Rome and live out your life. Once the fanatics of the Knights Templar realize that the Second Coming isn't going to happen now, your life will no longer be in danger."

"What are you two talking about?" Father William asked.

"Go ahead," Stefan Petrandriou said, nodding at Nikolai. "You've been itching to tell him, so do it."

"It's really elementary, my dear father," Nikolai said. "Brother Gerald is the last descendant in the family line of Mary and Joseph."

# CHAPTER 30

God went to Athens and transferred Stefan Petrandriou's money into an account at a bank there. Then, he paid a surprise visit on Petrandriou's distant cousin before departing from the old man's body in an Athens hotel. A slip of paper found in Petrandriou's luggage asked that the body be buried on the island of Naxos alongside those of his family members. Petrandriou's funds were left to the cousin.

Then, God returned to Heaven.

His long absence had consequences and things no longer could be the same. There was a shake-up in Heaven. Michael and Raphael had done what they could to keep all but a handful of their most trusted followers from knowing the details of the episode. That kept most of the rest of them in line. Gabriel was not as judicious. He all but openly sought support for the Second Coming. While he would remain the angel of prayer. But he also was given new responsibilities, this time on Earth rather than in Heaven. Ecstatic at first over his new assignment, Gabriel came to learn that God, indeed, can work in mysterious ways.

By comparison, the changes on Earth seemed innocent. Only a few people were directly affected. But depending on how these few reacted, the new paths that had been opened to them could go a long way to impacting the lives of many more, even for generations not yet born. The

*EARTHLY SPIRITS*

Almighty knew this more than any other being. By seeking to abdicate, He had unwittingly interfered in the natural course of events. There could be no retirement for God.

Because no person in Rome, except for Brother Gerald and Father William, knew what had happened and what would not, the Vatican was back to business as usual in a few weeks. Rumors persisted for a little longer, then faded into forgotten Vatican lore.

For the pope, the timing had been fortuitous. He had gotten the cancellation notice too late to avoid telling Cardinal Grosetti what he already had told Cardinal Sforza about his plan to call a world religious council. He dropped the plan a few days later and left Rome to spend a week at the papal retreat in Castel Gondolfo. Officially, the pope was there to rest. When he returned to the Vatican, he informed Grosetti and Sforza that he had misinterpreted a vision caused by the stresses of his job as the Holy Father of the Church. It was a weak excuse and Sforza bought it. As always, Grosetti the right to be suspicious.

Cardinal Sforza continued to do what they had done for so long. For a while, he relentlessly pursued his hunt for the identity of whoever had forged his and Cardinal Grosetti's names to the letter that had summoned Brother Gerald to the Vatican and the travel order that had sent them to Paris. An unexpected event that would startle much of the Vatican was taken by Sforza as a signal to abandon the search and focus on his work.

Cardinal Grosetti was convinced more than ever that some sort of cabal not only was operating inside the Vatican, but had expanded its intrigues to include him as a target. For one thing, he had lost the services of Father Monahan, who had left the priesthood to pursue a career as an information specialist with the United States government. For another, he no longer could rely on Father Shane, who had replaced Brother Gerald as head of the project of researching and writing a history of the Devil. Both priests fit into their new jobs like hands into custom-tailored gloves. Like Sforza, Grosetti had read the warning sign that a surprise Vatican event had raised. He ignored the consequences of persisting and decided to stealthily follow the trail. Cardinal Grosetti could not help himself.

Two weeks after the pope returned to Rome, Cardinal Verano was given the position that he was destined to fill. The Holy Father appointed him ambassador to a small African country where years of missionary activities had failed to produce the expected number of converts to the Church. He would live out the rest of his life there.

North America was not immune to the aftermath of God's adventure.

Father John was transferred from his position in Nova Scotia to New Mexico, where he would minister to the faithful as pastor of the only Catholic church in a small town surrounded by desert. He was replaced by a new priest at Saint Andrew's Church, where the secret room in the cellar was walled off, but not before being stripped of its contents, which were sent to the Vatican.

Ewan Sinclair resigned his membership in the Knights Templar. He surrendered his ring to Father John on the priest's last day in Nova Scotia. Once he was out of the order, Sinclair took a leave of absence from the legal profession, closed his office and sold his house. A few months later, he joined a law firm in Toronto.

Both Rick and Robin Erlandson, and Teresa and Chris Lucci briefly wondered whether they would have to move again. They soon realized it would be pointless because whatever unpleasantness had intruded on their lives in the past seemed to have a knack for finding them wherever they might go. When they heard the unexpected news from the Vatican, the four of them agreed to go to Rome together for a very special reunion.

Meanwhile, back in Rome, a couple of things still needed attention. Nikolai had been ordered to take care of them.

Penko Lazar was the most immediate problem. The Bulgarian assassin had been plotting for weeks to find a way to get to Brother Gerald. Few jobs had taken so long. To help pass the time, Lazar began visiting an internet café, browsing for property he dreamed about moving to when he retired. He already had more than enough money in his secret Swiss bank account to buy something that might appeal to him for occupancy when he retired. One day, he found his account was two-hundred and fifty-thousand dollars short. Someone had hacked into it and withdrawn the amount of the non-refundable deposit for his work in Rome. He called the bank, but no one there could help. He called the general, who told him that his fee also had vanished. The general called his

*EARTHLY SPIRITS*

contact, who called another. All of them denied knowing anything about the money. But the last contact down the line said he had been told the job had been cancelled. When he was told it was off, Penko Lazar left Rome for Switzerland to transfer his funds into another secret account at a different Swiss bank. Besides the deposit, he was out nearly ten-thousand dollars in expenses. He would make it up with the next job. First, he would try to find who took his money.

Nikolai's other problem was greater. Just before leaving for Earth, Gabriel was told that Lucifer would have the final word whenever the two of them disagreed. The Almighty knew that the two would be at each other's throats so often that they would have little time to interfere in worldly problems. That might give people just enough breathing space to work things out without the questionable help they had been unknowingly receiving for centuries. The Devil was not going to be undone that easily. To keep Gabriel out of his hair for at least a few decades, he assigned him to the one job that he could not ignore now. Because the Almighty wanted someone to watch over Gerald, Lucifer assigned Gabriel to be the monk's guardian.

Brother Gerald and Father William soon had new jobs at the Vatican. Instead of producing a new history of the Devil, Gerald was to take a fresh look at God. The emphasis of this new work was to be The Almighty's relationship to Jesus and the relationship of both of them to all people regardless of their religions. Gerald was given an office of his own and a small staff of a half-dozen priests and laymen to help him. Because the monk knew that he was no administrator, he appointed Father William as his chief of staff.

"Being a descendant of The Almighty really has its privileges," Father William said to Gerald in the monk's Vatican apartment the day before the big event. "Or are you still a doubter?"

"If I couldn't doubt, I wouldn't be me," Gerald replied. "But what's happened in the past year doesn't leave me with much room for doubt."

"Then you still have some doubt."

"Only with minor details. Even I have to accept my past. Imagine, my own father was someone else than the man I grew up believing was my father. My mother never said a word about it."

231

"She was just being a mother. If she had said anything about her one-night liaison with someone other than the man she married, it could have broken up your family. She didn't want to risk that for the sake of you and your siblings."

"I understand that. But how can I ever understand who I really am? My real father wasn't the man my mother married. I was conceived during a one-night affair she had with a defrocked Canadian priest, who also was a member of the Knights Templar. His father, who also would be my grandfather, was a fisherman. Then the further back I can recall, the more blurred everything becomes. It's almost like looking at an endless string of portraits on a museum wall. Bakers, carpenters, seamen, traders, knights, even thieves. And at the end of it all, which also was the beginning, Joseph."

"Which one?"

"Both of them, of course. Mary's husband and another of their sons, one of the brothers of Jesus."

"Do you think you'll ever figure out just where you are in the family line? A twenty-ninth cousin or a thirty-eighth nephew?"

"With so many different people, so many marriages and even a few births out-of-wedlock, I doubt even an expert in genealogy could trace the relationship accurately enough to find me the right family tree limb. Besides, there's also that other mystery. Whether God or Joseph was the real father of Jesus. He wouldn't tell us."

"I wanted to know that and so much more, too. Like the creation of the universe, life on other worlds, the location of Heaven. But we were told, and rightly so, that it all has to remain a mystery to us because too much of that kind of knowledge wasn't meant to be, unless science could eventually figure it all out on its own. But your creation was of a different life. Your conception was the first link in a different chain. If Joseph was the father, than you possibly could be a full twenty-seventh of thirty-first cousin. If he wasn't, then Mary is the direct link and you could be half thirtieth cousin. Or something like that."

"It's all too confusing for me."

"Then just take pleasure in being who you are and comfort in the knowledge that The Almighty doesn't have the heart of stone that you

*EARTHLY SPIRITS*

once believed He had. Now we know that He didn't want His son crucified and that He didn't want his only remaining earthly ancestor suffering death by an unnatural cause."

"I still find it hard to believe that I was a threat to the Second Coming."

"In a perfect world you wouldn't be. But in a world of earthly and heavenly fanatics, your ancestral ties would make you a surplus prince. And you've read enough history to know what used to happen to surplus princes. Remember what we were told about that Bulgarian assassin? You would have been eliminated before Jesus arrived in time to prevent it. In the end, it all worked out."

"I'm too tired to debate the subject with you. I probably should be thinking about what's going to happen tomorrow."

"There really isn't much to think about. The pope will say a few words and pat you on the head. You'll kiss his ring and that'll be it. I suppose after that I'm going to have to call you 'your eminence'."

"Don't you do any such thing."

"Has your promotion gone to your head already? I thought you'd at least wait until tomorrow to start giving me orders."

"I don't give you orders. Even if I did, you wouldn't obey them."

"Imagine, you'll be Cardinal Gerald."

"Only a cardinal dean."

"Cardinal dean, cardinal priest, cardinal bishop. In the end, there really isn't that much difference. They're all members of the College of Cardinals. And you know what that can mean. After all, the Pope is an old man."

"Don't go there. I've had more than enough of what you'd call luck for the lifetime of any priest."

"I wouldn't call it luck. It's been ten years since the pope elevated a priest to the rank of cardinal. And that was only because the priest was older than the pope and wanted the honor before he died. He had to petition the Holy Father for it. That's the only way priests skip past bishop directly to cardinal."

"I'd still like to think it was luck. I didn't submit any petition."

"There you go again. You damn well know who's responsible. I wonder if we'll ever see him again. Not as Nikolai, of course, but as someone else."

"I pray that we never will."

"You've got to admit he was fascinating."

"Next you're going to tell me he was a fun guy."

"That, too."

"More fun than me?"

"I'm not going to answer that. It might start another debate. It's getting late and you should try to sleep so you'll be ready for tomorrow's big event. I wonder if I'll cry."

Father William took a last sip from the nearly empty glass of wine in front of him, rose from his chair and said:

"One bottle's enough for tonight."

"Now there's a miracle," Gerald replied.

Father William waited until he reached the apartment door to reply. He opened it, turned back to Gerald, and said:

"I've seen you perform a bigger miracle."

"What miracle would that be?"

"You helped the Devil find God."

## The End

Printed in the United States
65845LVS00008BA/45